Caught Between Two Worlds

A J Hawke

Published by Mountain Quest Publishing, 2011.

This is a work of fiction. Similarities to real people, places, or events are entirely coincidental.

CAUGHT BETWEEN TWO WORLDS

First edition. July 25, 2011.

Copyright © 2011 A J Hawke.

ISBN: 978-0983450528

Written by A J Hawke.

To God who has blessed me with the ability and opportunity to write. And to my family and friends of encouragers. To my family of readers who build me up and help carry me on to write more novels. Thank you does not fully express my gratitude.

CAUGHT BETWEEN TWO WORLDS
Inspirational Contemporary Western Romance
A J Hawke

Chapter One

COLORADO ROCKY MOUNTAINS

August

Stephanie Wellbourne felt her ankle twist and tried to catch herself before she hit the gravel and dirt of the mountain trail, but landed hard. Pain slammed her right ankle and up her leg. She moaned as she brushed the dark hair out of her eyes. No way to tell how many bruises the impact with the ground had created. The stabbing pain intensified and gritting her teeth, she wrapped both hands around her ankle. She glanced in both directions, hoping to see someone who could help. Nothing but thick forest swallowed the trail in both directions. How long had she been walking on the path by the Retreat Center before she twisted her ankle? Why hadn't she turned back at the end of the paved walk instead of continuing through the forest?

Whipping her head around at an unexpected sound, she stared into the forest of trees that bordered the path. Was that a bird? Now she heard all sorts of noises.

With the help of a small pine tree next to the trail, she pulled herself upright and put weight on her right foot. Ouch! No way there'd be any walking on this ankle. Was it broken?

Queasiness rolled over her in waves, and she bit her lower lip. How could she make it back to the Retreat Center? Her corporate staff had the afternoon off, and she was stuck out here. She shoved her hand into her pocket searching for her cell phone. It wasn't there. Stupid! She should have accepted Sam Edwards' offer to walk with her. However, she had no desire to talk to the head of her corporate law division, and she'd been so angry with him. Angry at all of them! The entire management team refusing her solutions—how dare they? After all, it was her company.

She hopped on her left foot and made it about fifteen feet before stumbling to her knees. Pain surged through her lower right leg. She sat in the middle of the gravel trail, hugged her right knee close to her chest, and tried not to cry. This could not be happening. She fingered the tear in the knee of her black microfiber slacks. The red sleeveless sweater had been warm enough during the hike, but now she shivered in the stretching shadows of late afternoon. Looking around she felt the forest closing in on her. Where was her staff when she needed them?

The sun sank closer to the tree line. She struggled against the rising panic. The slight breeze brought a smell of pine and earth, and the effects of the wind had a different sound on the tops of the pine and fir trees. It didn't resemble her estate in the Hamptons in any way.

A sound that had been at the edge of her mind for several moments became a loud thump, thump of boots hitting the gravel. She turned toward the trail leading up the mountain. A tall man strode her way. Loaded down with a large black backpack, he pounded downhill with the water bottle strapped to his belt keeping rhythm with his steps.

His sudden stop sent a spray of small gravel fanning out in front of his heavy hiking boots. "Are you all right?" He seemed bewildered to find her sitting on the trail.

His short light brown hair looked as if it might be curly if allowed to grow. Why was she noticing his curly locks at a time like this? She shook off the thought. "No, I'm not. I may have twisted my ankle, and I don't have my cell phone. You wouldn't have one, would you?"

"Sorry, my battery's down." His voice was deep and mellow.

Nice voice. It wouldn't be hard to listen to, and he wasn't bad to look at either with his dark green T-shirt taut across the width of his chest and shoulders, snug-fitting khaki hiking shorts, and sporting sunglasses in the dimming light of day, although he seemed a little distant. Would he be like most men she met who gave her too much attention, especially when they discovered who she was? She would find out.

"Can you help me back to the Cedar Ridge Retreat Center? It's just down the trail."

Working his arms out of the straps of his backpack, he dropped it on the side of the trail. "Let's take a look at your ankle."

His square-jaw framed the lower part of his strong, handsome face. If only he'd take his sunglasses off so she could see the color of his eyes. She shook herself to focus on what he'd said as she lifted her ankle for his inspection. "I don't know what looking at it will do. I can tell it's sprained. I just need help getting back to my hotel room."

The man held out his hand. "Would it help if I introduced my-self? I'm Flint Tucker." His large hand swallowed hers in its warmth.

"Hi, I'm Stephanie Wellbourne of New York City." He towered over her from where she sat on the ground.

He squatted next to her, and more tenderly than she would have expected he palpated her ankle. "It's already swelling, and it's going to bruise." He slipped off her sandal.

"Ouch!"

"Sorry, but it'll feel better without the weight of the shoe." He glanced at her, and then down the trail. "It'll be dark in another hour and a half. I'll leave my pack here and carry you."

She felt control of the situation slipping away. "No, please. Just go get help."

"There's no time to get help and come back before the sun sets. I won't leave you alone on the trail after dark." Not waiting for her to respond, he turned to his pack and dug out a sweater. "Here, let's get you into this. The temperature is dropping fast."

A chill seeped into her bones. She shivered. When did it get so cold? She allowed him to pull the sweater over her head and upper body. "Thank you. I am cold." She smoothed the lightweight blue V-neck sweater down her body. At once, the fine microfleece warmed her.

He continued pulling various items out of his pack, which he shoved into his pockets. When he turned to her, he held an ace bandage. "I'll wrap the ankle for now. That should help with the pain."

"You seem to be prepared for anything." While he expertly wrapped her ankle tears squeezed out the corner of her eyes from the pain.

When he finished, he eased her foot to the ground, then sat back on his heels. "I've had a lot of practice. When out in the mountains it pays to think ahead."

Was he rebuking her for not thinking ahead, such as not having her cell phone or even a sweater? If he would only take off the sunglasses, she could see his eyes.

Before she realized what he intended to do, he slipped his left arm around her waist and his right under her knees. Without so much as a grunt, he lifted her as he would a small child. She wrapped her arms around his neck to steady herself.

Without another word, he trudged down the trail. With each step, the bouncing pounded excruciating pain in her ankle. Passing out would be a welcome relief. After what seemed an intolerable time, he stepped off the trail a few steps, then lowered her onto a stump.

"Why are we stopping?" She didn't try to keep the impatience from her voice. "It's getting dark. Let's get to the retreat center."

He removed his sunglasses and slid them into a pocket of his hiking shorts. "Would you like a drink?" He was even more handsome now that she could see his eyes.

"What?" She drew herself back from the depths of his amazing blue eyes.

"I'm thirsty and about to drink most of the water in my water bottle. I wondered if you would like a drink before I finish it off." He waited holding his water bottle.

"No, thank you. I just want to get to the Retreat Center." Yes, she wanted to get back to the center, but he was intriguing.

His muscles rippled under the veins and tendons that stood out on his arms as he drank the water and then hooked the bottle back on his belt. Even with the chill in the air and the darkening of the trail, a fine mist of sweat covered his face and arms.

"Ready?" he asked.

Forcing her wayward thoughts back to her need to get back to the lodge, she lifted her arms. "Yes."

He lifted her into his arms again, only this time he gave a slight grunt. She looked at his face and saw that the strain of carrying her one hundred ten pounds was more of an effort than he'd shown at first. "Are you getting tired?"

Keeping his eyes on his boots hitting the trail, he said, "Yes, you're getting a bit heavy but nothing I can't handle. It's just that I've already been hiking about eight hours today."

Wow! Eight hours. None of the men she knew could do anything like eight hours of walking, much less on a mountain. She couldn't imagine hiking that far in one day. "Why?"

He laughed and glanced down at her. "Why not? It's the only way I know to come down the mountain."

Talking helped keep her mind off the pain of her ankle. "You hiked to the top of this mountain and back in one day?" She tightened her hold on his neck to ease her weight on his arms. How thankful she was that he had come along the trail even though she also felt a little guilty at his effort.

He tightened his arm around her waist and lifted her higher. "I hiked up yesterday and spent the night on top. I took my time coming down and hiked off the trail some. Couldn't waste such a beautiful day."

As he hiked down the trail, she felt him lurch. His hold on her tightened, and he righted himself without dropping her. The stumble jerked her ankle, and an involuntary cry escaped.

HE TRIED TO PLACE HIS boots with care. A fall would be disastrous. His arms, back, and legs burned from carrying her. Her weight hadn't seemed much at first. In the growing darkness, he searched for the small side trail that led to the Retreat Center. He had never been there but had seen the sign pointing the way from the main trail. He knew the jostling hurt her ankle. Nothing to do but get her help.

She pointed toward the signpost. "There, that's the path."

He turned onto the side trail, glad that he would soon have her where she could get medical care. The warmth of her body felt good. Her petite figure, long dark brown hair, violet eyes, and lovely face all made for a vision of loveliness. He breathed the scent of her hair, a faint hint of flowers. It had been a long time since he had had a beautiful woman in his arms.

Ahead, lights from the retreat center glowed in the descending darkness. Relieved to be off the trail, he slowed his steps to ease his trembling legs.

Why had she been on the trail alone and without proper hiking gear? Her lightweight sandals were probably the reason she'd fallen. And not even having water with her, what had she been thinking? He chuckled to himself. Yes, she was a city girl with no idea of the danger of being hurt or lost on the mountain.

He stopped when the buildings came in sight. He hadn't realized that the retreat center was so large. A two-story main lodge dominated the space with several smaller buildings beyond each end. They looked rustic while at the same time having modern picture windows. "Where should I take you?"

She pointed a slender finger in the direction of the large lodge. "The main lobby. Some of my staff should be there."

"Your staff? You work at the lodge?" His words came out in gasps. His muscles cried out with fatigue, and his eyelids wanted to close and stay that way.

"Work there?" A soft chuckle escaped. She drew herself up straighter in his arms. "I'm the CEO of the Wellbourne Group of New York."

"New York, huh? What are you doing here in Colorado?"

She heaved a heavy sigh. "I'm beginning to wonder myself. My CFO talked me into bringing my management group for a three-day business retreat. And it's been fine except for the fall on the trail." She shifted her arms, which felt to him as if she massaged the back of his neck. Even though his shoulders and back hurt from the effort of carrying her, he liked the feel of her arms.

"Where do you live?" she asked.

"About thirty miles southwest of here." And he had hoped to be home tonight. Not much chance of that now with the delay of acting as a Good Samaritan. The gravel path became a paved sidewalk. Darkness descended, and he welcomed the foot-high lamps lighting the way. Ahead he saw people mingling about inside the brightly lit lodge.

A pretty woman with a blond ponytail ran up to them from the door of the lodge. Several people followed her. "Stephanie, are you all right?"

"I'm all right now. Just a sprained ankle. Brigitte Brower, this is Flint Tucker, who graciously rescued me."

Brigitte acknowledged him with a quick glance. "We've been so worried. You didn't answer your cell phone."

She shrugged. "I forgot my cell. And Mr. Tucker's cell didn't have a charge."

A man in his fifties dressed in walking shorts and a polo pullover opened the lodge door for Flint and his bundle. "Stephanie, do we need to get an ambulance?"

"No, Dan, I simply twisted my ankle. Get me to my room, and I'll be fine in the morning."

Brigitte motioned for Flint to follow her. "Stephanie's suite is on the second floor. Can you carry her that far?"

"Lead the way." He hoped they had an elevator—his leg muscles were ready to give up.

They did, and soon he laid her down on a king-sized bed in a large bedroom.

She relaxed with the pillow against the headboard of the bed. "Thank you so much for your help, Flint." She motioned to Brigitte. "Please, hand me my purse."

He wasn't about to accept pay. "I need to go. I'm late getting home. It was nice to meet you all. Hope the rest of your stay goes well." He edged toward the door.

"No, wait. I need to thank you." She sat up straight with her leg resting on a pillow.

He nodded. "You already have." He escaped out the door and took the stairs to the lobby two at a time.

He lumbered over to the reception desk. "Do you have a flashlight I can borrow?"

The young man reached under the counter and brought up an industrial-sized flashlight.

"Certainly, sir. Is there a problem with the lights in your room?"

"No, I left something on the trail." He took the flashlight from the clerk. "Okay if I return this in a couple of hours?" Why had he left his in the pack? Maybe the sight of a beautiful woman in distress had something to do with it.

"Sure, that'll be fine." The desk clerk turned toward a couple that had walked up to the counter.

He stopped by the men's room and then filled his water bottle at the water cooler. He looked at the couches in the lobby. Just to sit down and relax for a few minutes. No, if he did that he wouldn't get up until morning. With a sigh, he ambled out and up the path toward the mountain trail with the glow from the flashlight lighting the way.

Three hours later, he made it down the trail to his truck. When he left yesterday morning, the parking lot at the end of the trail had been full. Now, his red Ford F-150 was the only vehicle there. After throwing his backpack into the backseat, and the flashlight onto the passenger seat, he pulled himself up behind the steering wheel. His hand shook as he put the key in the ignition and turned it to start the big engine. He drove slowly onto the state highway.

A couple of miles down the road, he turned under the arched entrance onto the tree-lined lane to the lodge, intending to return the flashlight. But fatigue took over. He'd never make it home like this. It wasn't safe. He parked in the far corner of the lot and then laid his head on the steering wheel. Maybe he could grab a few winks. His folks wouldn't worry since he'd told them he might not be back until tomorrow. But would Allie be okay?

His little three-year-old daughter asked about him when he wasn't home. He didn't like that she would worry, but he couldn't keep his eyes open.

Throwing his sleeping bag open onto the backseat, he pulled off his dusty hiking boots and climbed in. The few inches of the truck's extra width allowed him to stretch out with only his knees bent. He barely positioned his backpack under his head before he fell into a deep sleep.

Chapter Two

SHE PICKED UP THE PHONE from the nightstand and punched speed dial for Room Service. "Yes, this is Stephanie Wellbourne in Suite 2020. I'd like to order the mountain trout braised in herbs and butter, vegetables, salad, and tea."

With thirty to forty minutes to wait before the meal would arrive, she hopped into the bathroom and turned on the water of the bathtub after dumping a generous helping of her favorite lilac bath beads. A soak in a steamy tub would ease her aches and pains. She laid out her new red silk pajamas. Discarding her dirty torn outfit, she tied her hair up in a bun on the top of her head. Gently she sank into the hot water now covered in fragrant bubbles. Whew. She'd managed the feat without bumping her injured ankle.

The clock on the bathroom wall helped her keep track of the time. She had fifteen minutes to soak and relax before she could expect the food. The hot water did feel good on the sprained ankle. At least she hoped it was only a sprain. It had taken longer than she expected to prepare her bath. Bouncing on one foot with stops to deal with the pain had slowed her down.

With a sigh, she leaned back in the tub and let the hot water rise up to her chin. How far did the hiker, Flint Tucker, have to drive before he got home to his bed? Would he drive the thirty miles back to his ranch? She revisited the feel of his strong muscular arms holding her so confidently. Was he married? He hadn't worn a ring. Was there a steady girl? Did he have thoughts of her?

The various men she had dated over the last few years seemed weak compared to the masculinity of the hiker. Most of them had been more interested in her fortune than in her. She rubbed her temple. Their betrayals still hurt. It would be nice to meet a man she could trust.

Shaking her head, she sat up and finished washing off the grime. Taking the handheld bath sprayer, she quickly washed her hair. Standing on one foot in the tub proved harder than she had anticipated. With care, she sat on the side of the tub and swung her legs to the floor. Using the large fluffy blue towel, she dried off and pulled on her pajamas.

Hopping with care to avoid the wet floor, she took the plush white bathrobe down from the back of the bathroom door and snuggled into it. Holding on to the wall and furniture, she unlocked the door to the hall. Just as she was trying to figure out how to keep it open, a young woman, wearing a polo shirt with the retreat center logo, arrived carrying a large tray with domed covers over the plates.

"Good, my supper. Just put it on the side of the bed. I'm going to eat there." She hopped back to the bed and climbed in, relieved to get her ankle up on a pillow. "Please, hand me my purse."

The young woman handed Stephanie her purse and waited patiently for the five-dollar tip. "Thank you, ma'am. Is there anything else I can get you?"

She glanced over the tray to make sure she had everything she needed. "No, this will be fine. Just make sure that you close the door hard, so it'll lock behind you."

"Of course, enjoy your meal." The young woman left and closed the door behind her with a definite click.

Uncovering the larger plate, she found a deboned mountain trout finely braised in herbs and butter. She spent the next fifteen minutes savoring her excellent meal.

Although the clock radio blinked eleven-thirty, her eyes refused to close. Might as well look over Dan's financial report. She snatched it up, turned to the second quarter, and read.

Images of a tall, handsome man bounding down the trail intruded between her eyes and the print on the page. She could smell the mixtures of cologne and sweat from his body as he had carried her. Flint, an interesting name. Who had come up with that? He had left so abruptly. Maybe she'd insulted him. That's what Brigitte said anyway. He could have waited and let her explain, but no, he had to rush out. She'd been polite, even gracious. Surely, he didn't think she was unappreciative.

Maybe people were different in this western state. He hadn't said much when he carried her down the trail. The pressure of his strong, steady arms around her waist and under her legs still lingered against her skin.

What was she doing thinking about how his arms felt again? She shifted her leg to ease her ankle. He'd looked so tired before he rushed off. She chewed on her pen, thinking she should have been more thoughtful and made sure he had something to eat and a place to stay. She had even forgotten to ask for his address or cell phone number. The least she could do was send a thank-you card.

She tossed the report down on the nightstand, then shoved files to the other side of the bed. Her ankle throbbed. Was it more than a sprain? Maybe she did need an X-ray. Brigitte had found some pain pills somewhere. She swallowed another one.

She pushed the covers aside after a sleepless and painful night. She'd had it with watching the time creep by on the clock radio. With each sleepless hour, the pain in her ankle had grown until she could think of nothing else. She snatched up the phone and dialed Brigitte's room.

A sleepy voice answered, "Hello."

"Brigitte, I need you to drive me into town to see a doctor. Come to my room as soon as you can."

A yawn traveled through the phone. "Is your ankle worse?"

"Yes, I want to get it X-rayed. Ask at the desk if they have a wheelchair. I can't tolerate any weight on my ankle."

"All right, I'll be there as soon as possible."

She hung up the phone, then glanced at the clock. Only six-thirty. No wonder Brigitte kept yawning. She hopped to the bathroom where she washed her face, brushed her teeth, and combed her hair. That would have to do for this morning. Returning to the bedroom, she struggled into a pair of brown slacks, and a light white sweater. She slipped on one sandal.

Brigitte arrived with a wheelchair and Granfield Wilson, her vice-president of marketing.

After helping her into the wheelchair, Granfield said, "I'll bring the car around front."

As Brigitte pushed the wheelchair out of the elevator and into the lobby, Stephanie spotted Flint exiting the lodge.

"Push me to the door, please be quick about it." Why was he still here? She peered through the double glass doors at the circular driveway outside the lobby in time to see him climb into a big red pickup truck and drive away. He had been wearing a windbreaker, which reminded her that she still had his sweater.

She turned to Brigitte. "Make a note to call Amanda in security. Ask her to have someone find out what they can about a Flint Tucker who lives within thirty miles of this lodge. We need his address to return his sweater."

Brigitte pulled out her Blackberry and started texting. "Do we know anything else about him?"

"No, but with a name like Flint, he shouldn't be hard to find."

HE DRANK IN THE SIGHT of the ranch house at the end of the lane. It had never looked so good. Sweat mixed with grime on his skin—a shower couldn't come soon enough. The night's sleep in the truck hadn't been too bad, but now the pit in his stomach needed to be filled. Three days of food bars were about his limit.

As he entered the big country kitchen, his mother set bowls of scrambled eggs and gravy on the table next to a platter of fried ham and a basket of biscuits.

A little brown-haired girl came running from the living room straight at him. "Daddy!"

He dropped his backpack on the floor by the door as he reached down and caught his sweet girl in his arms. How small and fragile she was. Compared to the weight he had carried yesterday, Allie was too slight, even for only three and a half years of age.

He planted a firm kiss on her soft cheek. "How's my little princess?"

She rubbed her face where the stubble on his chin had scrapped. "I'm fine. You need to shave, Daddy. You scratch."

He held her in one arm and rubbed his jaw with the other hand. "I need a shave for sure, and a shower won't hurt me either." He grinned before nestling his chin in the curve of her neck.

She giggled. "That tickles, Daddy."

The sound of his daughter's laughter filled every empty place in his heart. He nuzzled her and delighted to hear her squeal again.

"Stop teasing that child, Flint, and give me a hug." He didn't have to look at his mom to hear the smile peeking out from behind her stern words. His mother, Mary Tucker, always there to help him out. What would he do without her?

Holding Allie in one arm, he hugged Mom with the other. Allie reached a small arm around her grandmother.

"Everything all right while I was gone?" Mom understood his re-al concern. With the severity of Allie's heart condition, it was the main topic of their cryptic conversations.

"Yes, son, everything was fine. I'm glad you did your climb. You needed to get away for a change. How was it?"

He deposited his daughter in her wooden tray-less high chair at the table and then went to the sink to scrub his hands. "I had a great climb. I think I got some pretty good pictures." Should he tell her about the girl? Mom would ask all sorts of questions, but she'd be happy he'd at least spoken to a girl. Only in the last year had she start-ed mentioning various girls in the area, gently raising the question of his finding another wife. The three and half years since Valerie's death were still too short a time for him. He wasn't interested in dating.

His father came through the kitchen door from the barn, which saved him from having to decide. "Hey, son, glad you're home. How was the mountaintop?"

He grinned. "It's still there." At sixty-four, his father was still a tall, straight-backed cowman. Hair now liberally sprinkled with gray, he saw in Dad's face his own future aging.

Mom snapped a yellow bib apron with a picture of Big Bird around Allie. "Wash up Tom, and let's eat before the gravy sets on us."

Allie shot a serious glance at her grandmother. "Why would the gravy sit on us? That would be messy."

A grin broke across his face.

Mom put one hand on her hip. "I don't mean actually sit on us... I mean...oh you'll learn someday. I can't explain it." Mom settled across from Dad, smiled at Allie.

Flint pulled out the chair next to Allie, and then sat, taking her hand. Mary took her husband's hand. "Go ahead, Tom, you lead the prayer." Dad tucked his napkin into his flannel multi-colored shirt with one hand.

"Let's pray. Lord, we thank you for Flint's safe return. Bless this food to the nourishment of our bodies. In the name of Jesus, amen."

"Where are Holly and Benjamin?" Usually, his sister and her husband would have been at the table since it was the weekend.

"Holly had an early doctor's appointment, and Benjamin took her into town." Mom passed him the basket of biscuits. "Don't frown like that. It's just her normal check-up. Nothing is wrong."

But hunger had suddenly flown away. In its place, the image of Valerie's wan face flashed in his memory as she tried to reassure him that giving birth was a normal part of life. That reassurance had lasted until a few minutes before she died just after giving birth to Allie.

"Daddy, look at me." Allie had her napkin on the top of her head. She patted her head and grinned.

He saw his mom hide a smile behind her own napkin. "Allie, put that napkin back in your lap. You'll get food in your hair."

Tom grinned. "She just wants her daddy's attention."

If only Flint could freeze the image of his daughter in time, her lovely laughing face without a single concern. "Allie, sweetheart, finish your breakfast, and then you and I will take a ride in the wagon."

He forced himself to clean his plate and then patted his full stomach. "I'm in need of a shower. Then we'll play."

"Okay, Daddy, I'll go find Teddy. He wants to play, too." Allie climbed down from her chair and ran toward the living room.

He ran up the stairs to his room, grabbed clean clothes, then hurried into the shower in the hall bathroom. He'd spend this last day of vacation playing with his child. Only the Lord knew how many more days like this he'd get.

He got the large red wagon out of the garage. He glanced over his shoulder at Allie standing on the front porch. "Wonder if there're any little girls anywhere wanting a ride this morning?"

Allie clamored down the steps, yelling. "Me, Daddy, me." She dragged her old Teddy bear with her.

He put her in the wagon and pulled up the wooden railing.

Allie smiled while he pulled the red wagon round and round the yard.

After only thirty minutes, he noticed Allie yawning and her eyelids drooping, a sure sign that she was tired. He carried her into the living room. She made no protest. They lay on the couch while he read her favorite book, *The Velveteen Rabbit*. As usual, she fell asleep lying on his chest before he got halfway through the book.

He stroked her hair, a deep ache pulling in his chest. Times like this made it hard to believe how damaged her little heart was.

On their last visit to the Children's Hospital Heart Institute in Denver, the heart specialist, Dr. Whitehall, had been brutally blunt with him. "We've done what we can. Without a transplant, she won't survive past her fifth birthday if that long."

He simply stared at the doctor. What could the man say after such a pronouncement? He couldn't face losing his child.

Dr. Whitehall frowned and leaned forward. "Did you understand? I'm sorry, but we need to be realistic. You need to start the paperwork to get Allie on the donor list, but there's no way to predict when a matching heart will be available. If ever."

He tried to lick his lips, but his mouth was too dry. "What should we do while we wait?"

"I suggest you spend as much time as you can with your daughter and make the most of the time you have." Dr. Whitehall looked through a stack of papers on his desk until he found a brochure. "Read this over. When you leave here, go down to the transplant office and start the paperwork."

"Yes, sir." Start the paperwork, just as if his baby girl's new heart was a piece of property for which he should make an application.

Later on the drive home, he had gripped the steering wheel until his arms ached. All it would take to get his daughter on the transplant list was a hundred-fifty thousand dollars. To start. He would give his own heart to save his daughter. He'd give her the world. And that's all it would take, the world he didn't have.

"Flint, son? You asleep?" His mother's voice interrupted his memories. "What, Mom?" He raised his head and peeked down at Allie asleep on his chest. Her soft little breaths were so precious to him. Each one.

"I got lunch on the table, and Allie needs to take her medicine. I know you hate to wake her, but remember the doctor told us to keep a strict schedule." Mom smoothed back the hair from his forehead.

He nodded. "Hey, little princess, wake up." He rubbed his daughter's back as she began to stir.

"Morning, Daddy." Allie sat up and rubbed her eyes.

"Hey, silly bunny, it's lunchtime." He carried her into the bathroom, washed her face and tiny hands, and got her to smile.

Lunch consisted of soup, sandwiches, and for Allie, her medicine. He never ceased to be amazed how matter of fact this small child took her illness. With all the medicine she had to take and all the medical procedures she'd endured, she still managed to present them with a smile. But how much longer could he count on that smile?

Chapter Three

SHE MANEUVERED ON HER crutches from the car to the office lobby in New York City. Over the past two weeks, she gained proficiency each day.

The broken ankle still gave her pain, but she sighed with relief that the worst throbbing seemed to be behind her.

Edith stood and nodded from behind the reception counter as she crossed to the elevator. "Good morning, Ms. Wellbourne."

"Morning, Edith." She entered the elevator.

The ride to the top floor of the building was quiet and quick.

Brigitte stood in the hall to assist her as the elevator doors opened. She reached for Stephanie's purse and jacket. "You made it."

"I'm a little late getting here but did you doubt that I would?" She gingerly hobbled to her office chair and settled in. "Please put these crutches out of sight." She positioned her ankle with the cast on a low footstool that Brigitte that found somewhere.

Brigitte leaned the crutches against the wall in a corner behind a tall fern, then seated herself across the desk from her. "You have several phone messages. I put them in the order I thought you would want to respond. Let me know which ones you want me to handle for you. Oh, and the man, Wes Palmer, from security is here."

"Why?" She sorted through the phone messages, making notes and dividing them into two piles.

"Wes Palmer, he has the report on the hiker that rescued you." Brigitte stood. "You want me to tell him to forget it? You're not really interested are you?"

She gazed at her assistant. "You're teasing me, right?"

Brigitte grinned. "A little, is it too much?"

She smiled. "All right, I'll admit it. He interests me. He was awfully kind."

"He was also handsome and polite."

She handed her the larger of the piles of phone messages. "You take care of these, please. And send in the security man. Let's find out about this interesting hiker." Normally so serious in her work, she'd take Brigitte's little digs with good humor. Their eight years working together had been productive. Before she forgot, she pulled her cell phone out and made a notation. *Brigitte's birthday next week, get present.*

A bald, overweight man probably in his fifties carried a briefcase as he ambled into her office. "Morning Ms. Wellbourne. I'm Wes Palmer with the security division. Pleased to meet you."

She waved him toward the maroon wingback chair. "Thank you for coming. I can only give you a few minutes as I have a conference call coming in at the top of the hour." She glanced at the large sunburst clock dominating the wall behind her visitor.

He sat on the low chair and placed the briefcase on his knees. He pulled out a couple of black folders and handed one to her. "I'll spell out the gist of the report, and you can examine it in more detail later."

Brigitte entered the office carrying a tray of steaming cups of coffee, cream, and sugar cubes. She set the tray on the desk in front of Wes Palmer. Brigitte prepared her coffee and placed it in front of her.

"Help yourself, Mr. Palmer." She picked up the cup and took a sip. "Now, tell me about Flint Tucker."

Swallowing a gulp of black coffee, Wes shifted in his seat. "Flint Tucker was born in Winchester, Colorado to Tom and Mary Tucker, the fourth of five children. His oldest brother, Abraham, is a physician in a downtown clinic in Los Angeles. He's married with three children. His next brother Samuel works in Alaska as a petroleum engineer. He is not married. The next brother is Stephen, married with four children. He works with his father-in-law on a ranch not far from Tucker's ranch. The only girl is Flint Tucker's twin. Holly Baxter is married to Benjamin and with her husband she teaches school in Cedar Ridge." He took another swig of coffee.

She tapped her manicured nails on the desk. "That's interesting, Mr. Palmer." She couldn't imagine being part of such a large family. What must it have been like to grow up with three older brothers? She always wanted a brother or sister. "What else?" She wanted to hear everything about this man before the interruption of the conference call. She bit her lip at her own impatience. No matter that Wes Palmer was just doing his job.

"I'll continue, Ms. Wellbourne. Flint Tucker graduated from the University of Colorado with a degree in accounting and finance. He went on to get an MBA. His wife, Valerie, also attended the university and that is where they met. They married five years ago."

She leaned back in her chair. So, he was married. It was ridiculous to be disappointed.

"Then their daughter, Allison, was born three years ago and Valerie Tucker died shortly after the birth."

She leaned forward. "He's a widower?" Maybe that explained why he seemed so serious. That must have been awful for him.

"Yes, ma'am. With a superficial investigation, I couldn't find out if he is involved with anyone at this time. He works at Booker and Williams as a financial analyst. He has his CPA. I called his boss, Mr. Booker, but he wouldn't say much. I sensed he thought I was interested in hiring Mr. Tucker and wouldn't give any information. That may indicate how much Booker values Flint Tucker's work.

"He bought his ranch about four and half years ago which he owes on. He also has debt on his truck and other things. Evidently, he has a significant amount of medical debt, but I haven't been able to get details yet. He makes fifty thousand a year at Booker and Williams and some additional revenue from his ranch.

"His parents are in their sixties and live with Mr. Tucker. His mother cares for his daughter. His neighbors say he's hard working, always willing to help out, attends church regularly, is a volunteer firefighter for his county, and is well thought of generally. He doesn't seem to travel, and his only hobby appears to be climbing mountains.

"This is all that I could find out in the short time I had. If you want I can keep digging and give you a further report in a week or so."

She rubbed the side of her nose gently. "Yes, I want a more in-depth report, especially about his work experience. Keep me posted on what you find."

Wes dug into his briefcase and handed her a small red USB Flash drive. "Oh, here's a thumb drive with photos."

She stood on one foot and steadied herself with her hands on the desk. "Thank you, I'll look at these later. I'll expect another report by next week."

Wes fumbled with closing his briefcase and shoved his glasses up. "Yes, Ms. Wellbourne."

The door clicked shut behind him. She plopped into her black leather chair and shoved the thumb drive into her computer. Names of files popped up across the screen, each labeled nicely. Tucker Ranch 1; Tucker Ranch 2; Tucker's Truck; Tucker's Work and so on. Scanning the photos, Flint's handsome face covered her screen as she opened file after file. There was a series of photos of Flint pulling a little red wagon with a laughing child in it. She assumed that was his daughter, Allison. It was the only photo of him smiling. The love he had toward the child shone through the photo. Did the little girl look like his wife? It must be hard to raise a child alone after such a loss. Why had his wife died? She studied the photos of the child who had the smile of a little angel. It would be easy to love a child who looked like that.

After closing the file, she gazed out the window and stared across the New York skyline. Why was she so curious about this man? After all, she had only been in his company for a few hours. Somehow her heart was drawn to him, and he was in her thoughts constantly.

"Stephanie?"

She turned toward the office door where Brigitte stood. "Yes?"

"The conference call with the European directors? They're waiting."

"Thanks." She reached for the phone and pushed the button to place the call on speaker.

"Morning, or should I say afternoon everyone." Even though it was still morning in New York, it was seven hours later in Geneva, Switzerland.

As the meeting progressed, she began to have an uneasy feeling. The responses she heard seemed guarded, and she wasn't getting the information she wanted. Then she recognized Thor Swenson, Director of the North Sea Group. His voice was distinctive. She'd know it anywhere. What was he doing in Geneva? Moreover, why had no one informed her he was on the call? The meeting should have consisted only of the Middle and Southern European groups.

Might as well get it out in the open. "Thor, is that you?"

His deeply accented Swedish voice answered. "Hello, Stephanie."

"I hadn't expected you to be on the call today." How had he even heard about it? Who had broken her trust? Jacque Rossie from France, Paublo Martina from Spain, or perhaps Herman Buble from Germany? Pierre Limoge from Geneva she didn't question. But Thor Swenson she didn't trust.

"I'm here consulting, and we thought it might be useful for me to listen in on your call." The smooth sound of placating came through to her.

Thor had been a protégé of her father and probably had wanted to gain more control of the corporation after William W. Well-bourne's death. In subtle ways, he had let her know that he hadn't expected the old man to leave everything to his then twenty-six-year-old daughter. The fifty-year-old Thor occupied a seat on the Board of Directors, which gave him power.

She listened to the answers to her questions and decided she needed to fly to Geneva. Only by talking in private would she find out exactly what was going on in her company. Without giving a hint of her concerns, she finished the call.

After a few taps of her pen on the desk, she pushed the intercom button that summoned Brigitte. "Find a couple of seats on a flight to Geneva this evening. Do it quietly and tell no one. Go to my apartment and pack me a bag for three days and then one for yourself."

Brigitte had her iPad at the ready. "You don't want to take the company jet?"

She shook her head. "I want to keep this trip under the radar. And actually, two first class seats are cheaper than jet fuel, and the jet is due to be ready for a lease in two days." Her father had always kept the jet as part of a separate corporation that was operated as a leasing company. When she wanted to use the jet, she leased it back to the Wellbourne Group. Most of the staff assumed the jet belonged to the company.

Brigitte texted as she talked. "What do we tell the staff here about you being gone?"

"We can leak to the staff that I've gone to the Hamptons to rest my ankle and will work from there. Don't worry about it. You might be surprised how many people pay no attention to me being here."

"There's a flight at seven-twenty pm on American Airlines. We'll be in Geneva by seven am tomorrow. I'll get us a suite at the Hotel des Bergues." Brigitte continued to tap her iPad.

She took a deep breath. "All right, I'll get together the necessary documents and information. Let's go see what we can figure out."

SHE TRIED TO GET COMFORTABLE lying on the foldout seat in first class. The last thirty-six hours had been a whirlwind of appointments in Geneva. Thankfully, she and Brigitte were on their way home now. What she had learned in Geneva caused shivers of anxiety to crawl over her skin. A hostile takeover loomed. She could feel it. She had to get a handle on this. Somehow, they knew she was coming and yet neither she nor Brigitte had told anyone. What about the Board of Directors—were they maneuvering to get rid of her? Could they even do that? She wasn't sure. Two things she did know; she had to be wise, and she could not trust Thor. He was up to something. But what?

She pushed the button to call the flight attendant. The flight attendant appeared instantly. "May I help you?"

"I'm chilled. May I have another blanket?"

"Of course." The flight attendant reached up and opened the overhead bin. She pulled out a couple of the thin blankets and spread them over Stephanie's legs. "Is there anything else I can do for you?"

"No, thank you." She tried to re-position her ankle. It hurt again after the effort to get on the plane.

She needed an outside firm she could trust to come in and locate real numbers so she could figure out what was going on. An idea began to bounce its way around the edge of her thoughts. It just might work.

Chapter Four

HE DROVE CAREFULLY in the heavy early Monday morning traffic. Ben Booker's call for him to drive into town to the office was a surprise. He would rather have worked from his office at the ranch as he usually did, but Ben was the boss.

He turned into the parking lot of Booker and Williams just off Main Street. He pulled off his sunglasses and tucked them in the visor. Not only was Ben Booker's Escalade already in a parking space, but Tony Williams' BMW sat in its regular spot. Something was up for sure. Tony never came into the office this early.

He pushed through the lobby doors of the one-story office building. His pace slowed, the entire staff seemed to be at work. What's going on? A swift glance at the clock behind the reception desk revealed seven-fifteen. The call from Ben had come at five a.m.

Marcy looked up from behind the reception desk. "Hi, Flint." The forty-year-old woman had worked with the firm for years and knew everyone and everything.

"'Morning. What's going on?" If he could get a clue before he met Ben and William, it would help.

"I'm sure we'll all know soon enough. They're waiting for you in the conference room. There's coffee." The phone rang, and she turned away to take the call.

He stepped into his office and dropped his coat onto the back of a chair. He made his way to the conference room still carrying his new Rick Steves' Autobahn messenger bag, which held his laptop.

Only his mom would have ordered such a thing for him, but he was finding it useful.

"Flint, glad you could make it so early." Ben Booker's booming bass voice was almost painful so early in the morning.

"Well, you called, so I guessed it was important." He set his bag down on a chair then made a beeline for the coffee pot. He poured a cup, picked up a glazed donut from the Krispy Kreme box, and took a huge bite before making his way back to the twenty-seat rectangular conference table.

He grinned at the gray-haired heavyset man sitting across the table from him.

"Morning, Tony. I don't remember ever seeing you here this early."

"And I hope you don't see me again at this unreasonable hour." Tony took a drink from his cup of coffee and tapped the folder in front of him. "We've got a problem and a possible solution."

"Let's hear it." He finished off the donut and waited for Ben and Tony to tell him what was going on.

Ben spoke calmly. "The city of Denver has canceled our contract. They've decided to hire in-house."

He looked from one man to the other. This was terrible news for the firm. The city of Denver account was huge. What its absence would do to the bottom line of the firm, he could only guess.

"Did they give any reason for canceling?" He asked.

Ben shook his head. "No reason that has anything to do with us. It's the new Comptroller for the city. She wants to bring in some of her own people."

He rubbed his temple as if he had a headache. "But we do have another possibility for an even bigger account."

He opened his eyes wide and raised his eyebrows. "Oh?"

"The Wellbourne Group out of New York called me yesterday. They need an independent audit of some of their holdings on the q.t. They're willing to pay big for what they want."

Tony gave Flint a fixed stare.

"What exactly do they want?" Why did it feel like this would involve him somehow? Where had he heard of the Wellbourne Group before? The hair on the back of his neck stood up and he shook off the shiver. He wasn't sure he wanted to hear what they wanted.

Ben shifted in his chair. "They've requested that we do an audit of their entire European and American holdings. But quietly. They suspect a possible hostile takeover attempt. They've requested that we send someone to their New York office to liaison with them." Ben leaned forward and pointed his finger at him. "They've requested you for that position."

His first impulse was to say a definite no. He wasn't about to leave Allie and move to New York. "What did you tell them?"

Tony took over. "We told them to send the specs and contracts. What else could we do? The information arrived last night by carrier. They're offering two million dollars to hire the firm for the first six months with the possibility of another six months after that."

He drew in his breath. With the canceling of the City of Denver, a contract like this could save the company. "What do you mean they want me in New York?"

"One of the requirements for the deal is that you go to their New York headquarters and work with their CEO. They want to move fast. Evidently, they can't trust any of their usual people." Ben ran his fingers through his already unruly hair. "Flint, we understand the problem for you. We'll pay you a bonus in addition to what they're offering. We'll also pay your airfare to fly home as much as you need."

"What are they offering?" Not that it mattered, he wasn't going to do it.

"Your salary will be a hundred seventy-five thousand plus a living allowance. We'll kick in another twenty-five thousand dollars as a bonus. It means that much to the firm." Tony opened a folder in front of him. "They want you to fly up within the next two days."

Who would pay that much for his services? "Who is the CEO I'd be working with?"

Tony lifted a sheet of paper and read aloud, "Stephanie Wellbourne, daughter of William H. Wellbourne. She inherited the company from her father about three years ago."

He stared at the man. Stephanie Wellbourne. Surely not the beautiful woman he'd carried down the trail? "Do you have a picture of her?"

Ben frowned and leafed through the papers in front of him. "Here's one that was copied from a website about some charity do in New York." He slid it across the table to him.

As he examined the full-page photo of a stunningly beautiful woman in an emerald green tight-fitting evening gown, he recognized the girl from the mountain trail, the one who still had his sweater. "I've met her. It was about a month ago. She was at the Cedar Ridge Retreat Center with her management staff."

"You've met her? How well do you know her? I can't believe you know one of the richest women in the country and didn't tell us." Tony's voice held a note of reproach.

"I just met her once for a couple of hours. I don't really know her. It didn't register who she was." He rubbed his neck remembering the feel of her arms.

"Flint, will you do it for us? We really need this. We don't have a lot of European experience, but enough. We can do this. Tony and I will give you any support we can." Ben's eyes pleaded with him.

It made him uncomfortable to see his boss needing his help so badly. If it weren't for Allie, he would do it in a heartbeat. Heartbeat, Allie's heart.

Flint felt as if he was being sucked into something that would take control of his life. He couldn't leave Allie and go to New York. But the money ... If he was frugal, he could get enough for the heart transplant in one year. "I'll do it."

The rest of the day disappeared in a whirlwind of researching the Wellbourne Group, tying up loose ends and handing off his ongoing work, and arranging a flight to New York for Wednesday.

By five, he gathered his bag and jacket and climbed into his truck. Every mile he drove toward home made him more nervous. What would his parents say? He depended so much on them. And Allie, his baby girl. Clenching his teeth, he reminded himself of why he was leaving her. What if something happened to her and he couldn't fly back in time? He wouldn't think about that.

He parked his truck in the shed by the side of the barn, then sat gripping the wheel. Could he really do it? Leave his family with the day-to-day uncertainty they lived with?

His father thumped the driver's side window. "What's the matter, son? You look like you've seen a ghost. Why don't you get out of the truck and come into the house?"

He climbed down, shut the door, and then looked at Dad's strong face. His sixty-five years of working in the open showed in the lines. He needed Dad's support in this decision.

"What is it, son?"

He grabbed him in a hug.

The older man wrapped his arms around his youngest son and held tight. "It's all right son. You're home, and I'm here."

He pulled back. "We need to talk. Let's take a walk out to the creek."

"All right." Dad turned, and they strolled toward the back of the barn, then across the pasture that led down to the creek.

He told him about New York. "It's a way of getting the money for Allie. You know I don't want to go, but I don't see any other way."

Tom Tucker squatted on his heels by the creek, plucked up a piece of grass, and started chewing on it. "Allie will miss you. It might even make her worse. Have you thought of that?"

He kicked at a stone, and it rolled into the creek. "Yeah, I thought of that. But without the transplant, she'll die." His words caught in his throat and he swallowed to keep from throwing up. "We can stay in touch, and I'll come home every couple of weeks. I can fix up a webcam and talk with her every day."

Tom stood and put his hand on his shoulder. "You sure this is the best thing?"

"Dad, I don't know what else to do."

Tom rubbed the back of his neck. "Your mother sure isn't going to like this. Let me tell her."

"If you think that's the best way." He didn't want to face his mother's accusing eyes. All his life he had tried to avoid doing anything that caused his mom to turn hurt-looking eyes his way. No, he'd let Dad take on that chore for him. After all, he had offered.

"Sure, son. Let me do that for you."

He tried to be his usual self through supper. But he couldn't help staring at his little girl feeling that time was running out.

Allie said little and sat limply in her chair. In the evenings, as the fatigue of the day caught up with her, she often acted like a rag doll.

He carried her up to her bed and tucked her in. "What story do you want tonight?"

Allie slid her little hand into his and held on. "Tell me about Mommy." Not tonight. He wanted Allie to know her mother if only through stories he told, but there were times when it was almost too hard for him to talk about Valerie. However, Allie asked to hear the story over and over.

"Your Mommy was the most beautiful girl I ever met. When I saw her sitting in that college math class, I knew she would make you the best mommy in the world." He smiled at the memory of Valerie sitting among the other students in jeans and sweatshirt and her hair tied up in a ponytail.

He spent the next hour telling his little girl everything he could think of about her mother. Finally, Allie drifted off to sleep, and he pulled the covers up around her. Lying down beside her and watching her sleep, he prayed.

Fifteen minutes later, he descended the stairs and found his parents sitting in the family room. "Allie's sound asleep. I think she'll be all right for a while."

His mother patted the seat next to her on the couch. "Did you tell her about leaving?"

He slumped down next to Mom and shook his head. "No, I'll wait until tomorrow evening. I want the next twenty-four hours to be as normal as possible for her."

Mom sighed. "Well, son, your dad told me all about it. I understand you have it to do. We'll be all right here."

He put his arm around her shoulder and gave her a kiss on the cheek. "Thanks, Mom, I couldn't make it without you all."

Dad sat in his recliner. "I told your mom about the web thingy, the camera thing."

He had to smile. Dad absolutely refused to move into the computer age. Now, Mom was different. She spent hours on the computer e-mailing her children and grandchildren. Mom used the Internet to purchase clothes for him and the rest of the family. Her favorite website was Amazon. The UPS truck knew the way to their ranch better than the postal carrier.

"Tell me about the webcam. Can you install it?"

"Sure, it's not difficult. I bought one for the computer here at the house, and my laptop already has one. I'll install it in the morning and show you how to use it. What we can do is set a time each day. You and Allie can be in front of the one here, and I'll be on the laptop in New York." He hoped Allie would be willing to sit still long enough to talk to him over the webcam.

"How are you going to manage in New York without your truck?" Ever the practical one, Dad scratched his head.

"I'll probably ride the subway."

"Where are you going to live?" Mom asked.

"I thought I would inquire through the church in New York and see if I can find someone who has a room to rent. I don't need much." He placed his elbows on his knees. "I've already talked to Richard Anderson, their preacher. He went to school with Dave."

"I hope this Richard Anderson is as good a preacher as Dave. Being away from home you need the church there to be a strong one." Mom sighed deeply. "I know God will watch over you, but I really don't want you to go."

"And I don't want to go either, but if I can make enough money for the heart transplant, it'll be worth it." If Allie could get her new heart, it would be worth it for sure. But the image haunting his dreams was that another child had to die for Allie to have a new heart.

The next day passed too quickly what with packing, completing last minute chores around the ranch, and spending time with Allie.

With an hour before supper, he took Allie out to the little pond where they sat on a bench he'd built for her.

Allie patted his cheek. "Why do you look sad Daddy? Did I do something bad?"

He gathered her close in his arms as he had when she was a small baby. "No, honey, you haven't done anything bad. But Daddy is a little sad, and I need to tell you about it."

She wrapped her arms around his neck and gazed at him with a serious expression. "Okay. Is it a story?"

"Sort of. You know Daddy has to work so we can have money to pay for food and things. Well, I need to go away to work for a while.

I'll be back often, and we will talk every day over the computer. It won't make any difference except I won't come home every night." He didn't know if he was using the right words or not. How did you tell a three-year-old you were leaving?

She tilted her head and looked at him out of the corners of her eyes. "You go far away?" The sound of worry in her voice made him want to forget the whole thing.

He had to do this so his beautiful darling little girl could live. "Yes, to New York, a very big city."

She looked at him with a frown. "I'll come too. We will go together to the big New York."

He smiled at her simple solution. "I wish you could, but someone has to stay here with Grandpa and Grandma. If you don't stay here, who will take care of them?" The little frown between her eyes and the way she twirled a curl of her brown hair told him she was trying to work it out.

"You will come back, you promise?"

He swallowed the lump in his throat. "Yes, sweetheart, I promise you, I'll be back as soon as I can."

"Okay, Daddy, I'll take care of Grandpa and Grandma."

"I know you will. I love you, little bunny."

She wrapped her arms around his neck again and squeezed as hard as she could. "I love you, Daddy."

He returned her hug. "Let's get back to the house and see what Grandma has for supper."

AS HE PUT ALLIE TO bed, he combined his good night with goodbye. He didn't think she realized he wouldn't be there when she woke the next morning.

By three a.m., he had his bags loaded into the truck. He'd spent a sleepless night, and the strained lines on his parents' faces indicated they had too.

"You ready to go, son?" Tom Tucker pulled on his coat as he waited for him to say goodbye to his mother.

"You call me any time. I'll always have my cell. I can grab a flight and be home within six to eight hours." He was repeating himself. His mother knew what to do.

"You go with peace of mind. We'll take care of Allie." Mom hugged him one more time. "Now, go on with you. You don't want to miss your flight."

He climbed behind the steering wheel while Dad took the passenger seat. As he drove down the lane toward the highway, he looked in the rearview mirror for one last view of the ranch house. He heaved a Rocky Mountain-sized sigh, then turned left and headed through the dark early morning toward the Denver International Airport, an hour and a half away. Was he doing the right thing?

The burden of unshed tears at leaving Allie intensified the ache in his chest. If only he could find release, but he hadn't been able to cry since Valerie died.

Chapter Five

SHE WOKE WITH A SENSE of excitement. Flint Tucker's scheduled noon arrival had her acting like a teenager. Why she was so sure he could help make a difference in her corporation, she didn't know. Something about him drew her, and she wanted to trust someone. Maybe more hope than reality.

She rummaged through her closet, then chose a pair of black silk slacks and a red silk shantung shirt. This was her first day to wear regular shoes, although she still had her ankle wrapped in an ace bandage. Slipping her feet into a pair of Italian leather mules with an antique map printed on the top, she decided to let her hair flow loose. Moving to the bathroom, she picked up the brush and brushed her hair smooth and straight with it parted slightly on the side and falling alongside her face and down her back. She applied her make-up lightly and finished her preparation by putting on a pair of drop pearl earrings and a gold necklace with five pearls. Stepping back from the mirror, she surveyed her appearance. It was the best she could do. With a shrug, she turned to go.

WHEN SHE ARRIVED AT her office, she found Brigitte already at work.

She laid a stack of folders on the corner of Stephanie's desk. "Here are the faxes, reports, and emails. The phone messages will be ready in about ten minutes." She slid into her chair. "Pretty blouse. Red's your color."

"Thanks, Brigitte. You don't look too bad yourself." She grinned at her. Brigitte's brown velveteen slacks and white tailored blouse looked great on her. She had arranged her blond hair in a French twist. She sat in her chair at her desk and slipped out of her shoes. She could tell that her ankle was going to be more painful today in regular shoes.

"What time does he get here?" Brigitte asked.

"Who?"

Brigitte leaned forward. "The mountain man who will save the corporation."

She tipped her chair back to gaze at her assistant. "His flight arrives at noon. George will meet him. Is his office ready?"

"Want to see?"

"Sure." She slipped the mules back on.

They walked down the hall, passed three offices and stopped at the corner one.

Brigitte stepped back to let her enter. "Since he comes from the west and the wide open spaces I thought he would like more windows."

She surveyed the room. The large walnut desk, complete with a lamp and phone, commanded the center of the room. A matching credenza behind it, flanked by bookcases on each side, gave this manly office a rich ambiance she hoped would please him. Two couches, two wingback chairs, and end tables with lamps made a nice informal area against the eastern wall. Two of the office walls, actually floor-to-ceiling windows, opened to a panoramic view of the New York skyline—a city she loved and hoped he'd come to enjoy.

Brigitte had the responsibility of getting everything ready for Flint Tucker to begin work. Her ability to organize and delegate amazed Her. She turned to Brigitte. "You've done well. I'm sure he'll be pleased."

"I hope so. We were fortunate that Jim Henry retired and this office became available."

She nodded. "I know other people were jockeying for it. I hope everyone will welcome Flint and help him do his job."

Brigitte frowned. "The problem is no one knows exactly what his job will be. What should I tell them when they ask?"

She led the way back to her own office furnished in modern, bright chrome décor. "We can say he's a financial strategist hired to work with me personally to develop a long-term plan for the company. That should cover it."

"I didn't want to tell you, but you might want to know. Dan told me Thor Swenson called and asked questions about this guy coming in to work with you."

She sat at her desk and stared at Brigitte. "Thanks for telling me." She drummed her fingers on the desk, frown lines creasing her forehead. "But several things really concern me. What was it he really wanted to know from Dan? And who told Thor about my hiring Flint? Who is in the home office that I can't trust?"

Brigitte's words disturbed her a great deal. But She didn't want to let anyone know how much. She had relished the challenge of taking over from her father, but at times, she really wished he were here. One of her goals was to keep her employees from knowing how scared she felt sometimes. She must maintain a hard businesslike exterior. No one was going to know that inside she was still a frightened child.

HE SLEPT ON THE FLIGHT from Denver to Kennedy International. When the plane landed, he made his way slowly carrying his backpack and messenger bag with his laptop. For once, he was thankful his mother paid so much attention to his clothing. If it had been up to him, he would have worn jeans with a western shirt and boots. His business attire blended in with the other men getting off the plane.

At the unsecured baggage area, he pushed the glass door open. When the luggage came around on the carousel, he grabbed his two checked bags. Looking toward the exit, he saw a man in a black suit holding up a sign with the name FLINT TUCKER printed on it.

Dropping his bags onto a luggage cart, he stopped in front of the man. "I'm Flint Tucker."

"I'm George. I drive for the Wellbourne Group. I'll take your luggage. Just follow me, sir."

He followed half a pace behind to a Lincoln Town car parked in the limo lane, where George held the door to the backseat.

The drive into the city took nearly an hour. He had no idea where they were, as this was his first visit to the New York. As he looked out at mile after mile of the cityscape, he couldn't hold back a shudder. He didn't want to be here.

George pulled up in front of a tall office building. Taking a deep breath, he got out in front of the skyscraper where letters on a big sign announced the Wellbourne Group.

Lord, I'm here. Help me do my best work and take me home soon.

SHE MET FLINT TUCKER at the elevator in the hallway outside her office. "Welcome to the Wellbourne Group."

She tried to glance over the tall, tanned man without his noticing. He wore black microfiber corduroy slacks with a gray herringbone sports coat that set off his broad shoulders nicely. The blue silk tie with his white cotton dress shirt made him look like a successful businessman in his thirties. Not at all like the wilderness hiker she envisioned from their first meeting. The silk tie was a little crooked, which added to his charm, though she could still see him looking more comfortable in his mountain man clothes.

Flint enfolded her hand in his large one. "Ms. Wellbourne. It's nice to meet you again."

She extracted her hand to wave him into her office. "Please, I'm Stephanie. And may I call you Flint?"

"Yes, ma'am, please do." He set his bag on the floor and settled in one of the wingback chairs in front of her desk.

She sat behind the desk. "Just Stephanie. No ma'ams here." Brigitte entered carrying a tray containing a tall chrome carafe of coffee and china cups. "Hello, Mr. Tucker. I don't know if you remember me or not. I'm Brigitte, Stephanie's assistant." She set the tray on the desk.

He stood and shook hands with Brigitte. "Yes, I remember you. Please, call me Flint."

She poured coffee into two cups. She couldn't help noticing that Brigitte's face lit up as she talked to Flint. Someone else was attracted to this handsome westerner.

Brigitte left, and he sat across from Stephanie again. He reached for the cup of coffee she slid across the desk.

How should she start? She cleared her throat. The best bet would be to plunge into it. "I'm sure you have a lot of questions about the sudden hiring of your firm and me asking you to liaison. I need to tell you a story to give you the full picture. Then you'll better understand what I'm up against and can develop a plan to help me."

He raised his eyebrows and leaned back holding the cup with one hand and the saucer with the other one. "All right, I'm listening."

She explained her suspicions about recent events within her company. She described the various players and how much money was involved. "Basically, I can't trust anyone. I need to know in a hurry if the numbers coming out of Europe are solid and if not, how much is fabricated. I need to know who is buying stock and who is giving proxies. I've asked, but I'm not getting clear answers. Can you and your company help me?"

He set the empty cup and saucer on the tray, leaned back, and crossed his leg over the other. "We can do an external audit with no problem if you give us access. Also, I can analyze the audit and tell you whether it makes sense regarding the holdings you have. I'll need records going back several years to use as comparisons and to find what doesn't make sense."

He spoke with such confidence. She felt as if a weight around her heart was lifting. "What about the movement of shares?"

He nodded. "We can start tracking the shares and see if anyone is gathering a sizable number and behind what proxies. I'll need a complete list of stockholders."

She nodded. "I can get that. I've tried to track them myself, but I can't seem to follow through with where some of the buying and selling is ending up."

He looked around the office. "You have somewhere I can work?"

She sent him a smile and stood. "Oh, yes. We have an office ready for you. Have you arranged for a place to stay? We can get you a hotel room temporarily."

He followed her out of the office and down the hall. "I have a place for a couple of nights, and after that, I'll need to find something."

She opened the glass door to his new office and stepped back. "Here's your office. You'll have Brigitte as an assistant. She'll still be helping me, but she's the only one I completely trust right now. Also, she can help you find a place to stay."

He walked behind the desk and sat in the leather chair. It didn't look as big with his large frame in it. "This will work just fine."

"Good. Then I'll leave you to it. I'll send Brigitte in to get you set up with passcodes and access to the databases you'll need." She turned to leave but stopped. She looked at the man who was really a stranger. "I feel good about you being here. I hope it wasn't too disruptive for you to come, but we really need the help."

He smiled at her for the first time. "I'm glad I can help out. I won't promise you anything, but we'll do our best to help solve your problem."

She nodded and then carefully walked the long hallway back to her office, trying not to give in to the weakness of her ankle. He never really said whether the move to New York was disruptive or not.

Chapter Six

HE GLANCED AROUND THE spacious office. What would the fellows at Booker and Williams say to him if they saw his workplace? He put his bag with his laptop on the credenza and opened the top-of-the-line Hewlett Packard laptop on his desk. After booting it up, he scanned its programs when he heard a voice from in front of the desk.

"Flint?" Brigitte stood by his desk, waiting for his attention. He had not really looked at her before. She was as stunning as Stephanie. Brigitte was a classic blond beauty, and Stephanie was dark haired. He couldn't decide which he liked looking at more.

"Yes?" He leaned back in the black leather executive chair, luxuriating in enough comfort to make him consider smuggling the chair home.

Brigitte handed him a stack of folders. "Here are the passcodes and access data. Also, a list of names, phone numbers, email addresses, and positions of the upper management of the Wellbourne Group. These cover both the U.S. and European Groups."

He placed his hand on top of the pile. "I'll need to keep these secure."

Brigitte nodded. "May I suggest something?"

"Of course."

Brigitte glanced toward the closed glass door leading to the hallway. She stepped closer to the desk. "I don't know who to trust, but I wouldn't put anything on the company server that you want to be kept secure. Even the encrypted files may not be safe. With the amount of money involved, I'd not be surprised to learn they'd tapped the phone and bugged the walls. Of course, Stephanie says I watch too much television. But something is going on."

He was intrigued. "Just how much money is involved?"

She lowered her voice even more. "If someone could get control of the European group, we are looking at maybe five hundred million in assets." She paused and looked over her shoulder at the closed glass door again. "If someone could get the Board of Directors to vote Her out and take over, they would be in charge of close to a billion dollars in assets."

He rubbed the side of his nose as he thought over her statement. "That kind of money could buy a lot of dishonesty." He met Brigitte's gaze. "That's what you are trying to tell me."

Brigitte took a deep breath. "Yes, and I think Stephanie is too trusting and has been for a long time."

"Why do you trust me, Brigitte?" He was glad she did trust him, although he was basically a stranger.

She fluttered her hand to her throat. "I don't know. I just sense that I can. I care about Stephanie. She's been good to me, and I don't like the idea of someone trying to hurt her."

He nodded. "You can trust me. The only investment I have in the outcome of this job is to help Stephanie and to get paid. Maybe we can make a commitment that we'll work together to do just that." It wouldn't hurt to have this woman on his side and on Stephanie's team.

Brigitte smiled, revealing perfect white teeth. "I can do that. Is there anything else you need right now?"

He returned her smile. "Is there any way I can get a sandwich? I missed both breakfast and lunch. I guess I could go out and hunt some food, but I'd rather get going on this." He nodded toward the files on the desk.

Brigitte's smile had disappeared, and a frown now bordered her blue eyes. "I'm so sorry. We just didn't think. I'll have some food here in a few minutes. What would you like?"

He almost felt bad about mentioning the need for food, but he was hungry. "Something easy. A sandwich, pizza, whatever is handy. And could I get some more of that coffee?"

Brigitte nodded. "I'll order the food and bring in the coffee. Please don't hesitate to ask for anything you need."

"Thanks, it's nice to know I have a friend here." He held out his hand to her, and she shook it.

"You do have a friend here." Brigitte released his hand and left the office, only to return within a couple of minutes. She carried a tray with a coffee maker, cups and saucers, a tin of coffee, sugar cubes in a bowl, and a carafe of crème.

"I gather that you're a coffee drinker so I'll just leave this here for you." She set the tray on the credenza and quickly plugged in the pot. "It should make in about three minutes."

"Thanks, that's great. I do drink a lot of coffee." He didn't add that he seemed to drink more when he hadn't been to bed in thirty-six hours.

Brigitte straightened the cups, gave him a brief smile, and left the office.

He began his search through various files and databases. From his experience, he knew it would take a couple of days or maybe even weeks to figure out what was going on in a company as large as the Wellbourne Group.

Thirty minutes later, Brigitte returned with a young man carrying a large tray. "Put it down on the corner of the desk, Charles."

With a nod, Charles slid the tray onto the desk, then left the office.

She lifted the tray's metal cover and revealed a full meal, including rolls and butter. "I hope you like beef medallions in sauce over noodles with vegetables on the side and a salad."

"Wow, this sure beats a sandwich. Thanks, Brigitte." He almost felt faint from the aroma of roast beef filling the office.

"I hope you enjoy it." Brigitte left the office, closing the door behind her.

He dug into his meal like a starving man. It only took ten minutes to clean the plate. He poured a second cup of coffee and sighed in contentment.

He remembered Brigitte's warning that anything in the office might be compromised and took a CD player out of his bag. When he turned it on, the office filled with the sound of jazz. If there were bugs in the office, the music would mask any conversation.

He picked up his cell phone and punched a couple of numbers.

Ben Booker answered on the first ring. "Flint, did you make it all right?"

"I made it fine and have settled into my office." He walked over to the glass wall through which he gazed out over the city. "I need to tell you some things. First, there's a real possibility that Wellbourne has one or more spies. Therefore, I suggest we go into full security mode. I'll only call on this phone and only to your cell and Tony's. We must assume security is compromised in both this office and ours in Colorado. I'll be sending some files later today. I'm going to put them on my laptop and then find a Wi-Fi some place away from the office. I'll send them to the outside e-mail address. I'll be using level-three encryption. You need to go outside our office to download them onto your laptop."

"You think it's as bad as that?"

He thought about how to answer. He had no facts yet, just a hunch. "It won't cost us anything but time and energy to go for full security. And if I'm right, it could save millions."

"Did you talk to Stephanie Wellbourne?"

"Sure did. She gave me an overview of what has been going on and her thoughts about what might be happening."

"What's she like? You think you can work with her?"

He grinned. "Yeah, Ben. I can work with her. She's assigned an assistant to help me out."

"Good. Complete the job and get back as fast as possible. We need you around here." Ben's voice held the gruff friendly tone he often used when he was serious but trying to soften his words.

He looked out over the city. Nothing he wanted more than to complete the job and get back home. "I'll do what I can, but this is a huge corporation. It's going to take a while to acquaint myself with their holdings, much less what someone is doing to subvert the situation."

"I know it'll take you weeks, maybe months. Just do the best you can."

"I will and thanks for your support."

"And get some other kind of music to play to mask your phone calls. I'm tired of that jazz."

As if Flint hadn't heard that a billion times. He grinned at his boss although no one could see it. "If you find a country western CD that works as well, send it over. Meanwhile, look for those files in about two hours. I'll keep my cell phone on so you can reach me."

"Okay. Watch your back and call me in the morning. I want a call at least twice a day, you hear?"

"Sure, I'll keep you informed. Talk to you in the morning." He hung up and looked at his watch. Six o'clock New York time made it four o'clock Colorado time. It would be better to call Allie now before she ate supper and started to get sleepy.

He took off his jacket and tie so he would look his usual self to her. He positioned his personal laptop on the desk so he could look directly into the built-in Web camera. Making sure the computer was connected to the

network, he entered the Internet address to call his computer at home. He then dialed his mother's cell phone.

His mother's voice was tentative. "Hello?"

"Hi, Mom, it's Flint. Is the computer on?"

"Oh, yes, it is."

He smiled. Mom always had the computer on. "Get Allie, please, and open the Web meeting button I put on your desktop."

"All right, just hold on a minute." The sound of the cell phone hitting the desk came through Flint's phone.

Allie's serious face appeared on his computer screen. Then he couldn't help but grin from ear to ear.

"Daddy? You in the computer?"

"Hi, sweetheart. I'm in New York, the big city."

Mom's face appeared on the screen. "Just a minute, let me turn up this volume. There, now go ahead and talk to your daddy, Allie."

For the next several minutes, he talked and laughed with his little girl. At one point, she disappeared and returned with her stuffed bear. He obligingly said hello to Teddy. Finally, he had to end the conversation with a promise to call the next day and read her a story.

Just as he closed the laptop, Stephanie tapped on his door and entered. "Wanted to check on you and see how it's going."

He appreciated her flawless beauty, which was undisturbed after a day at the office. "It's going all right. You understand that it may take days to sort things out?"

"Oh, yes, I understand that. I'm not expecting any results for a while." She sat in one of the leather-covered chairs in front of his desk and crossed her legs. "Actually I wanted to know if you needed any-thing."

He nodded. "I need to talk to you but not here. Is there some-where we can go to get some coffee and talk?" He took a piece of pa-

per and wrote on it telling her that they might be bugged, and he also
needed a Wi-Fi connection outside the office.

Her eyes widened, and her eyebrows shot up. "Yes, I would like
that. Do you want to go now?"

"Whenever you're ready." He stood, tied his tie, and put on his
jacket. He grabbed his bag and stuffed his computer into it.

"Let me get my jacket and handbag, and I'll meet you at the elevator." She hurried from his office.

He watched her leave. He didn't mind spending a few hours with
a beautiful woman. Did she have a steady fellow? Shaking his head at
such foolish thoughts, he headed out of his office.

Chapter Seven

HE AND STEPHANIE MET at the elevator. By the time they arrived at the lobby, he had spotted George outside nosing the Lincoln Town car up to the curb. Perfect timing.

He let her slid into the back seat before he got in beside her.

"I never drive myself in town. And George knows where everything is located."

She told George they needed an Internet café. He nodded and pulled into traffic.

Five minutes later, George stopped in front of an upscale restaurant that advertised Wi-Fi connections at the tables.

He followed her into the restaurant, and the waiter showed them to a booth. He took out his computer and turned it on. In a matter of seconds, he connected to the fast, smooth Internet connection. He plugged a Flash drive into his USB port. After a few taps on computer keys, he connected with the web server that he and Ben used for such purposes. He downloaded all the files he had copied from the Wellbourne Group so that Ben and the others back at Booker and Williams could get busy with the inquiry on their end.

She sat quietly.

He glanced up at her. "It'll take a few minutes for the files to download. I copied several gigabits off your sites this afternoon. I'm sending them to Ben Booker. He'll know what to do. By tomorrow a major audit of your firm's holdings will be in process."

She nodded. "I feel sort of exposed with all my business being sent to an outside firm. It's probably just my paranoia."

"I'm sorry that it's necessary." He noticed the way her dark brown hair flowed like silk over her shoulders. He shook his head to get back on track with the business at hand. "I discussed the situation with my firm, and we decided to treat this as a full-fledged attack on your company. This means we won't trust any avenue of communication attached to your computers and assume there's a possibility that Booker and Williams may also be under attack. If you have spies in your firm, then whoever is behind this will know you've hired us."

She glanced at the waiter as he approached the table. "We might as well order something to eat unless you have other plans."

"I have no plans for supper." He had a meal late in the afternoon, but he could eat again. He glanced at the waiter. "What's really good here?"

"Our lasagna is excellent. Actually, any of our pasta dishes are good." The waiter stood patiently with his pen and pad at the ready.

He glanced at the menu, then up at the waiter. "I'll have the chicken pesto pasta and a house salad with honey mustard dressing and water."

The waiter turned to Her. "And for you?"

She looked up and smiled. "I'll have a duplicate of his order."

The young man responded to the charm of her smile with one of his own. "That's easy. I'll be right back with your drinks."

He watched the waiter hurry toward the kitchen, then turned to find her eyeing him. "What?"

"You seem very different from when I met you on the mountain."

"Different environments call for different clothes and attitudes." He could have said the same thing about her. The sophisticated woman seated in front of him was far more intimidating than the casually dressed fallen hiker

on the mountain had been. "What caused you to contact our firm for this job? There are many other, larger firms right here in New York that could do the same work."

The waiter brought their water and salads.

"Thank you." She took a sip of water then looked back at him. "I wanted someone that wasn't part of the mainstream. I remembered our meeting and researched Booker and Williams. I also checked on other companies they've done work for. You may be small and located in a strange place to do international work, but I believe you are the right one for this job at this time."

He nodded. "We couldn't function without the technological advancements of the last few years. It makes smaller firms like ours viable. Ben Booker and Tony Williams would not have agreed to take on the project if they hadn't known we could do it."

"Are you a partner?"

"No, I'm just an employee." He wished he was an owner. Ben and Tony had offered to let him buy in as a partner, but he could never get the money together. Medical bills did that to a person's bottom line. But she didn't need to know the details.

She poured honey mustard dressing over her salad. "Ben Booker said you came on board just out of grad school. Is this the only company you've worked for?"

"Yes, as a fulltime position. Of course, I've worked on the ranch. One summer I drove eighteen-wheelers for a trucking firm. I also rode snowmobiles patrolling for avalanches on my Christmas breaks from college. I did other work through high school and college."

"And I understand you're a firefighter for your county."

He swallowed a bite of salad. "Only part-time. Of course, most of us do it on a volunteer basis."

"Why do you do it?"

"Someday it may be our ranch that needs help. Most of the callouts are for range and forest fires after lightning storms." He didn't add that there was also something exhilarating about it.

"Oh good, here's our food." She pushed the salad bowl aside to make room for the large plate of chicken pesto layered on top of angel hair pasta. "This smells delicious."

He leaned back as the waiter placed the plate of food in front of him. He folded his hands, bowed his head, and prayed silently. *Lord, bless this food and bless Stephanie in her troubles. Help me to be a Christian example for her. Bless my Allie. In the name of Jesus, Amen.* When he raised his head, he found Her staring at him.

"If it's not rude, what were you doing?"

He shifted in his seat. "I was giving thanks for the food."

"To God?"

He smiled. "Yes, to God." Her question raised more for him. What sort of beliefs did she have that she couldn't tell when someone was praying?

"Do you really believe he's there and even cares to listen?"

He leaned forward. "You don't?"

She shook her head. "No, I've never been spiritual. It's not something I think about."

Surely there must be some sort of belief in her background. "How about your parents?"

"No, they didn't have a religion. I don't know much about it. What about your parents?" She twirled her fork gathering pasta.

He smiled. "My parents are Christians, my grandparents were Christians, and I consider that one of the great blessings of my life." Yes, they definitely came from two different worlds. He'd have to be careful to be an appropriate example to her.

"One day I'd like to meet your parents. I understand they live with you."

"Yes. Another blessing. They help me out a lot." A lot didn't begin to describe the help his parents had provided him in the last four years. How could he ever fully express his gratitude to them?

"With your daughter?"

"My little Allie," he nodded. "Mom especially is there when I can't be. She's practically raised her. Of course, Dad has also been a big help."

"You have a picture of Allie?"

"Sure." He opened the computer again. With a few taps on the keyboard, several pictures of Allie's beaming face appeared.

She laughed. "That's one way to carry around pictures of your daughter."

He grinned and ducked his head. Pride for this fantastic child flushed over him. His flesh and blood, she was a continual miracle in his life. With another click, he set the slideshow in motion. View after view of Allie, his parents, the ranch, and Flint appeared.

"Wow, these are great. I feel I've had an introduction to your family. Can you play it again?"

He shrugged, smiling. "I'll play it all evening."

"She's very special to you." Her voice softened.

"Allie's my life," he said.

"Did you take the photos? They look professional."

"Most of them. Mom likes to get a hold of the camera at times. You'll see me with a camera often. It's sort of a hobby."

The waiter returned to their booth. "Everything all right here? Either of you care for dessert?"

She shook her head. "Not for me. The chicken pesto pasta was excellent. You Flint?"

He spread his hands out palm down. "Not for me. I am officially full."

"Put the bill on this." She handed the waiter a credit card. She turned to him "The tab is on the company since we've been conducting business. Tomorrow Brigitte should have a company business credit card for you. It will have a limit of a hundred thousand. Ben Booker was very insistent that you fly back to Colorado to consult every two weeks. I'm not sure why he wants you back so often, but use the credit card for all your expenses. I expect you to fly first class as it's more restful. Also, rent a car if you need, although George will be available whenever you need him."

"Thanks, I'll be sure and keep a record of expenditures." Warm gratitude filled him for the thoughtfulness of his boss and friend Ben Booker, for making it possible for him to see Allie so often.

She tried to hide a yawn behind her hand. "You ready to go?"

He closed the computer and slipped it back into his bag. "Yes, it's been a long two days."

She had her cell phone to her ear. "Hi, George. Outside in five minutes?" She dropped her phone into her purse. "George will drop me off, and then he can take you on to where you're staying."

"Thanks." He followed her out to the sidewalk. Moments later George drove the car alongside the parked cars on the street.

Flint quickly opened the door to the back seat and then slid in after her.

Forty-five minutes after dropping her off at her apartment, George stopped the car in front of a restored brownstone along a street of many such row houses. The old trees between the sidewalk and street, and the architecture of the homes indicated the age of the neighborhood. He took his backpack and message bag from George. "You sure it's not a problem to leave my other bags in the trunk?" Until he knew where he would be staying, it would help to leave them in a secure place.

"They'll be fine for a day or so. What time should I pick you up in the morning?"

"I'd like to get into the office early. Six o'clock too early?"

"I'll be here." George closed the trunk. "Good night, sir."

He extended his hand. "Good night and thanks for your great service this evening."

George shook his hand. "You're welcome. I do my best."

Flint climbed the steps to the brownstone and rang the doorbell. He heard the sound of footsteps heading toward the door.

When it opened, an older balding man stood just inside. "Flint? I'm Richard Anderson. Come on in, we've been waiting for you."

AT SIX O'CLOCK THE next morning, by the light of the street-light, George helped him carry his bags up the steps into the brown-stone.

"Just put them down here, and I'll carry them up to the bedroom my friends have offered me." He reached to grab one of his suitcases, but George shook his head.

"You lead the way, and we'll take them on up." George stood waiting holding the bags.

He shook his head. "All right, but its two floors up." He started climbing up the two flights to the guest bedroom that was his free of any rent, as long as he needed a place in New York. Richard and Nancy Anderson were proving to be as wonderful a Christian couple as Dave, the preacher back home had promised. He thanked God for the blessing of free housing for the stay in New York. It would help put him that much closer to his goal of funds for Allie's heart.

Chapter Eight

SHE SAT BACK AND CLOSED her eyes as George drove her back to the office after dropping Flint off at the airport. What was the matter with her? She had come very close to asking him if she could go with him. How silly was that? Something about the man made her feel safe. The two weeks since he arrived had passed so quickly.

Sighing, she rearranged her legs in the spacious back seat of the Lincoln, which only moments before had seemed full with Flint's tall, muscular body next to her. She spoke to George. "Take me to my apartment, please."

She pulled her cell phone out of her purse. Punching the speed dial, she waited. "Brigitte, its Stephanie. I've decided not to come back to the office."

Brigitte's voice came through the phone. "Is something wrong?"

"No, nothing is wrong. I just don't feel like coming back. Is anything pressing?"

"No. It's Friday afternoon, and the place is emptying fast. Of course, the European Group is asleep, so all is quiet."

She nodded. "I'm in the mood for an evening off. You have any plans?"

Brigitte's laugh came through gently. "No, I only turned down four or five guys waiting in line to take me out to dinner. But none of them were interesting enough."

"Then come on over. We'll grill steaks, have a salad, and watch an old movie. I'll get the tissues out."

THE DOOR ATTENDANT had rung up to announce that Brigitte was on her way. She opened the door just as the elevator doors parted.

Brigitte carried a large shopping bag and tugged a carry-on bag on wheels behind her. "I stopped at Eli's and picked up some goodies and a couple of movies."

"Great. I have the grill heating and the steaks marinating." She led the way through the entrance gallery and large living room to the spacious kitchen.

Brigitte left her carry-on bag and purse by the small elevator that rose to the living quarters above. "What can I do to advance the serving of dinner? I'm starving. I was going to order for myself when I sent out for Flint's lunch, but he never asked me to order him anything. So we both missed lunch."

She shook her head. "And I'm not sure the flight he's on to Denver will serve a meal or just a snack. It bothers me that he has obviously lost weight since being here." She pointed to baby spinach and tomatoes on the counter. "You make our salads, and I'll start the steaks."

Brigitte pulled an apron from a drawer and covered her white silk blouse and navy blue slacks. She had her blond hair up in a ponytail.

Twenty minutes later, She put a steak on a china plate for each of them. "Let's eat in here." She carried the plates to the table and finished setting out napkins and silverware.

"Sure, I love the view out over Central Park and beyond from your kitchen. It's like glittering jewels with the darkness and all the lights."

She grinned. "Brigitte, do you realize how many of your sayings have to do with jewelry?"

"Well, I love pretty things, especially gemstones." Brigitte set the salads and a couple of baked potatoes on the table.

She sat and placed her napkin in her lap. She had the sense of waiting for something that was missing.

Brigitte sat across from her. "What's the matter? You look like you're listening for something."

She shook her head. "It is the oddest thing. For the last two weeks, I've eaten dinner with Flint almost every night so we could talk outside the office. I guess I was waiting for the blessing he always says before the meal. Never in all my life have I sat at a meal that was started by prayer, and here in two weeks I've come to expect it."

Brigitte sliced open a baked potato and slathered it with sour cream and butter. "He bows his head and closes his eyes before he starts to eat at his desk, too. I assume he's praying then. He must be very spiritual."

She cut into her steak. "Yes, he seems to be although he hasn't done any preaching. He knows I don't believe in God as he does. But he did tell me that he comes from a religious family. Maybe that's why he seems so nice compared to most men I meet."

Brigitte frowned. "Maybe that's why we're sitting here without a fellow on a Friday evening. We're looking for something beyond the usual men we meet."

She nodded. Men asked her out, but she seldom dated anymore. Brigitte dated much more often, but no steady guy. What was the problem? She had assumed through her early twenties that she would be married by now. Was she just not meeting the right men?

After they ate, they put the dishes in the dishwasher, and then got comfortable on the living room couches. She pushed the button to open the wooden panel that revealed the fifty-inch television. They voted to watch an old movie, *An Affair to Remember*.

Her thoughts wandered as the scenes played out with Cary Grant and Deborah Kerr. Flint should be getting into his office soon.

Would he drive on to his ranch after the meeting? How would he get there? Would his father drive in and pick him up? Would his little girl wake up to greet him?

"Stephanie." Brigitte's voice finally penetrated. "Yes?"

"The movie is over. Where were you?" Brigitte leaned back on the plush cushions.

She stretched and yawned. "I was wondering whether Flint had made it to his firm's offices. It's two hours earlier there, so they're still working."

Brigitte nodded. "It's going to be a long day for him. He got into the office this morning at six. I don't know how he does it." She looked around. "Can we talk here?" She asked in a whisper.

Rubbing her temple, She didn't answer at once. Could they talk in her own apartment? Surely, no one would bug her private residence. But then she hadn't anticipated that someone might try to take over her company. "Let's watch this other movie." She put her finger to her lips and then to her ear, hoping Brigitte would understand.

"Great, I'd love to watch South Pacific again." Brigitte stood and took the disk. She loaded it into the DVD player. Soon loud music filled the apartment. Brigitte came back and sat next to her on the couch.

She pushed back her hair. "I think this may be silly, but Flint seems to take it seriously." She kept her voice quiet under the noise of the movie.

"I don't think you can be too careful. Just the little he shared with us indicates a serious problem."

"I know. I just don't like it."

"One of the smartest things you've done lately was to hire Flint and his firm. Like that meeting he's in right now, all those people analyzing what's going on and hopefully no one in our group knowing about it. Almost like Flint is your secret weapon."

She shrugged. "It was an impulse really. I can't take credit for actually realizing how useful he would be."

"Who do you think is behind the takeover, if that's what's happening?"

"I'm not sure, but I do suspect Thor Swenson is in the middle of it. For it to go very far, someone from here in New York must be involved too. I hate to think of Dan, Granfield, or someone else maneuvering behind my back." She sighed. "It's times like this I wish my father were still alive. He would relish such a fight."

Brigitte leaned forward. "And you don't? That surprises me."

"Maybe I'm a little burnt out. When Father died, and I had to take over, it was like an adventure. Find out where the money and the power were, and go after it. But now, I really don't care. What's the point? So we figure all this out, and I fire a bunch of people and make another bunch mad at me. For what? More money? I can't spend all the money I'm making now."

Brigitte nodded. "I've been thinking a lot about my life, too. Is it our age? Are we having a middle-age crisis?"

She laughed. "I hope not. I'm only twenty-nine years old. Surely this isn't middle age."

"I find myself looking wistfully at couples on the street or restaurants. Maybe what we need is to find a man and get married." Brigitte sighed. "But it seems like all the good guys are either taken or not interested."

She glanced at her friend. "Are you referring to Flint? You two have spent a lot of time together these last two weeks. Are you interested in him?"

Brigitte gazed back intently. "I'll be honest with you. I think I could be. He has been nothing but nice. Such a gentleman, he compliments my clothes, thanks me for every little thing I do for him, teases, but very gently. Yes, I could fall for him. However, I have no idea what he's thinking. For sure, he hasn't asked me out. With the hours he works, he doesn't have time for a personal life." Brigitte looked down at the Van Cleef & Arpel bracelet Stephanie had given her on her birthday. "And you? Are you interested in him?"

She raised her eyebrows at the question. Was she interested in Flint? She certainly enjoyed his company. "He's very nice, but like you, he has never made any attempts to make it more personal. Maybe he has a girl back in Colorado."

"That's always a possibility. Well, at least he'll be around for several more months. I really enjoy him being in the office."

She rubbed her temple again. The loud music was giving her a headache. "What dessert did you bring? Let's eat some and then go on to bed. Since you brought your bag, I assume you're staying over. I'm glad because I don't want you going home this late in the evening. It's not safe."

"My feelings exactly. Besides, by staying here you motivate me to get up and out on a Saturday morning. I stopped for some raspberry and pecan cheesecake and apple Danish for our breakfast. That suit you?" Brigitte grinned.

"Considering that's my favorite cheesecake it will suit me just fine. Of course, I'll have to hit the gym first thing in the morning." She patted her flat stomach.

Brigitte rubbed hers also. "And I'll be right behind you on the treadmill."

She stood and walked to the DVD player to stop the movie. The sudden cessation of noise in the apartment revealed a vague, distant roar of the city traffic. She led the way into the kitchen.

As she watched Brigitte cut the cheesecake, she wondered if maybe both of them were more interested in Flint than they wanted to admit to each other. Brigitte's voice had sounded more than a little wistful. Would she be willing to stand back for Brigitte to have more of an opportunity with Flint? That was something to consider.

SHE WOKE ON SATURDAY morning wondering what Flint was doing. She felt vaguely uneasy and wasn't sure why. After she showered, she headed downstairs to find coffee.

Brigitte sat at the kitchen table drinking a cup of tea. "Morning, did you sleep well?"

"I'm not sure. Let me get a cup of coffee, and I'll let you know." She prepared the coffee maker. While the coffee brewed, she called the spa. She booked a One-Hour Body Massage and a Classic European Facial each for herself and Brigitte. Before ending the call, she turned to Brigitte. "You want a manicure and pedicure?"

"Just a manicure."

She finished the call. "We need to be there by ten o'clock. I'm looking forward to the massage. Maybe it will help me relax. But first, let's head to the gym, and later this afternoon let's stop by Christi Harris MakeUp."

Brigitte swallowed the last of her tea. "Great, I'll go get ready."

Putting the dishes in the dishwasher, She wondered what Flint would do on a Saturday back home in Colorado. Why did this man she barely knew fill so much of her thinking?

Chapter Nine

AFTER THE LONG FLIGHT from New York to Denver and then the airport shuttle to the office in Cedar Ridge, exhaustion nibbled away his ability to concentrate. Nevertheless, concentrate he must. As the meeting ran down, they studied pages of printouts detailing the Wellbourne Group's financial records and stock movements. Here was hard evidence that someone, or some group of people, were rearranging the holdings. And not to her advantage.

As Ben and Tony discussed what the data revealed, he agreed with their assessment. The problem now became what to recommend to her.

Ben removed his glasses and rubbed his nose. "I don't think she can save the whole company. She doesn't own enough shares to dictate to the other shareholders. Her best bet might be to get rid of her European stock and to consolidate her American holdings. She would end up with a smaller company, but it might secure it from a hostile takeover."

Tony shifted his bulk in the chair he had occupied for three hours. "I concur. Cut and burn. And do it quickly before whoever is behind this gets wise." He glanced at Flint. "How capable is she of doing that? Is she emotionally invested in keeping all her father's holdings together?"

He sighed and threw his pen onto the pad in front of him. "She's capable, but you're really asking is she tough enough. And the answer is, I don't know." He leaned on his elbows with his chin resting on his folded hands. If he closed his eyes, he could easily fall asleep. "The question is important. How emotionally invested is she? That makes a big difference. Will she make decisions based on logic and reality, or based on her feelings about the company? It's easy for us to say she should do such and such. It's not our company."

Ben stood and headed for the coffee maker. "Blast it, we're out of coffee." Returning to the conference table, he sat in his chair. "All we can do is give Stephanie Wellbourne our best advice, and let her take it from there. Flint, you take the weekend off and go see Allie. We'll keep working and see what we can draw up regarding strategy."

He raised his arms high above his head to stretch and yawned. "Sounds good to me. Dad should be here shortly to drive me to the ranch."

Tony slapped Flint's shoulder. "If you have any brilliant ideas, give us a call this weekend. We can use all the help we can get. I think we've figured out what has to be done. If we can convince Stephanie Wellbourne, we'll earn our money. It's just too bad it isn't what she wants to hear."

"Yeah, and I guess you're planning for me to tell her." He put his hands out palm up in surrender.

Ben nodded. "You're our man in New York. You get the fun part of the job."

They all flinched as the buzzer from the front door sounded.

He stood and put on his sports jacket. "That'll be Dad. I asked him to be here by ten p.m. I'll leave you fellows to get on with it. Call me if you have to. Otherwise, I'll see you early Monday morning."

Ben stood and extended his hand. "Thanks for the job you're doing, especially under the circumstances. It's way beyond what we have a right to expect."

He shook hands with Ben and then with Tony. They were right. He had done good work in the last two weeks. What they didn't know was just how tired he was.

He left the building, greeted his dad, and climbed into the passenger seat of his truck. "You mind driving? I'm bushed."

"I don't mind, son. You go on to sleep if you want. I'll get us home." Dad started the truck, and soon they were on the dark highway heading out of town.

He closed his eyes meaning to rest for only a couple of minutes.

"SON, WAKE UP, WE'RE home." Dad shook his arm.

Realizing the truck was parked in the shed, he struggled up from his slumped position. "Why didn't you wake me? I could have driven part way."

"I don't think so, not as hard as you were sleeping. My, but you must be tired. Come on, your mother's waiting up to see you." Dad grabbed Flint's backpack and headed toward the house.

He followed carrying his messenger bag with his computer. He breathed deeply of the pine scent in the cold mountain air, which had a hint of frost. Doves cooed in the distance. How he had missed his home.

After greeting Mom, he went to Allie's bedroom. Slowly opening the door so as not to wake her, he knelt by the side of her bed and watched her sleep. Brigitte had sent a little, stuffed bear for him to give Allie. As he laid it alongside her, the sleeping child murmured in her sleep and wrapped her arms around it.

He gently pushed Allie's dark brown curls back from her face. "Sleep well, little bunny. Daddy's home. Love you." He watched for several more minutes, then went down the hall to his bedroom. Too tired to shower, he pulled his clothes off and tumbled into bed. If it weren't for Allie's heart, he would never get back on that plane come Monday morning.

HE BRUSHED THE FLY away from his nose, but it came back. He swatted at it again and heard a giggle. Opening one eye, he looked at the little grinning face behind the feather brushing his nose. "What do you think you're doing?" he said in a gruff voice as he reached out and tickled her under the chin. Her laughter was his reward.

"It's time to get up and play, Daddy. You've been asleep too long. Come on, get up." She grabbed the sheet and pulled.

He caught it before she could get too far. "Go away, little girl. I want to sleep."

She shook her head, which set her curls bouncing. "No, Daddy, you got to get up."

Mom came into his bedroom. "Morning, son."

He stretched and yawned. "Morning. What time is it?"

"It's almost eight. Allie was anxious to see you." She picked up the little girl—who was dressed in overalls, long-sleeve red shirt, and cowboy boots— and put her on the bed beside him. "Give your daddy a big hug and kiss. Then we'll go get his breakfast ready while he showers and gets dressed."

Allie giggled. "You ready, Daddy? It's going to be a very big hug."

He opened his arms. "I'm ready for the biggest hug ever."

Allie threw herself onto his chest and wrapped her arms tightly around his neck. She squeezed as hard as she could.

He hugged her back and rubbed his unshaven chin on her neck, which always made her squeal with laughter.

"All right you two, enough of that. Time to go get some breakfast going." Mom scooped Allie up and carried her out over her protests.

He lay in the bed staring out the window at the mountains. It felt good to be home. Allie seemed all right. Maybe his being gone hadn't caused any harm. Deciding not to waste more of the day, he climbed out of bed and headed for a hot shower.

The day went by too fast. He focused on whatever his daughter wanted. It was a relief after the last two weeks' hard mental work.

Even as he pulled Allie in the wagon, the corner of his mind worried with Wellbourne's problems in New York. What did She do over the weekend? He missed knowing she was just down the hall in a nearby office.

After supper, he carried Allie to her room and read to her. She clutched the soft brown stuffed bear that Brigitte had sent to her.

"You have a new friend?" He asked as he pulled the covers up to her shoulders.

She held up the bear for him to see. "He came last night, all by himself. Can I keep him?"

"Sure, sweetheart. Actually, he flew on the airplane with me. A pretty blonde haired lady named Brigitte sent him to live with you."

"Okay, he can stay. Is he a big New York bear?" She patted the stuffed bear's plush fur.

"Yes, he's a big New York bear. Goodnight, little bunny." He kissed her soft cheek and left the door open a crack.

Once downstairs he chose the recliner since Mom and Dad side by side on the couch.

"Is Allie asleep yet?" Mom asked.

"She will be in a few minutes. I'm afraid I tired her out with all the playing today." He stretched out and tilted the recliner back.

She smiled. "Don't worry. She can catch up on her rest after you leave. That is if you must go back?"

He adjusted a small pillow behind his head. "I'm afraid so. We made a lot of progress in the last two weeks, but there's more to do if we are going to help Stephanie Wellbourne save her company."

Dad put his arm around the shoulder of his wife and pulled her close. "Tell us about New York. Is it as wild and wooly as they say?"

He smiled at Dad's show of affection and marveled that after forty-five years they still could act like a couple just dating.

For the next hour, he described his life in New York, mostly about Richard and Nancy Anderson and the people he had met at church the two Sundays he had been there.

His folks told him news about Allie, the ranch, and the rest of his family. It surprised him how much could happen in one family in just a couple of weeks.

"It doesn't seem like Allie has gained any weight since I left. In fact, she feels a bit lighter." He had to say it.

Mom nodded. "Yes, she's lost a couple of pounds. I don't know if it's your being gone or what, but she won't eat much. She has another visit to Children's Hospital in a couple of weeks. Are you planning on being here?"

He ran his fingers through his hair. "What day of the week is the appointment?"

Dad spoke up. "It's on Monday, November tenth."

He nodded. "I'll make a point to be here. You can count on it. And then two weeks later I'll be back for Thanksgiving."

"Good. We're having a quiet Thanksgiving. But Christmas will be fun. All the kids are coming." Mary smiled at Tom. "Your dad's going to wait to decorate the outside of the house until all the boys get here."

Dad winked at him. "She's afraid I'll fall off the roof if I try to put the Christmas lights up alone."

"I wouldn't want you to bother with decorating if it wasn't for Allie," Flint said.

Mom nodded. "For Allie especially, and for all the grandchildren. They're the reason we put up the decorations these days."

"Dad, why don't we put up the Christmas lights on Thanksgiving? And Mom, I want pumpkin pie for Thanksgiving and pecan pie for Christmas. And I mean a whole pie, just for me. I'm putting my order in early."

"But not as early as your brother Samuel. He wrote the other day with an order for lemon meringue pie for Christmas. And your sister wants a fresh apple cake. I better start my baking next week." Mom looked pleased at the requests for her special desserts. "By the way, did you buy that Steiff Teddy bear for Allie?"

He raised his eyebrows. "The what?"

Mom chuckled. "That new bear Allie's got, son. It's a Steiff classic teddy bear from Germany. It sells for at least two hundred dollars."

He shook his head. "No, you're kidding. For a stuffed bear?"

"I am not kidding. I've seen enough of them on the web to recognize it, and then I saw the button in its ear. It's a Steiff all right." Mom looked first at him and then at his dad, in that way she did that ended arguments.

"Brigitte, my assistant in New York, sent it to her. I thought it was a nice gesture and thanked her. I had no idea it was so expensive. Should we let Allie sleep with it?"

Mom nodded. "Let the child enjoy it. She won't hurt it."

He knew that wasn't true. How about the Barbie Allie had taken apart? But he also knew what his mother was really saying. Allie might not have that much more time so let her have her toys.

"Tell Brigitte we appreciate her kindness. She sounds like a sweet lady."

"She is, Mom, and she's taking good care of me. I don't even have to leave my office for lunch. She orders in full gourmet meals." He knew his mother would appreciate that sort of detail. Sure enough, she began to ask one question after another about this Brigitte woman.

In self-defense, he stood up and retrieved his computer. "I have something to show you." He began a slideshow of photos he had taken in the last two weeks. He saw his mother raise her eyebrows at both Brigitte and Stephanie's pictures. Surprisingly, she didn't ask more questions after seeing their photos as if their sheer beauty had hushed her.

He didn't know what to think, but he was glad not to answer more questions. He was attracted to her, and if he let himself, he could spend way too much time thinking about her. She was the first woman to invade his thoughts like this since Valerie. But nothing would ever come of it. Too many differences. They were each caught in their different worlds.

He soon went to bed and fell asleep alternately thinking about two dark-haired beauties—Allie and Stephanie.

Chapter Ten

"WAKE UP SON."

He swam out of a sound sleep to find Dad leaning over the bed. He woke instantly. "Allie?"

"No, the fire brigade. There's a callout. If you don't respond, no one will say anything. But knowing you, I thought I better tell you before heading out." Dad already wore his orange jumpsuit. "It's Ted Bonner's place. Lightning on that side of the mountain probably sparked some leaves or a pine tree."

"Give me ten minutes, and I'll be ready to go." He climbed out of bed and vigorously rubbed his head to get more alert. Just short of one in the morning and ink black dark outside.

"All right, I'll wait for you. Your mother is preparing sandwiches and a couple of thermoses. I'll get the truck ready to go." Dad hurried away.

He opened his bedroom closet and took out his old orange jumpsuit, helmet, gloves, and heavy boots, all treated with fire retardant. First, he put on the ultra-light microfiber long underwear and undershirt that his mom had ordered over the Internet. It absorbed sweat and kept the skin dry. She had also ordered a headband and thin microfiber gloves to wear inside his heavier ones. Over the underwear, he pulled on jeans and a long-sleeve cotton shirt. Last, he climbed into the orange jumpsuit and heavy boots scuffed from other firefights. The jumpsuit was a hand-me-down from his dad, and he wasn't sure how fire resistant it was. He had meant to purchase a new one but kept putting it off.

Carrying his helmet with its attached light and the two pairs of gloves, he walked as softly as he could into Allie's room. She was sleeping peacefully with the new teddy bear clutched in her arms. Bending over her sleeping form, he kissed her little soft cheek. *Lord, watch over my Allie. Let me come back to her.*

HE DROVE AS FAST AS the county road would allow. "Which way is best to get there?" The country roads were dark except for the shine of the headlights.

Dad leaned forward in the passenger seat peering into the midnight sky for the first glimpse of the fire. "Take this road east to the county road leading north past Perkins' store. That should put us around the mountain and straight into Ted Bonner's place. Thirty minutes at the most."

"Too bad we can't go the way the crow flies straight over the mountain. It's only about fifteen miles north, instead of thirty." More than once, he had wished for a helicopter.

He kept his eyes on the road. When he was within a couple of miles of the Bonner place, he glanced to his left. "There, you see it?" An unnatural orange light glowed in the distance.

Dad nodded. "Yeah, it looks to be moving away from us, maybe a couple of miles wide. I hope enough men respond to the callout to get it out quickly."

As he drove to the Bonner's ranch house, his team captain, Hank Johnson, hurried up in the light from the headlights.

"Hey, Flint, I thought you were off working in New York. Glad you and Tom could make it. If you don't mind, leave your truck here and catch a ride with Darwin. His truck has a higher axle and can make it up the old timber road. You all go up about three miles and start digging, making a fire line along the creek. We got another crew working on the other side. Maybe we can stop this fire tonight." He banged on the hood of the truck and dashed toward another vehicle that had just arrived.

"You ready, Dad?" He looked at his father in the glow of the overhead light in the truck.

"I'm ready. Let's get that fire out."

They gathered their gear and located Darwin, the local postal carrier. His old flatbed truck with the high sides had five men standing in the back already. All of the men were neighbors or men from town.

"Hey, Flint, Tom."

"Howdy, boys." Tom accepted a hand up from one of the men.

Flint nodded and concentrated on getting into the truck with his gear. Darwin started the noisy diesel truck and careened up a winding road if it could be called that. Fifteen minutes later, they stopped beside a creek and climbed out of the truck.

As the oldest man there, Tom Tucker took charge. "Bill, pick a couple of fellows and start from here. Darwin, you take two others and work in the middle. Flint and I will hike down to where the creek branches into two streams and work our way back. Keep an eye on the wind and if it gets away from you, cross the creek and find a place to ride it out. Let's go men."

The three groups divided shovels, axes, and chainsaws between them. He grabbed the chainsaw before his father could get to it and put it up on his shoulder. He also took an ax. "Dad, take a shovel for me, please."

"All right, we got everything?" His father checked their belts to make sure they had their breathing masks and water bottles securely fastened. "Let's go."

He set out at a fast pace down the side of the creek with the light from his helmet leading the way. They needed to make it down about a mile to where the creek branched into two smaller streams. He could hear Dad's boots crunching on the grass that grew along the bank. The smell of acrid smoke drifted through the night. They didn't waste their breath on talk.

The smoke-laden air decreased visibility by the minute, and as they reached where the creek branched, the burn line approached faster than he anticipated. The loud whoosh of the ponderosa pines bursting into flames surrounded him.

He beat out the little river of flame that crept toward the creek. Dad handled the chainsaw to cut down the trees and smaller shrubs along the creek itself. He could barely hear the buzz of chainsaws from the other two groups of firefighters. Stopping the conflagration moving toward them was imperative. If it jumped the creek, it had a straight shot across the pastureland all the way to the road. Ken Bonner would lose all of his winter pastures.

Finding a rhythm, he shoveled dry dirt onto the little flames systematically devouring the grass. He wore his breathing mask, as the air was dense with pungent smoke. Scooping up a shovel of dirt, he dumped it over his boot as he was standing in fire.

After a couple of hours, an area of brush and grass suddenly blazed in front of him. He had to back off. Moving toward the creek, he searched through the hazy darkness for his father. The fire lit the blackness just enough to see vague shapes. His helmet light wasn't much use in the smoke. Flint heard the chainsaw to his left. Through the haze, he could barely make out Dad cutting down a medium-sized tree.

He pulled the air mask away from his face and yelled. "Get back to the creek. It's getting away from us."

Dad looked up and then at the fire behind Flint. He nodded. Slinging the chainsaw over his shoulder, he started for the creek.

He spotted Dad's shovel in the beam of his helmet light, picked it up, and headed after him. The wind stirred, urging the fire closer and closer.

Dad waded across the two-foot deep creek managing to keep the chainsaw dry. He turned and looked back at him and started yelling. "Run, Flint!"

He picked up his pace until he was running. All of a sudden, he heard the familiar whoosh of a pine tree igniting close by. Too close. Without thinking, he raised his left arm to protect his face. Intense heat caught the back of his left arm and shoulder. He reached the creek and fell flat into the water, hearing the sizzle of flames being extinguished. Dad's hand pulled him toward the shore. The searing pain settled across the back of his left arm and shoulder.

"You all right, son?" Dad sat on the creek bank holding his head out of the water.

"Yeah, Dad. Just a little singed. Not sure how bad." He lay for a minute coughing, getting his breath. "The wind? What's it doing?"

"It died down as fast as it came up. The fire is burning back on itself. We stopped it for now along the creek. We'll need to do some cleanup and make sure it's all out." Dad helped him stand and then turned the flashlight on his arm. "You've got some burns along that arm and shoulder. We should have bought you a new jumpsuit long time ago. This one is no good. If you had been wearing one like mine you wouldn't have burned. Let's get back to the truck. You need some first aid."

"I'm all right, Dad. I can help with the cleanup." He tried to shrug off the mounting pain.

"Come on, follow me." Dad started up the creek.

He had never disobeyed his father and didn't intend to start. The blue-gray light of the dawn peeked over the mountain. Tired to his core, he staggered up the embankment after Dad.

They walked a short distance when they met another crew of men materializing out of the dark as they pounded down alongside the bank of the creek.

John Abrams, the high school football coach, was barely recognizable in his firefighter gear. "Tom, what's the status?"

"Fire's contained, but we didn't get any clean up done. Flint's got a burn, and we need to head back." Dad paused. Taking the cap off his water bottle, he drew a long drink.

"Then you keep going. We got this." John waved the crew of six men forward, and they tromped past.

Signs of daylight trickled into the sky as he, and his dad reached the truck. Parked alongside the grass track that passed for a road were trucks, jeeps, and cars.

Hank Johnson met them. "What's the matter?"

"Flint has a burn. We need first aid." Tom set the chainsaw on the truck bed.

Hank ambled over. "Let me take a look."

He turned so Hank could see the back of his left arm where the pain seemed to be localized. "I can't see it. Don't know if it's anything to worry about or not."

Hank took a look and hollered over his shoulder. "Doc Gonzales."

"Here." A short, olive-skinned man came hurrying up. "What have you got?"

He turned his body so the doctor could see his back and arm. "What do you think, Doc? I can tell you it's hurting pretty good."

The doctor turned on his helmet flashlight and examined the back of the left arm and shoulder. "Well, Flint, you've got a second degree and possibly some third-degree burns. Let me put a dry sterile bandage on it until you get to the hospital."

He twisted his neck trying to see the burn. "You think I need to go to the hospital? Can't you just bandage it?"

"You go to the hospital and get this treated. You've already got blisters. If you mess around and it gets infected, it won't be good."

Doctor Gonzales turned to Dad. "I assume you'll drive him to the hospital. Watch that he doesn't go into shock."

"No problem. We'll be at the hospital within the hour."

He sighed. The decision had been taken from him. He really didn't mind going to the hospital as long as he didn't have to stay there. They would have something for the intense pain that was rising by the second.

The next couple of hours were definitely no fun as they traveled to Ted Bonner's place in the back of a pickup. From there, his father drove ninety miles an hour to the hospital at Cedar Ridge. They could have waited for the ambulance, but Dad said he could get him to the hospital faster than the ambulance.

Not long after walking into the hospital emergency unit, he lay in a bed with a doctor tending his arm and shoulder, feeling no pain which was the miracle of morphine.

"How bad is it, Doc?" Dad asked.

"It's not bad at all compared to what it could have been. It is only blistered. It'll take time. If you keep it clean and let it heal, you might not have any scars. Of course, I'm not saying it's not painful, because it is. Any burn is painful. We'll keep you for observation for a day or so. In a week or so you should be right as can be."

"What if I don't stay in the hospital and instead fly back to my job in New York tomorrow?" He asked.

"Well, if you see a doctor there immediately, you'll probably be all right. But, and this is a major but, the pain will be intense. Traveling will make it worse. I can give you a prescription for pain medication, but absolutely no driving." The doctor finished his work, put a sling around his neck, and gently rested his arm in it.

Dad's face creased with worry. "Son, don't you think you should stay in the hospital for a couple of days?"

"I need to be with Allie today, and tomorrow I have to get back to work. I need to finish that job so I can be paid as soon as possible.

A little pain will be worth it." His voice sounded a little groggy as it echoed in his head. He felt shivery and just wanted to get to his bed and lie down.

Dad took care of the hospital dismissal. After stopping by a pharmacy to fill the prescription for the pain medicine, they drove to the ranch arriving before noon.

He climbed out of the truck with care as the first pain shot was definitely wearing off.

Mom took one look at his face and guided him to his bedroom without a word. Dad helped him out of his clothes and into pajama bottoms. He didn't bother with the top, as the bandage was around most of his chest.

Dad peered closely at his face. "You need more pain medicine?"

"Yeah, I need it bad." Burns always hurt worse than any other kind of injury. He'd had several minor burns from other firefights. It was just one of the rewards for volunteering since he was sixteen.

His father gave him a couple of pills and a glass of water.

He swallowed the pills down. He didn't want to sleep the rest of the day. What kind of day could he have with Allie now?

"Mom, where's Allie?" He had expected her to come running before he could get to bed.

"She's taking a nap. I fed her early, and she was tuckered out, so I rocked her to sleep."

"Is she all right?" He couldn't keep the anxiety from his voice.

"She's tired from yesterday. Anything extra tires her out these days, but she needed the time with you two playing. Don't worry about it. She'll be in here later trying to figure out what happened, so you better come up with a good story." Mom kissed his forehead and then stood, smoothing his hair back.

One of his earliest memories was this gesture from Mom. As always, it was comforting. He felt the medicine start to take effect. The pain from his arm receded, and he soon relaxed into sleep.

Chapter Eleven

HE SHIFTED HIS INJURED arm onto the armrest, thankful that She had insisted on his flying first class. In the meeting with Ben and Tony, before he left on Monday morning, they finalized the strategy to present to Stephanie. Then Dad drove him to the Denver International Airport to catch the flight to New York. He exhaled deeply, letting go of tension in his shoulders. The plane was due to land at one twenty. Getting on the ground would be a relief.

After he disembarked, he made his way toward his meeting point with George who stood ready to assist him as he stepped off the escalator onto the main floor of the terminal.

Reaching for his backpack and messenger bag, George asked. "Problem, sir?"

He smiled at the calm question. "You might say so. Got a little injury fighting a forest fire this weekend." He added the last part when he noticed concern overtake George's face. "Also, on the way to the office, I'd like to stop at this address if that's possible. If not, I could take a cab."

George glanced at the address Flint handed to him. "That's between here and the office. Please follow me. The car is just over here."

It only took forty-five minutes to weave through the traffic and reach the fire station. He opened the door to climb out. "I shouldn't be too long. You mind waiting?"

George unfolded his New York Times. "No problem, sir. I'll just read."

He approached the side entrance next to the massive garage doors blocking the fire trucks from view. He pushed the doorbell, and within minutes, the smaller door opened.

A tall, muscular man in black sweatpants and a white T-shirt stood in the doorway. "What can I do you for?" His Bronx accent coated every syllable.

"I'm looking for Alberto Romero. Tell him Flint Tucker needs to speak with him." He cradled his left arm in its sling while the man looked him over.

"Wait a minute." He closed the door.

Shortly, the door opened again. A short, broad and muscular man stood in the doorway. "Flint, come on in. What are you doing here?" Alberto's black hair and dark eyes spoke of his southern Italian heritage. "What's the matter with your arm?"

He grinned, once again thankful that God had arranged their growing friendship through the church. Had he only known Alberto for two weeks? "That's why I stopped by. I remembered your fire station number but didn't have a phone number to call you."

"Well, come into the ready room and meet the guys." Alberto led the way past the huge fire truck to a large room at the back. It was a combination kitchen and living room. Six men sat sprawled on semi-circle couches in front of a large screen television watching a baseball game.

"Hey, you guys, meet my friend Flint Tucker from Colorado. I'll let the guys introduce themselves." Tony motioned him to sit in a comfortable chair.

He greeted the men. "I didn't have Alberto's cell number, but I do need some help. The night before last I got a burn while fighting a fire in the mountains back home. The only way the doctor would release me to fly back here to work was if I saw a doctor today. I figured you might help me get an appointment. I could go to an emergency room at a hospital, but I really don't want to do that."

Tomas—the man who had opened the door initially—said, "Hey, you thought right. We can get you in to see the doctor we use for minor burns. Emmanuel, go get Doc's number."

A younger man jumped up. "Sure, always glad to help a fellow firefighter. I want to hear about the fire, so wait until I get the number before you tell us what happened."

He grinned at the young man. He hadn't realized they would want details.

Alberto handed him a cup of coffee. "You look a little peaked. I noticed you weren't at church yesterday. Richard said you had flown home for the weekend to see your daughter. How is she?"

He always had a problem knowing how to answer such a question. Did he say she's dying? People didn't want to hear that. "She's doing about the same. I enjoyed being with her for a couple of days."

"You mind telling the guys about her condition?"

He looked around at the group of firefighters. "My little girl, Allie, is almost four years old. She has a serious heart condition, and we're waiting on a transplant." The simple explanation made the problem sound uncomplicated, too. If only it were.

Alberto nodded. "My preacher here and Flint's preacher out in Colorado are friends, so our church family has prayed for little Allie since she was born and Flint lost his wife."

A gray-haired man who had introduced himself as James and captain of the shift asked, "You mind if my wife and I pray for your little girl?"

He raised his eyebrows and smiled. He hadn't expected such a request. "Not at all. I covet all the prayers I can get for my daughter." He took a deep breath. "Time is running out. We're praying for a miracle."

Emmanuel came back with a name and phone number on a slip of paper.

James held out his hand. "Let me have the number. I'll call Doc." He pulled out a cell phone and walked to the other end of the room.

He told the men about the fire on Ted Bonner's place. "The Lord blessed me that I had the creek right there and could just fall into it. Otherwise, the burn would have been much worse."

Tomas nodded and grinned. "Yeah, we could use a creek every once in a while at a fire, but we don't seem to have many in the middle of the city." He got a laugh from the men.

James came back and gave him the slip of paper. "Doc is only a few blocks from here. He lost a brother on 9/11 who was a New York City firefighter and is always ready to help. He said to come right over, and he'll look at your arm."

He put the paper into his jacket pocket. "Thanks, James. I appreciate this. You're mighty kind to help me out this way."

"It's the least we can do for a fellow firefighter. We may fight fire in the city, and your fires are in the mountains, but we have the same enemy," James said. The other men nodded.

Alberto stood and motioned toward the door. "I'll walk you out."

AFTER MEETING DR. ROBERTSON, he gave him the letter from the doctor in Colorado explaining what treatment he had already had.

"The first thing I want to do is start an IV of saline and antibiotics to guard against infection," Doc called for his nurse to bring him the equipment to start the IV.

"Is that really needed?" He didn't relish such a thing.

Dr. Robertson nodded. "You have second-degree burns and infection is a danger. You may even have a touch of third degree. You probably should have gone to the hospital and stayed a few days."

"You're probably right, but I needed to get back to my job here. I'd appreciate it if you could take care of it."

"As long as it heals and there are no complications. That means you come here every day and you keep this ace bandage on it. Take the pain medication because there's no benefit in being in so much pain."

"Is it possible for you to see me early in the morning?"

"What time works for you? I can be here as early as seven."

"That would be perfect. How long do you think I'll need to come to see you?"

"For at least ten days to two weeks. You need to drink a lot of fluids. Also, expose the burn to the air for a couple of hours every day."

He wasn't sure how he could accomplish that. He couldn't very well walk around the office without a shirt. Sleeping might be a problem, as he tended to roll over on the burn and that always woke him.

Back in the car, George drove to the office, and he gulped down one of the pain pills. He really wanted two, but he would have to endure some pain to keep a clear head. He glanced at his watch. Already four. Where had the day gone?

When he stepped out of the elevator with George a few steps behind him carrying his laptop in the messenger bag, he was prepared for Stephanie and Brigitte's concern about his injury as George had called ahead.

She met him and then walked him to his office. "George called and said you had an injury and that he had driven you to a doctor. How bad is it? Should you be here?"

"I'm fine, Stephanie. I just have to change the bandage each day. Don't worry about it." He wished she could have the same reaction as Mom. But then, his mother had years of experience with her husband and sons coming home with injuries. He supposed She hadn't had to deal with much in the way of burns.

"You don't look fine. You look like you've been run over by a truck. Exactly how much pain are you in?" Her voice was sharp with anxiety.

He looked at his gray sports jacket and dark slacks. "I didn't think I looked that bad." He grinned at her.

"Oh, you. I'm not talking about your clothes. You're pale, your eyes are sunken, and you look like you've lost more weight. Don't make light of it. Besides that, you have your arm in a sling, and you're holding yourself like someone who's afraid to move."

He eased himself into his chair behind the desk. He felt a lot weaker than he wanted to admit. "Don't worry. Honest, I'm fine. Now we need to get some work done. We on for supper tonight?" They had decided on the language of two friends spending time together until they could deal with the possibility of the office being bugged.

"Of course. What do you need to get done here before we go?" She asked.

"I just want to go over some things before I call it a day. Give me about an hour, then we can leave." He had to be sure of his figures before he gave her the information he and his firm had decided on.

"Brigitte took the day off to go to the dentist and run some errands, but she'll be back in the morning," She said.

He glanced around his office, which suddenly seemed empty without Brigitte hovering. "I wondered where she was."

"I'll make a couple of phone calls and meet you at the elevator in an hour." She left his office without a backward glance.

He watched her click away on three-inch heels. In the emerald green silk blouse above her ankle-length flowing black skirt, the back view was almost as appealing as the front. He drew in his breath as he felt the shock of her beauty hit him anew. Corralling his thoughts of her, he forced his mind back to the job he must do.

Chapter Twelve

GEORGE STOPPED THE car in front of the Wi-Fi Express Cafe. He held the door for her to enter before him. After being shown to their booth and being seated, he opened his laptop and got online. He downloaded e-mails and files from Ben and Tony. Then he uploaded several of his own. Finally, he set the computer aside and looked up at her. Time to be honest with her. If only he had different news for her. He swallowed and rolled his shoulders back and winced as the movement set the pain from the burn to a higher level.

She had ordered dinner but asked the waiter to wait and to serve them until he finished work. She smiled. "It's good to have you back. You were missed this weekend." Her smile nearly stopped his breath, and her beauty struck him like a spotlight.

"Thanks, I missed you all."

"Tell me about your injury, your daughter, your family, and your trip. Then we'll talk about my business." She put her elbows on the table, rested her chin on her folded hands, and gazed into his eyes.

Disconcerted by her gorgeous violet eyes, he wanted to forget the talk and just stare into their depth. With an effort, he drew himself back to reality. He told her of the firefight and how he had received his injury. He made it simple without much detail. "The doc back home said I'd be fine to return to work if I got the bandage changed every day. So I stopped by a friend's workplace, and he referred me to a doctor who specializes in burns and injuries to firefighters. That's why I was a little late getting to the office. I'm due to see him again in the morning."

She took a deep breath. "Wow, you talk about going to put out a forest fire as if it is an everyday phenomenon."

He grinned. "Well, out our way it's not an everyday thing, but it happens often enough to keep us in practice."

"What's the doctor's name here in New York?"

"I saw Doctor Robertson. He seemed to know his business. He was definite about me seeing him every day for the next couple of weeks. He seems invested in keeping the scarring to a minimum."

She frowned. "You know I would have gotten you a doctor."

"I know you would have, but I felt comfortable asking my fire-fighter buddy for a referral. The doctor lost a brother on 9/11. One way he seems to deal with that loss is by treating firefighters."

The waiter brought their meals of smoked salmon, steaming vegetables, and salad.

He said a blessing, and then they both ate in silence for several minutes. He was hungry, having missed lunch. While he ate, his fatigue grew, as did the pain from the burn—now more of a searing pain. He had expected it to hurt, but the pain wore him down. But he didn't dare take any more pain medication until he reached his room for fear of falling asleep.

"Were you able to visit with your family?" She took a sip of water.

He nodded and thought of Allie waving at him in the rearview mirror of his truck when he left for the airport with his dad. How he hated to leave her again. "They're doing fine. Which reminds me, when I go home in two weeks I need to stay over until Tuesday. I have business to attend to on Monday." He didn't want to tell her it was Allie's visit with the heart specialist.

"Sure, whatever you need. Now, tell me about The Wellbourne Group. What have you learned?" She gazed at him with a look of expectation.

He pulled a folder from his bag and pushed it across the table to her. "Here's a summary of the preliminary audit. With more time, we'll have a complete audit. There's no doubt that someone is moving shares around, especially your European holdings. As far as we can tell, you have several million dollars that appear to have simply evaporated. We're still looking. Because your holdings are so vast with numerous groups and offices, it's hard to tell who is doing what. But to say that you have enemies in your own camp is to simplify the issues." He paused and sipped some of the hot decaf coffee. What did she think as she heard such news? And how would she react to what else he had to tell her? "Bottom line, we can't see a way for you to keep your European holdings. The German group bidding for a takeover will be successful because they've garnered enough stock options through proxies." He paused as her porcelain skin blanched and her eyes widened. She stared at him unblinking.

She swallowed and drew in a deep breath. "I had no idea it was that bad. Are you saying I'm going to lose control of Wellbourne International?"

He nodded and softened his voice. "We don't see any way for you to stop the takeover."

"Well, if it's going to happen, at least I'll be prepared." She wiped a tear from the corner of her eye. "Sorry, I know it's only money. But my father spent his life building this company and now I can't keep it together."

"Maybe that's okay. Building it was your father's life. Perhaps it's not your life. And if we can act quickly, you may be able to hang on to your American holdings. Please understand, I'm saying maybe. There's no guarantee you'll be able to make even that happen."

"What do you mean? How could I lose control of Wellbourne Group of New York?" She stared at him as if frozen in place, not knowing which way to run.

He reached to cover her pale hand with his. "A lot of shares are being moved around and where it will end up is unsure. You have a shareholders' meeting just after Thanksgiving. That doesn't give us much time to find out who owns all the shares. You only own forty-two percent. If someone can get fifty-one percent of the shareholders' stock options, they can vote you out and take over the company." Her eyes looked stricken. "I'm sorry, but I have to tell you the truth."

She grabbed his hand and held on. "You don't think it can be stopped, do you?"

"No, I don't think there's time. If we'd been aware of what was happening a year ago, we might have stopped it. You can try to sell your European shares, and use that money to buy enough shares to take control. Of course, that depends on whether there are any to be bought. They may already be tied up in proxies." He didn't mind that she held onto his hand. He just wished it was for a different reason than the need for an anchor.

"What would you do?"

He winced at the grief in her voice. "I would let it go and not fight it. Sometimes in life, it's better to be realistic and stop fighting. You can act to pull out money and still be an incredibly wealthy young woman, or you can use your wealth to try to keep the company." He squeezed her hand to emphasize his point. "Of course, the danger is you'll risk losing everything. I would let it go, and start again with my own company—one I built myself, not one my father handed to me. He had his success. You can have your own success if that's what you want."

She rubbed her temple with her free hand. "What you're saying is I have to make a decision about whether to fight or just walk away."

He shook his head. "Not just walk away, walk away with most of the money. If that's what you decide, I'll let my firm know, and we'll immediately start working to help you sell off your European Group and find what shares can be purchased toward your North American holdings. Then over time, sell it off. You can't get it all done by the vote of the Board of Directors' meeting in December. But enough to be in a solid position."

She let go of his hand and leaned back in her chair. "I knew something was going on, but I could never get a handle on it. The truth may be that I didn't want to see it nor believe it."

She took her napkin and wet it from the glass of water. She dabbed at the corners of her eyes with the cloth. For a moment, she covered her face with the napkin. Then she heaved a deep sigh and replaced the napkin on the table.

"Are you all right?" He leaned toward her. How could he give her support through this?

"Yes. It's not what I wanted to hear. I'm wise enough to know that none of this would be, nor could be happening, without some of my so-called friends betraying me. That hurts more than losing control." She sighed again. "But in a way, I feel relieved. The uncertainty is lifted. It's almost as if it's a relief to give up the responsibility. There are some people in the company that I will make sure are given bonuses. If they stay with the company, great, or if they leave they will be all right, too."

"Do I hear you say you want to follow the suggestions my firm is making?" He didn't want to mention it was primarily his suggestion, although Ben and Tony agreed with him.

"Yes, but let me sleep on it. I'll tell you for sure tomorrow. Right now I'm too upset to make a decision." She rubbed her arms as if needing to protect herself.

He wiped at a spot on the table with his napkin. "I have another suggestion. To make life easier, I suggest we get a security firm into your offices, your car, and your apartment to search for electronic bugs. I know of someone here in New York that could do a good job for you."

She nodded. "I'd like to know whether my apartment is bugged."

"If bugs are found I would leave them in place for a while. Sometimes they stop functioning on their own. If some are found, leave them alone for a few days and then neutralize them one by one. That way you aren't alerting whoever is listening that you're wise to the surveillance."

"When can you get this done? What will we tell them in the office that these people are doing?"

He thought for a moment. "I can ask them to scan the office at night. And you are the only one who has to know they're scanning your apartment. You can trust George about the car."

"Yes, I'd trust George with my life. He drove Father and has been with me since his death."

He rubbed his face with his right hand and then held his left arm gently. "There's not much we can do this evening. I'm a little tired." He scrutinized her face. She seemed to be holding up under the news he had brought her better than he would have thought. What he had expected he wasn't sure. He couldn't protect her from the hurt of the world, just as he couldn't protect Allie.

She put her hand up to her mouth. "I'm so sorry. I should have realized. Of course, let's get you home and to bed."

He shook his head. "It's all right. I think some of my weariness is from the pain medicine. I just need to get a good night's sleep."

"Are you in pain now?" She leaned forward, her hand gently stroking his right arm.

He wanted to deny it, but couldn't lie. "Well, some."

"Tell me the truth, exactly how are you feeling." Her voice had taken on a commanding tone.

"All right, I'll tell you. The pain in my arm and shoulder is pretty severe. And I'm tired to the bone. What I want to do is get to my bed, take a couple of pain pills, and pass out." He didn't know why he was so honest with her. Maybe it was the pain medicine.

She pulled out her cell phone. "George, we're ready. In five."

"I'm meeting the doctor at seven. I should be in the office by eight-thirty or nine at the latest." He slid the computer back into the bag but had trouble with the zipper. The pain in his arm rendered his left hand useless.

"Here, let me." She reached across, zipped the bag, and picked it up.

He couldn't argue with a little help. "Thanks."

When they climbed into the car, she instructed George to take him home first.

"That's not necessary. Let him drop you first." He hoped she wouldn't listen to him, as he wanted to get to where he could lie down.

She shook her head. "I've got too much on my mind and won't be able to sleep for a while. The ride will do me good."

He gave in to her logic. "Thanks again. The sooner I make it to my bed the better."

"Why don't you lay back and rest. I'll let you know when we get there." She suggested.

He hiked his good shoulder. "All right. Thanks." He leaned back on the soft leather seat and closed his eyes.

Chapter Thirteen

SHE WATCHED FLINT SLEEPING in the seat next to her. He looked tired. The car hit a pothole and bounced. He moaned softly but didn't wake.

She had a strong desire to take him into her arms and kiss away his hurt. Never had she felt like this with any man she had dated. Was she falling in love with this westerner?

"Miss Stephanie?" George parked the car along the curb and looked over his shoulder at her and Flint.

"Yes, George?"

"We're at Mr. Flint's place, ma'am. Should I help him to his room? It's on the third floor."

"That's kind of you. Maybe you should at least walk up with him and carry his bags. Let me wake him." She gently patted Flint's right arm. "We're here."

He jerked awake. "What?"

"We're here. George will carry your bags up."

He rubbed his face. "Thanks, I didn't mean to fall asleep. Goodnight. God's blessings on you."

She didn't know how to reply. "George will be here to take you to the doctor in the morning."

With his arm in the sling held tight against his body. Flint slowly unfolded his tall frame from the back seat. He climbed the steps of the brownstone with George behind him carrying his bags.

An older baldheaded man stood in the open doorway to welcome them. She watched as the door shut. Loneliness smothered her as the weight of what Flint had shared descended on her shoulders. She began to cry.

AFTER A SLEEPLESS NIGHT, she called George. "Please swing by and pick me up before you get Flint."

George's deep voice came through the phone. "Yes, ma'am. I should be there in thirty minutes."

"Good, I'll be waiting downstairs." She hung up the phone and then hurried to finish dressing, as she thought of several questions for Flint. The drive into work by way of his doctor's appointment would be a good time to talk. How would she avoid being overheard if there were listening devices in the car?

George tapped the car horn before She noticed he drove a different vehicle, a pale blue Cadillac.

She slid in the back seat. "What is this, George?"

George closed her door and then positioned himself behind the steering wheel. "Mr. Flint is worried about listening devices. So until I get the car checked, I thought a rental would be best."

She had to smile at the simple solution. "Thank you for your proactive wisdom." She would check his wages and bonus. He deserved more pay.

At least she and Flint could talk freely. Pulling her laptop computer out of her purse, she added to the list of questions and notes she had compiled at three this morning.

Flint waited at the curb. He raised his eyebrows as he greeted her. "Morning, I didn't expect to see you this early."

She felt a tingling in her stomach as she searched his face. He looked much better this morning. "I thought we could talk while riding to your appointment if you don't mind."

He placed his messenger bag on the car floor. "That's a good idea. We don't have time to waste."

She nodded. "I've thought of nothing else since we talked last night. Sleep wasn't possible with so much on my mind."

He turned sideways on the seat so that he looked directly at her. "All of this must be a major stress. I'll do what I can to help you through it."

"How about you? Did you get any sleep?"

He nodded. "Yes. Of course, the pain medicine probably helped. Also, I talked a bit with Richard Anderson."

"That older gentleman I saw at the door?"

"Yes. Richard is the minister of the church and has become a good friend. His wife, Nancy, is a lovely lady. They opened their home to me for as long as I need it."

"They must be good people." She thought of her large apartment and the mansion in the Hamptons. Would she open her home to a stranger?

"The best." He looked out the window at the busy traffic surrounded by tall buildings.

After a few moments, She said, "I have some questions about the actions I need to take for the company. You feel like talking about details?"

He turned back to her. "Sure."

In the forty-minute ride to Dr. Robertson's office, they discussed the procedures needed to sell her European holdings. It seemed surreal that she was really going to break up what her father worked so hard to build.

He opened his laptop and began typing notes. "Let my firm discreetly initiate securing buyers for your shares. If you've made up your mind, then you might as well see who will bid highest. You have five weeks until the Board of Director's meeting, and I suggest you sell off as much of the European shares as possible by then. In the meantime, I'll track down shares of your North American holdings. You should know before the meeting where you stand."

A headache threatened, and she rubbed her temple. Not near enough sleep last night. "Have your firm send me the authorization statements giving them the power to act for me. If we're going to do it, let's get started."

He patted her arm. "I know this is difficult. I'll help where I can." She placed her hand over his and held on. "Thanks, you're being the rock I need through this."

George looked into his rearview mirror at her. "We're almost there. Another two minutes."

"Thanks, George." She removed her hand from over Flint's and straightened in her seat.

He returned his laptop to its case. "Want to come into the doctor's office with me?"

She was surprised and pleased he would suggest it. "If I may."

George stopped in front of a door with a small sign announcing the offices of Dr. Carl Robertson.

"I'll call when we're finished." She climbed out of the car and followed Flint, who moved slowly and carefully.

"Yes, ma'am." George shut the rear door and then got back behind the wheel.

Flint punched the doorbell.

Moments later the door opened, and a gray-haired man in a white lab coat stood there. "Come on in, Flint."

He let her enter first. "This is my friend, Stephanie Wellbourne."

She was surprised that he gave no more information and he referred to her as his friend. "Dr. Robertson, I'm glad to meet you."

"Come back to the exam room. My nurse isn't here yet, but I can handle changing a bandage." He led the way.

She hesitated at the door to the room. It was small with an examination table, two chairs, and a sink counter. "Should I wait out here?"

Dr. Robertson raised his eyebrows. "Not unless you're squeamish." He turned to him. "Do you mind?"

"Not unless you're going to do something more than changing the bandage." He smiled at her and nodded toward the chair in the corner.

The doctor asked him to slip out of his coat and shirt. He sat on the exam table while the doctor cut the bandages off.

Surprised at the many layers of bandages, she noticed how tightly Flint gripped the edge of the table with his right hand until his knuckles turned white when the last one was lifted from the wounds. Sweat broke out on his forehead, and he breathed shallowly through his mouth.

"Doing okay?" Dr. Robertson asked.

"Yeah, I'm okay. It always hurts a little more than I expect."

Dr. Robertson picked up a syringe and plunged the needle into Flint's right arm. "Just some more antibiotics."

Flint grunted.

She swallowed and hoped she could control the queasiness in her stomach.

"Well, you've got a pretty nasty burn here. I need to be thorough in treating it to protect against infection. I'm going to spray it with something cold. That'll help with the pain while I clean it and apply a fresh bandage." He picked up a silver can and sprayed the red, blistered area. "This is already looking better than yesterday. If we keep it clean and the pressure bandage on, it should heal all right."

She stood and walked to the sink. She pulled several paper towels out of the holder and wet them. She stood next to Flint and carefully dabbed the sweat from his forehead.

Dr. Robertson smiled at her. "Thanks, usually my nurse would do that. Just keep still for another couple of minutes, Flint, and I'll be done. If you want, I can give you a shot for the pain."

He shook his head. "I'll pass. Once you stop poking, it'll feel better. I need my mind clear today."

He looked into her eyes and nodded.

She didn't know how much it helped to wipe his face. But she felt good to be of some use.

The doctor finished wrapping Flint's arm and then used an elastic bandage to capture his left arm tight against his chest. "Leave this on until morning, then a couple of hours before I see you, take it off but leave the gauze bandage on. In a day or two, we'll start leaving the bandage off entirely."

In the outer office, a phone rang. Dr. Robertson turned to her. "You mind helping Flint into his shirt and coat? I need to grab that phone."

"Of course, take your call." She picked up his white shirt and helped him slip his right arm into the sleeve. She couldn't help but notice how muscular his chest and arms were. She wrapped the shirt around and buttoned it for him, leaving the left sleeve empty.

"Thanks, I didn't realize you would need to help." He grimaced as he tucked his shirt into his pants. "I've got a tie in my coat pocket. Could you tie it for me?"

She found it and stood close in front of him. Feeling his breath on her face, she tied the tie and adjusted his collar. It brought back memories of her father teaching her to tie his one summer when he broke his wrist. She'd had to tie it from the front, as she was too short to do it any other way. The faint scent of Polo by Ralph Lauren also brought back memories of her father. She patted the shirt in place. "There, that looks good."

"Where did you learn to do that so expertly?"

She picked up his coat and held it while he slipped his right arm into the sleeve, and then she draped it around his left shoulder. "From my father." She wanted to continue to stand so close and draw in the masculine scent, but stepped back and picked up her purse.

Dr. Robertson came back into the room carrying a prescription, which he handed to Flint. "Get rest, drink water, and keep the bandage on. Get this filled so you'll have plenty of medicine for the pain. It'll ease off in a week or so. I'll see you in the morning." He picked up the sling and handed it to Stephanie. "If you do take the pressure bandage off, use this sling."

"Thanks, Doc. I appreciate your seeing me this early."

"Glad I can help. Thanks, Ms. Wellbourne, for helping out."

"Thanks for letting me assist. We'll be here at the same time tomorrow morning." She led the way out of the clinic.

When George saw them, he got out of the Cadillac and opened the back door. As they rode to the office, she glanced several times at Flint who was pale and had a strained look on his face. "Are you sure you're all right to work today?"

He nodded. "I'm fine. We have things to do. Thanks for coming this morning. I didn't know it would be so intense. Sorry about that."

She smiled. "The most useful thing I've done in a long time."

Chapter Fourteen

HE ENTERED THE LAST of the data he needed to downsize Stephanie's holdings. Now he could begin the real work of reorganizing the company. Flexing his left hand, he tried to relax the tense muscles in his recuperating arm. It had been a hard week, both physically and mentally. Could he be any more tired?

He looked up as Dan came into his office. "Morning."

"Flint, we haven't had much time to get together. How about lunch?"

"Thanks, but I've already ordered lunch brought in. I plan to work while I eat."

He didn't mention the rest of the reason, that he wanted as little contact with Dan as possible. He now knew that it was either Dan or Granfield who had instigated the betrayal against Stephanie by feeding confidential information to the German group. One of these two men would sell her out, and he needed to be on guard.

Dan shuffled from one foot to another as if uncertain what to do next. "That's too bad. Granfield suggested the three of us should get together."

He walked around the desk to face him. "Why don't we plan for lunch tomorrow?"

Dan's eyes darted around the room, but he nodded. "All right, I'll let Granfield know." He hurriedly left the office.

He turned on the CD player. Jazz filled the office with a heavy beat. He stood by the window and dialed Ben's cell.

"Hey, Ben. I need you to do something for me as quickly as possible. Call Harlan Wolf at Deep Cover and get a financial report on Granfield Wilson."

Ben's clear and firm voice came through as if he were in the next office and not eighteen hundred miles away. "Granfield Wilson, the Head of Marketing?"

"Yeah, I have a feeling about him. We may have found at least one person who has been sabotaging Stephanie's efforts."

Ben hesitated a second. "How would the Head of Marketing have enough clout to make that much difference?"

He rubbed between his eyes and moved to the window. "The damage has been caused by the transfer of knowledge to the wrong people at the wrong time. Granfield can access all the data. He doesn't have to have decisional power."

"But what does he get out of it?"

"That's what we need to find out. And who he is communicating with. That will determine the extent of the damage." He scanned the city panorama spread before him out the windows. What a beautiful sight. If he squinted his eyes, he could almost see the mountains. "Sorry Ben, repeat that please."

"I said, what's our next move?" A hint of impatience clouded Ben's voice.

"We keep to our plan and try to consolidate the North American holdings. I'm tracking the shares of stock, but so far, I can only get forty-eight percent ownership for Stephanie. I've got to find more shares she can pick up. With the selling of the European holdings, she's got the funds." He turned and saw Brigitte through the hall door. "Need to go. I'll call again this evening."

Brigitte held the door so Charles could carry in the tray with Flint's lunch that he set it on the edge of the desk.

"Thank you, Charles." She smiled at him as he left the office.

He turned down the music. "Thanks, Brigitte. As always, I'm hungry."

Brigitte rearranged items on the tray. "Good. I ordered pork loin with vegetables."

He sat in his chair and pulled the tray toward him. "This smells great."

"I'll leave you to it. You need anything else?"

He picked up the napkin and sent her a smile of appreciation. He took in her perfect complexion, classic bone structure, and bright blue eyes and couldn't help but notice what a beauty she was. "No, I'm fine."

After she left, he ate his lunch while scanning reports on the computer. He went into the personnel files and studied all of the upper management who worked out of the New York office. He actually only wanted a couple of them but knew he would leave cyber footprints in his search. By pulling up about twenty files, no one would know which ones he really wanted to check.

Granfield Wilson. How close was She to him? He wanted to protect her from any more hurt. But the nature of the game meant he couldn't protect her from much of it. To sell off her European holdings meant nothing to him, but it did mean a lot to her. As they met each evening, he watched her put on a brave face to deal with the breakup of her father's company. How could he protect her and still protect his own heart? It was getting harder.

Two weeks before Thanksgiving, he flew back to Colorado. Driving his truck onto the ranch land with Dad seated beside him, seeing the aspens turning yellow, smoothed a healing balm on his spirit. He drew in a deep breath of the mountain air. He'd come home.

By now, he only needed a small bandage on his shoulder where the deepest burn was. Without the pain medication, his mind functioned more clearly. He spent the weekend with Allie, his parents, and his sister Holly and her husband, Benjamin, who came from town. It was a relaxing time away from computers, finances, and the crowded city.

As he played with his dark-haired child, he thought of a dark-haired woman far away. Why couldn't he keep Stephanie out of his mind? Nothing would come of such an obsession but a friendship. They were too different.

On Sunday after church, he and his parents drove Allie to Denver. They spent the night in a hotel, which delighted Allie. He would have enjoyed the trip except for the reason they were there. He dreaded the next day with the doctors. In his anxiety, he couldn't eat but did his best to hide it from Allie.

They spent Monday morning Allie having an MRI and an echocardiogram. He was relieved the doctor decided not to do a MUGA since Allie had one in June. Allie did well except when the phlebotomist had to insert the needle to draw blood. Then she cried and begged her daddy not to let the people hurt her. It was all he could do to keep from gathering up his little child and running from the building. Instead, he held her and let them do what they had to do.

Dad took Allie to a play area in the lobby of the building while he and Mom met with the doctors.

The doctor looked from him to Mom. "We've compared all the tests with those in August. Allie is definitely losing ground. I could give you the exact figures, but what you need to know is that without a transplant she'll have maybe six months to a year at the most."

Mom gripped his hand harder. "What do we do until we can get a transplant?" she asked.

"Continue with what you've been doing. Don't let her overdo, but let her do what she feels up to doing." He glanced at Flint. "Any questions?"

He swallowed hard, but it felt like a rock stuck in his parched throat. "When do we bring her back?"

The doctor glanced at his notes. "I'd like to see her in January. We'll monitor her condition. I'll give you a prescription for oxygen at the house. Have her sleep with it. Her oxygen absorption is borderline, only 90 this morning, and more oxygen might help her sleep better. The oxygen absorption level will have a tendency to drop throughout the night while she sleeps. Other than that, keep her on the same medications. With winter coming, keep her out of the cold and away from people with infections."

He didn't remember much of the rest of the talk. All he could think was that he only had six months with Allie, maybe a year. Each month his bank account grew. He barely spent anything during his time in New York, thanks to the generosity of Richard and Nancy Anderson and Stephanie. But it would still be another eight months before he had enough money to get her on the transplant list. He was willing to sell the ranch if that would have helped, but he owed too much on it, and the land wasn't selling.

On the drive back to the ranch, he sat in the back seat of the truck beside Allie in her car seat. She soon fell asleep from the exhaustion of the day of medical tests. He brushed her curls back and tried to memorize each detail of her face. The ache in his chest threatened to choke him. If only he could cry.

His folks talked softly in the front seat. Mom explained to Dad what the doctor had told them. It was nothing new. Except that each visit and series of tests meant Allie's time got shorter.

He almost couldn't leave on Tuesday morning. He hated to miss any more of the time left with Allie. He gritted his teeth and kept his mind on the hope of a transplant ... if he could get the money.

Each time the plane landed back in New York, his life went on hold until he could get back to Colorado.

SHE DIDN'T SLEEP WELL, waking several times during the night. Each time, a vision of a tall brown-haired man filled her mind. Untangling the covers, she got out of bed and headed to the kitchen to start the coffee pot. Only five-thirty. Too early to go into the office. He wasn't due back until noon. Looking out the kitchen window into the early morning darkness, she watched the traffic lights blinking amid the steady white streetlights. Had she come to the point where every minute of her day revolved around him?

Beeping indicated the coffee had finished brewing. The rich aroma filled the kitchen. She poured coffee into a mug and added a little cream. Taking it upstairs, she set the mug on the nightstand and fluffed the pillows against the headboard. Making herself comfortable sitting in bed, she opened the report she had been reading the evening before.

Reading the information Flint's firm had gathered of which shares had been bought and sold and who held what proxies, soon made her tense. However, the pattern of sales and buyouts, along with the notes Flint had added, helped her understand who controlled the shares. Clearly, someone was systematically raiding her company and garnering shares to force her out of leadership. She examined her feelings. Was she sad? Angry? Surprised? She didn't really care about losing the European Group. It would simplify her life in many useful ways.

She drained the last of the coffee as her spirits rose. He would be back by noon, and they would begin the work of saving her position with her Board of Directors. She quickly showered, dressed, and headed downstairs to meet George.

He drove the light blue Cadillac alongside the cars parked on her street. She quickly entered the backseat as horns blared behind the car. As soon as she was settled, George pulled into the stream of traffic.

"What time are you due at the airport?" she asked.

George looked at the rearview mirror and nodded at her. "Mr. Flint arrives at twelve-twenty, ma'am."

"Good, I look forward to his return. By the way, did you ever get my car checked for listening devices?" She watched his face in the mirror.

"Yes, ma'am. I had it checked, and there were two devices in the back seat." George shrugged. "Mr. Flint said to leave them and drive a rental. Tomorrow I'll turn this one back in and get another at a different company. I'll keep doing that until this crisis is over."

"That's a great idea. Thank you for thinking of it."

"I didn't think of it, ma'am. Mr. Flint did."

She smiled. It gave her a warm feeling of contentment to know that Flint looked out for her. Even with her father, she had never had someone genuinely concerned with her welfare.

In front of the office building, she climbed out of the car, then turned to speak to George. "Please give me a call when you pick up Mr. Tucker and let me know when you'll arrive."

"Yes, ma'am."

The almost serene calmness with which George did his job never ceased to fascinate her. She wished all her employees were as dependable.

The elevator took her straight to the twentieth floor. She had settled into her office chair when Brigitte bustled in and sat in the chair in front of her desk.

"Morning, you're looking more chipper today."

"Thank you, I'm feeling better." She felt much more optimistic than she had for several weeks. Almost as if she had been freed from a weight.

Brigitte lifted her eyebrows. "Did Flint tell you why he needed to stay in Colorado yesterday?"

She shook her head. "No. He said he had business that couldn't be done on the weekend. I didn't question him. He's worked so many hours during the last month, he could take a week, and I'd still owe him."

Brigitte twirled her necklace. "I need to say something, but I don't want you to misunderstand."

"Sure, Brigitte, say whatever you want." She leaned on her elbows and rested her chin on her folded hands.

"I know we are both drawn to Flint. He's become important around here." She paused and then nodded as if coming to a decision. "But I want you to know that although I've come to care deeply for him, it isn't in a romantic way."

She shifted in her chair. "What are you trying to tell me?"

Brigitte smiled. "As I've gotten to know him, he and I have become true friends. I've watched you, and I suspect that you care a lot more for him than you want to admit."

For a couple of seconds, she sat and stared at her friend. She couldn't think what to say. She did have strong feelings for him.

"Well, I wanted you to know that you don't need to worry whether I'm interested in him that way. You have a clear path, and I wish you well."

She finally found her voice. "That is so sweet of you, but there's just one problem with your reasoning."

"What's that?"

"He has not shown one single indication that he's interested in me as more than a friend." Even as she said it, it stung a little. She had never spent so much time with a man who paid absolutely no interest in her. "Either he has a girl back in Colorado, or I don't appeal to him."

Brigitte grinned. "My friend. I've never known you to be so unobservant."

"What do you mean?"

"His eyes follow you, and whenever he comes into the office, he's on high alert until he spots where you are."

"You must be wrong. He's never said anything to indicate any interest in me."

Brigitte sat back in her chair and crossed her legs. "He may not have said anything but all the signs are there."

"Well, until he makes a move, I won't count on anything."

"That's wise. There may be a reason he's not free to let you know how he feels. Maybe he has a rule about dating someone from work."

"I never thought about that, but it would fit." She tapped the desk with a manicured nail. "Please don't say anything about this to him. I need to get through next month."

"I understand. Rest assured I won't say another word about it. You didn't mind me bringing it up, did you?"

"No. I appreciate it. That's one of the many things I like about our friendship. We tell the truth."

"I didn't want any misunderstandings between us." Brigitte stood and smoothed her skirt. "I have a few things to do before Flint gets here. I want to be ready to take care of whatever he needs me to do."

"Thanks. You've been great taking care of him. Be sure to ask him if he's eaten and if not, order lunch for him."

Brigitte nodded. "My guess is he'll need lunch." She closed the door on the way out of the office.

She couldn't contain her relief that Brigitte had no interest in Flint. But why should she care one way or the other? As she had told Brigitte, he was the perfect gentleman and had given no indication of the slightest interest in her. Frowning, she rubbed her forehead. What did Brigitte see that she missed?

Chapter Fifteen

THURSDAY AFTERNOON She sat at her desk with another opened file folder. She couldn't believe how fast the week was passing.

She had worked for several days with Flint and Brigitte going over spreadsheets and trying to understand rows of figures.

Brigitte entered her office. "Something just happened that I need to tell you." She looked around at the walls of the office and mouthed. "Is it safe to talk in here?"

She raised her eyebrows and put a finger to her lips. "What have you got for me?" She turned on a CD player and filled the office with an instrumental rock song. Then she stood and walked over to the chairs and couches arranged in a conversational grouping. With a gesture to Brigitte to sit, she settled on the couch. "Flint says music masks low conversation. There's still an active bug at my desk but not in this part of the office."

Brigitte looked around again and then leaned toward her. "Charlie went out and picked up lunch for several of us. When he came back, he saw Dan and Granfield leaving the building and getting into a car. He swears that Thor Swenson was in the back seat. Sort of casually he asked me if Thor was still working with The Wellbourne Group now that the company has split." She shook her head. "I don't think Charlie was suspicious or anything. He was curious, as he had met Thor on other visits. I told him that they were meeting to clear up some loose ends, but he shouldn't mention to anyone else that he had seen them."

She didn't know what to say. Thor Swenson no longer worked with the company in an official capacity, but he still holds a seat on the Board of Directors. "Why do you think Dan and Granfield are getting together with him?"

Brigitte shook her head. "I'm not sure, but it seemed odd."

She agreed. "I'm glad you told me. I'll talk it over with Flint. Are you available to go to the Hamptons for the weekend? I'm asking him to go tomorrow so we can have several days without listening devices. I've had the house checked, and it's bug free. We can get a lot done. I only have three weeks until the Board of Directors meets."

"Sure, I always like going to your place. What time do you want to leave?"

"Early in the morning so we can arrive by eight or nine and have the whole day to work. I'll ask Flint and make sure it's all right with him." She was relieved that Brigitte could come, as she wasn't sure he would feel comfortable with going away for the weekend with her alone. "I'll go talk to him and let you know."

"Great, I'll plan on it. I'll gather the files we might need." Brigitte stood and headed toward the office door.

"Brigitte, give George a call, too and see if he can drive us, and call Maria to alert her."

"No problem." Brigitte disappeared out the door.

She stepped into the bathroom that opened off her office. She ran a comb through her hair and checked her makeup. Then she headed to his office.

He waved her in. She noted he was speaking to someone on the phone. Jazz filled the large office.

As she walked toward him, she heard him say, "Yes, the Patterson shares. Can you tell if they've been put under a proxy?" He listened for a couple of minutes and then nodded. "That's what I needed to know. I'll call you back tomorrow, Tony." He clicked the phone off.

"You still trying to track down the last few shares?"

He nodded and smiled. "It's a slippery little slope because it changes every day. Just when we think we have every single share-holder tracked down, someone else decides to sell, buy, or shift shares. With a company this big and the number of shareholders in-volved, it's a challenge to get and keep a handle on transactions."

"I came to ask you to consider a weekend at my house on Long Island. We need to talk some of this through so I can understand my situation. I'm tired of trying to do it with this music blaring and just in the evenings. There are no listening devices there."

He gazed into her eyes. "Who else would be there?"

She knew she had been right. She needed to include Brigitte for him to feel comfortable. "I have a couple who live there and take care of everything. Then Brigitte will come. Of course, George will drive us. Is there anyone else you think I should ask?"

He shook his head. "I don't think you should trust anyone except Brigitte. When do you want to go?"

"I'll have George pick us up at the regular time in the morning and drive directly there. Depending on traffic, we can be there by eight-thirty and have the day to work. We can stay until Sunday evening, and be back in the office by Monday morning." M usually went to church on Sunday. What would he do about that?

"All right, I'll be ready in the morning. Are you set up with Wi-Fi at your house?"

She nodded. "Yes, the house is both wired and has Wi-Fi so we can use our computers and access the company computer system. But bring whatever we need to work on for a couple of days. I especially want us to develop a strategy for the board meeting."

He raised his eyebrows. "You're right. We need to get you pre-pared for that, and it's coming up on us fast."

"I'll admit that I'm a little scared about what may happen. I'd like to be as prepared as possible." She felt the tightening of her chest that let her know that she was more nervous about the whole thing than

she wanted to admit to anyone. Only to him had she verbalized her
fear.

HE WAITED ON THE CURB as George eased an extended-
length black limo to a stop outside Richard and Nancy's brownstone.
George exited the car and opened the door for him.

"Morning, George." He handed over his duffle bag but kept the
messenger bag with his computer.

"Mr. Flint, fine morning to you. We'll stop for Ms. Wellbourne
next." M settled into the plush seat back seat. He enjoyed the luxury
of plenty of space for his long legs. A fella could get used to this.
He was curious about what type of house someone as wealthy as
Stephanie had two hours from the city.

It took another forty-five minutes to collect both Stephanie and
Brigitte. M noticed that each woman brought a couple of bags for a
simple work weekend.

Stephanie, dressed in corduroy slacks, a blue cotton shirt, and
suede jacket, sat next to him. Brigitte, more formally dressed in a
black pants suit with a beige silk blouse, sat with her back to George
facing them.

"Would you prefer to face forward? I'll switch with you." He offered to Brigitte.

She smiled and shook her head. "No thanks, but I appreciate you
asking. I normally sit here on the rides to the house in the Hamptons."

He turned to Stephanie. "Do you have a list of what we need to
discuss?"

"No, I have questions, but I'm not sure what I need to be ready
for at the meeting."

He studied her for a moment. Her lovely violet eyes could trap a
man in their lush interior. He forced his thoughts back to this busi-

ness at hand. "Then we need to start by covering what we know and brainstorm all eventualities. I can bring you up to date on the shares and what holdings you currently own."

She nodded, and Brigitte took out her laptop.

He let his mind scan through all he had learned in the last five weeks. In many ways, his time in New York seemed so much longer. Each day separated from Allie was painful, knowing it could never be retrieved.

"We've finally been able to track all the shares, but not necessarily who holds all the proxies. You still have the forty-two percent you have always owned. We know several of the major shareholders hold another thirty-six percent. It's the sixteen percent held by proxies that'll make the difference. I've personally spoken with several of the shareholders about purchasing more, but so far no one is selling, or if they are, not to you. So I can only assume that someone is gathering proxies and shares with a base of funds that is beyond what we would expect." He handed Brigitte a thumb drive. "Here is a list of shareholders. I think it would be worthwhile for you to call, Stephanie, and encourage them to vote with you."

She shifted in the leather seat. "So you're convinced it'll come down to a vote of confidence?"

Flint noted her troubled eyes. He wanted to tell her not to worry and that all would be well. But he didn't believe that. "Yes, it'll come to a vote—one you may lose."

"Why do you say that? A lot of the older shareholders are friends of my father and have known me all my life." Her tone sounded argumentative.

He nodded. He didn't mind her tone as it wasn't directed at him. "That's why I want you to call and talk with them. But be realistic. Others are also talking with them and arguing that they can offer better management, more profits, whatever to turn them against you."

She stared out the window at the passing landscape of trees, lawns, and, where the immaculately trimmed hedges allowed, the stately homes.

What did it mean to her? The money? She had more money than she could ever spend. Was it the power? That was something he couldn't relate to, as he had never had much power, especially over circumstances of life.

She turned to face him. "In some ways, I just want to get past the board meeting and know where I stand. Then I'll deal with it."

"Ma'am?" George's voice came through the sound system. "Yes, George?" She leaned forward.

"We'll be there in a few minutes. Do you want to stop in the village or go straight to the house?" George's voice came back.

"Let's go straight to the house."

"Very good, ma'am."

She smiled and turned to him. "The house we call the End of the Pointe will be on your right. The property sits on the waterfront, but you can't see the bay except from the back of the house. We have ten and a half acres with a heated outdoor and indoor pool, tennis courts, and stables. The house has twelve bedrooms and twelve bathrooms so obviously it's too big for me. But my grandfather bought it over a hundred years ago, and it's part of the family."

He had a hard time wrapping his mind around such an enormous place for one person. They drove down a narrow tree-lined road with tall hedges blocking the view. Then George turned the limo through an arched gateway, and he saw what he could only describe as a mansion with a three-story central section and wings extending out from both sides. All of a sudden, he understood why they were called wings—the main house looked like a giant eagle sleeping on the ground with wings outstretched. Any moment it might rise into the air and flap those massive wings. George drove the limo around the circular drive and parked under the portico at the double front doors.

George opened the door for Stephanie to exit from the car. He indicated for Brigitte to follow her and then stepped onto the brick driveway.

The front door opened as if by magic and Stephanie led the way inside. "Maria, saluta!" She embraced a heavyset woman with Italian features.

He glanced around the massive foyer with its circular grand stairway leading to the second floor. The chandelier alone was impressive. As he looked through to the far glass wall, he glimpsed the bay.

"Flint, this is Maria. She and her husband Enzio live in the caretaker's cottage and manage the place for me. They also worked for my parents."

He shook hands with Maria. "I'm glad to meet you."

"I have your rooms ready. Ms. Brigitte you know which room you'll have. And I thought we should put the gentleman in the corner suite at the back so he could see the water."

She nodded. "That's perfect, Maria. And we'll be working out of the third-floor salon."

"Yes, ma'am. It's ready." Maria stepped back.

She climbed the broad stairway. "Flint, I'll show you to your room. We have an elevator for the house, but I usually take the stairs as it gives me more exercise."

As he reached the top of the stairs, he stopped to look out tall windows at a manicured lawn with a swimming pool, and beyond over a dune to a sandy beach on a bay. The water sparkled from the bright sunlight. After so many days cooped up in an office, the expanse of water leading to a far horizon took his breath away.

She turned back. "What's the matter? Your room is down this hall."

He took a deep breath of sea air. Even with the windows closed, he could smell the sea. "I'm just taking in the enormous beauty of your place and the water."

She stepped to the window next to him and looked at the sea. "Yes, it's beautiful. I've seen it so many times I forget to look. Thanks for reminding me."

He felt the warmth of her body so close to him and smelled the faint scent of flowers in her hair. He wanted to put his arms around her and draw her close, but instead, he stepped back. "Let's see my room and then where we're going to work."

She opened the door to a bedroom decorated in shades of yellow and with two walls of windows where he had a view of the sea.

She pointed into the bright and open room. "This has always been one of my favorite rooms. You look out those windows and see the bay, and you turn to these windows, and you're looking at the sea." She pointed toward another door. "Through there is the bath."

He set his messenger bag on the bed and removed his jacket. "This'll do just fine. You have any problems with me leaving the windows open so I can hear the sea?"

She laughed. "Not at all. That's what I do, although with this being November, it'll get cold tonight. But we have German comforters on the beds so you'll stay warm." She put her hand on the doorknob. "I'll leave you to freshen up and then we'll meet in the salon on the third floor. Maria will have coffee and breakfast laid out for us."

She hadn't been gone three minutes when someone knocked on the door.

He opened it to find a short, strong looking man in his fifties holding the duffle bag.

"Your luggage, sir." He entered the bedroom and walked into the bath suite. "I'll just put your things here in the closet." He unpacked the duffle bag with deft fingers and placed Flint's clothes on the shelves of the walk-in closet.

He stood, not sure how to respond. He wasn't used to someone waiting on him.

"Sir, where would you like this?" He held up a small leather satchel.

"Call me Flint. I'll take that." He took the satchel and put it beside his laptop, which was still in its bag.

"Very good, sir. I'm Enzio. You need anything you ask me, or my wife, Maria. That red button on the phone signals us, and we'll call you to find out how we may be of service."

He placed the empty duffle bag on a high shelf, closed the closet door, and walked to the center of the bedroom. "Is there anything special you like to eat? Or anything you need?"

He started to shake his head but changed his mind. "Yes, I understand we'll be working in the salon on the third floor. I like my coffee fairly strong."

"No problem, sir. I'll make sure we have some stronger coffee. Ms. Stephanie likes hers smooth and mellow, as does Ms. Brigitte. But we can have an extra pot of stronger coffee. In fact, I have some nice coffee beans from Italy that make a strong brew." Enzio smiled as if he and Flint had a private understanding that men drank more robust coffee.

He laughed. "That'll be great. Thanks."

Enzio left the bedroom, and he went into the bathroom to splash water on his face and check his hair. With its waves that were almost curls, it sometimes did its own thing.

He grabbed his bag with the laptop and mounted the stairs to the third floor. He marveled at the antiques everywhere he looked. They were probably furniture pieces that had been in her family for years. He could hear his mom exclaiming, "Would you look at that." He would take pictures to show her. For such a large house, he was impressed with how bright and cheerful it seemed.

Thinking of his mother brought a stab of guilt about the weekend with Allie he was missing. How many more weekends would there be? He needed to finish this work as soon as possible. He gripped his laptop and strode up the stairs.

Chapter Sixteen

HE FOUND THE SALON easily—a large room where an entire outer wall of glass doors led to a balcony overlooking the backyard and farther out to the sea. A large oval table commanded the room's center with chairs pushed around it. He assumed that was their working area, so he placed his laptop bag on the table. As if drawn by a magnet, he wandered onto the balcony and leaned against the railing taking in the view. The sea air carried by the stiff breeze blowing off the water left a faint taste of salt on his lips and there was a faint smell of that must have been the natural scent of the sea.

Someone entered the room behind him, and he turned to see Maria rolling a service cart to a counter at the far end of the room. Without acknowledging his presence, she emptied the cart of dome covered bowls and plates producing a buffet of breakfast foods.

He turned back to the view. What would Allie think of the sea? A fist closed in his chest. His daughter might never see such a sight. So many things he wanted to share with his little girl. Would he ever get the opportunity?

With a sigh, he pushed off from the rail and ambled back into the salon. He glanced around the room at comfortable chairs and couches, tables and lamps, a fireplace at one end with a large flat screen TV above the mantel, and a wet bar where Maria had set up the food. A salon—precisely what kind of room is that? Just how many living areas would a house of this size have? This salon would make a nice large living room for a family.

Stephanie entered from the hallway with Brigitte behind her. "Oh, good, Maria has breakfast ready. I'm hungry." She held up a plate. "Flint? You ready to eat?"

He walked over. "I'm always ready, but you ladies go first."

After they had filled their plates with scrambled eggs, ham, fruit, and toast, they sat around the oval table and ate.

For the next four hours, he and Stephanie discussed the business situation. Brigitte took notes and produced files as needed. He was impressed with Stephanie's knowledge and mental quickness. If it hadn't been for the seriousness of the matter, he would have found the time enjoyable. How often had he had two beautiful, intelligent women hanging on to his every word?

Maria served a soup and salad luncheon, and they continued to work. Toward the middle of the afternoon, Stephanie leaned back in her chair and stretched her arms over her head. "I need to get out of this room and take a break. Why don't we relax for a while and start again after dinner?"

He cut his eyes away from her stretching body and reined in his thoughts. "That would probably be a good idea. Let's give our brains a rest."

She stood and gazed out toward the waterfront. "Who wants to go horseback riding with me?"

"Not me, I want to go for a swim and then a nap," Brigitte responded quickly.

"You have horses on the property?" He felt a surge of energy at the thought of getting on a horse. "Where do you ride?"

She brushed her hair back from her eyes. "I keep four horses here. We can either ride on the bridle path or on the beach."

He grinned. "I'll vote for a ride on the beach. That's something I've never done."

Brigitte stacked several files and set them aside. "You two go and enjoy. That's too athletic for me."

Stephanie laughed. "It's just you and me then. I'm going to change clothes. I'll meet you at the front door in fifteen minutes."

He watched her leave the room. She still walked with a slight limp. He turned to Brigitte. "Is her ankle well enough for riding?"

Brigitte cocked her head. "I think so. She's probably putting on her boots. She should be fine."

"Then I'll go change as well." He took the stairs two at a time down to his second-floor room where he changed into jeans and a western shirt—now glad that he had packed them. He was already wearing flat-heeled boots.

She waited near the front door. "Enzio has saddled a couple of horses. The stables are a short walk down the road."

"Let's go." He eyed her clothes. "You look like an English rider."

She glanced at her riding outfit and then at his jeans and western shirt. "We're a contrast, aren't we? East meets west? I used to ride in competitive dressage, and also jumpers. This outfit is a left over."

"Why did you stop?" He shortened his long-legged step to fall in with her daintier stride.

"Too busy. When my father died, I suddenly had a huge corporation to manage. Competitive dressage takes a daily commitment. I enjoyed it but responsibilities interfered."

"I know how that is. When I was in high school and college, I was part of the school rodeo team. But as you say, responsibilities interfered." He fingered the buckle on his belt won riding bucking horses. He had others for bull riding.

They walked together to the stables with a well-cared for paddock where two thoroughbred horses stood saddled with Enzio holding the reins.

She strolled to the gray dappled gelding and patted its nose. "Hello, Dandy. How're you doing, boy?"

The horse twisted his neck to muff at her.

She pointed to the other horse. "You can ride Mr. Rupert."

He quietly walked to the big black horse and rubbed its muzzle. "What a beauty. How old is he?"

"He's eight years old, strong and healthy." She bent her knee and Enzio gave her a leg up.

He checked the length of the stirrups and then the tightness of the girth. He mounted the horse and settled into the saddle with a sigh of pleasure. It had been weeks since he'd ridden.

She must have noticed because she grinned. "Feels great, doesn't it? Let's ride out to the beach." She reined her horse around and trotted down a path that led over the dune and onto the flat sandy beach. She kept the horse at the edge of the water just out of the waves.

He guided the black horse, following her, but not too closely as her horse kicked up sand and water. The big horse had a smooth gait.

She looked back and shouted at him over the surf and hooves. "Want to race?"

He grinned and urged his horse alongside hers. "Sure. How far?"

"We have a clear mile before we hit a drift fence. We'll turn around there. Ready?"

"Let's go." He tightened his hold on the reins and prepared to squeeze a signal to the horse with his knees.

"Okay, on three. One ... two ... three!" She let out a yell and flicked her horse with the reins.

He laughed aloud at the joy in her face and the challenge and kicked his horse in the flanks. After a couple of jumps, the black horse galloped down the beach. Her horse stayed even with the black horse, but gradually he drew ahead. Before he was ready, he saw the drift fence approaching and pulled back on the reins. He guided the black horse in a turn and faced back to meet Stephanie. She turned her horse, and they rode side by side in a slow walk to let the horses cool down.

"Wow, I knew you rode, but mister, you can really ride."

"You're not a bad rider yourself. But you gave me the faster horse. No wonder I won." He leaned on the pommel slouching in the saddle and watched the wind blow her dark hair into her face.

"I have never seen Mr. Rupert run like that and he's not even breathing hard. You won because you rode him better than I rode."

"Thanks, that's nice of you to say. These are fine animals." He patted the horse's neck.

"My mother was a rider more than my father. She insisted on having great horses. Otherwise, she didn't want to ride."

"When did your mother pass away?" He hoped he wasn't too forward.

"She died a few months after I graduated from college. I miss her more than I can say. My father was the strength in our family, but my mom was the heart." She looked out at the sea.

"I'm sorry if I brought up a painful subject." He should have been more thoughtful.

She turned back and met his eyes. "It's not really painful, and I don't mind talking about my mom. I just miss her."

"It has to be hard to have lost both of your parents and not have any brothers or sisters. I can't think what that must be like." He thought of the last time his family had been together. On July Fourth, twenty family members were at the ranch enjoying a time of talking, laughing, and food. He couldn't imagine not having that in his life.

"I'm glad you can't imagine it. It must be wonderful to have a big family like yours with everyone still living ... Now I'm sorry. I almost forgot about you losing your wife. That's something I can't imagine."

He nodded. He couldn't say it wasn't painful to talk about Valerie because it was. They both had suffered loss.

They walked the horses slowly as they talked. By the end of two hours, they turned back toward the stable. He wanted to change the subject. "What time do we meet for supper?"

"We'll eat at seven in the dining room, and then we can go back to the salon for a couple of hours." She pulled back on the reins, the horse stopped just outside the stables, and she dismounted.

He followed suit. He rubbed the black horse on the nose and wished he had an apple to offer as thanks for the pleasure of the ride.

As they walked back to the house, he said, "Thanks for the ride. I really enjoyed it."

She intertwined her arm with his. "I did too. It's been too long since I let myself have so much fun."

He covered her hand on his arm. "Me, too. Fun isn't something I have much of these days."

She glanced at him as she walked toward the house. "Why not? Don't you play with your daughter?"

"Yes, I play with Allie as much as I can. But there are always responsibilities waiting in the wings." He didn't know why he held back the information of Allie's heart condition. He loved his time with his little girl, but there was always an undercurrent of sadness and fear of time running out.

With reluctance, he let go of her hand to allow her to enter the front door first. But he knew it was best. He couldn't afford to start liking her any more than he already did. "I'm going to go shower before supper."

"Me too. I'll see you at seven. I just need to check with Maria."

He climbed the stairs to his room. He undressed and entered the big walk-in glass shower. He turned on the faucet and stood under a soothing massage from six showerheads. Closing his eyes, he reveled in the luxurious feeling. He could get used to living like this.

After dressing in slacks and a long-sleeved polo shirt, he returned to the salon and powered up his laptop. Punching the speed dial number for his mother's cell phone, he waited.

"Hello."

"Hi Mom, it's Flint." He smiled.

"Oh, hello son. You ready to talk to Allie?" Her voice sounded strong as usual, but he heard the stress nevertheless.

"Sure, but first how are you?"

"It's Allie. She hasn't had a very good day."

He felt as if he'd been punched in the chest. "What's wrong?"

"Oh, nothing specific. She's just tired and weak. You know if she wants to lie on the couch with her stuffed bears instead of going outside then she's not feeling well."

"Does she feel well enough to talk to me?" *Oh, God, please let my baby be all right.*

"I'm sure she'll want to speak to her daddy. Let me get her in front of the computer."

He waited, staring at the computer screen waiting, then he saw his Allie's face. "Hi sweetheart, it's Daddy." He could see tiredness in the dark splotches under Allie's eyes. She lacked her usual sparkle, and she didn't speak at first.

"Allie? Can you hear me?"

"Hi, Daddy. Why are you still in the computer? When are you coming home?" Her voice was small and weak.

"Soon baby, I'll be home in a few more days."

"I want you now. Please, Daddy." Her eyes filled with tears that ran silently down her cheeks.

"Don't cry, baby. I love you, little bunny." His chest ached with tears he couldn't release as he watched his little girl cry. He wanted to reach into the computer and gather her in his arms to comfort her, but there was nothing he could do.

"I love you too, Daddy. Please come home soon."

"I will, I promise." How long would it take to get a flight home? Suddenly, Mom's face appeared on the screen. "I think that's about all Allie's up to, son."

"Mom, should I come home? I can get on a plane and be there by morning."

She shook her head. "No, son. Allie just needs some rest. Stay and do your work, but call in the morning."

"All right, but you call me if she gets worse. I love you, Mom."

"Love you, son. I'll sleep with Allie tonight, and if need be, we'll call the medivac helicopter. I'll talk to you in the morning."

He closed the laptop, dropped his head in his hands, and prayed from the depths of his heart. *Dear God, please give Allie more time.*

Chapter Seventeen

SHE LEANED AGAINST the doorframe of the salon and watched him as he sat with his eyes closed and supporting his head in his hands. Was she intruding on something that wasn't her business? Was he in despair or maybe in prayer? "What's wrong, Flint?"

He jerked, blinked at her, and rubbed a hand over his face. "I just talked to Mom. My little girl, Allie, isn't feeling well."

She settled across the table from him. "How ill is she? Do you need to go home?"

He shook his head. "Mom said she'll call if I need to go." He rubbed his temple. "Is there a helicopter service nearby I could take to Kennedy Airport if it comes to that?"

"Yes, it only takes twenty minutes." She studied his lined face. He looked older than he had shortly before and she sensed that he was truly concerned. "If you need to go, just say so."

He heaved a heavy sigh. "Mom and Dad can look after Allie. They've been doing it all her life. If I'm needed Mom will call, no matter the time. But thanks for being concerned."

"I've fallen in love with that beautiful little girl just from her pictures. Anything I can do, you let me know."

"Well then, let's eat. I'm hungry." He closed the computer before standing.

She led the way to the stairs. "It seems to me that you're always hungry, but you never put on any weight."

He smiled. "You're right. My mom says I get that from my dad's side of the family."

Brigitte waited at the bottom of the stairs.

They entered the dining room where a long mahogany table was formally set.

After the meal of sirloin tip roast, baked potatoes, glazed carrots, salad, and hot yeast rolls, they returned to the salon for two more hours of work before scattering to their bedrooms for the night.

When She was finally in her room, she drew bath water, poured in her favorite lilac bath beads, and slid into the hot water to soak in her oversized bathtub. Just how ill was his little girl? He had seemed so much more somber after the call from his mother. Would he be that worried if she had a simple cold or the flu? Of course, she was a small child. She had no experience with sick children, but she regretted that the little girl wasn't feeling well.

He had appeared so tall and masculine riding the black horse along the edge of the surf. Getting out of the tub, she dried off, slipped the long blue silk nightgown over her head, and let it pour over her body. Padding barefoot on the plush carpet, she climbed into bed. Instead of drifting contentedly to sleep, however, thoughts of Flint swirled through her mind. If only when the job was completed, he could stay on. He never said anything that could be interpreted as personal interest, although he seemed to enjoy being with her. She slammed her fist into her pillow. If only he would speak about his feelings.

SATURDAY MORNING AS they worked in the salon again, she began to understand how much she had to lose. Not in terms of money, but in power. If she lost the position as CEO and head of the Board of Directors, she would lose her positional power. Listening to Flint and Brigitte discuss her finances, she felt curiously removed. Could it be she no longer wanted to be in charge of the Wellbourne Group? She wouldn't mind if she were no longer responsible for the lives and finances of so many people. The fun of meeting the challenge that had been a part of her life for the last several years had dissipated as the burden had increased.

"Stephanie, are you listening?" Brigitte peered at her over a file.

"Sorry." She straightened in her chair and pulled her shoulders back. "What are we talking about?"

Brigitte frowned. "Flint asked how badly you wanted to retain control of The Wellbourne Group?"

"I'm not sure how to answer that. I hate that it's being taken away from me. However, I don't know if I want to fight for it. I keep asking myself, what would my father want me to do? If it were my personal decision to let it go and move on, I'd possibly be fine. It's the betrayal I don't like."

He nodded. "I can understand that. You want it on your terms. After all, you worked long and hard to keep it together after your father's death."

She leaned forward. "Yes, and what right does someone have to come in and take it away?"

"Greed."

"What did you say?" She wasn't sure she heard him.

He scratched the back of his neck. "I said greed. Someone wants to make money and have the power to control it. Between the banks your company owns, the real estate, and the manufacturing, there's a lot of financial gains to be made and controlled."

"I'm not sure I want to fight over that. Let them have it. I've never truly wanted to be in control. I inherited control." She tapped a pen on the table.

"So if the Board of Directors voted to put someone else in your place, you'd be okay with that?" He stared at her with intensity as if he was trying to read her mind.

She returned his gaze. "I'll grieve it, but I'm not going to let it destroy me."

He leaned back and slapped his hands on the table. "Good for you."

She smiled at his reaction. "That doesn't mean I won't enter the board meeting with the intent of winning."

"Okay, then let's decide how you can fight."

They spent the morning discussing the possible outcomes of the meeting. Finally, she brushed a stray strand of hair from her face. "Let's stop for lunch and do something fun this afternoon and then meet again after dinner."

Brigitte gathered up files and papers. "What do you want to do?"

"Let's take the sailboat out and spend time on the water. Maria will put together a picnic, and we can eat on the boat. Then maybe when we come back, we'll have time for another horseback ride." She glanced from him to Brigitte, waiting for their responses.

Brigitte smiled. "I would love to go sailing. You know I'm always up for that."

"I'm willing, but I need to confess before we get on a boat, I'm not much of a sailor." He seemed almost embarrassed. "I've only been on a sailboat a couple of times on small lakes, but never the ocean."

She reached over and patted his arm. "Don't worry. Brigitte and I have sailed since we were children. We can handle the boat."

THE REST OF THE DAY and evening passed with laughter and fun as she and Brigitte taught Flint the rudimentary skills needed to sail the boat. She was amazed at how quickly he picked up on the ropes and rigging. By the time they sailed back to the dock, he helped as much as Brigitte.

Before he went to his room for the night, he spoke to her. "I hope you don't mind, but in the morning I'd like to borrow the car and go

to church. I asked Enzio about the location, and there's a congregation about ten miles from here. They have services at nine."

"Of course I don't mind." She wasn't surprised by his request, as
he seemed to go to church every Sunday.

"Would you and Brigitte like to come with me?"

She examined his face. She couldn't tell if it was important to
him or not. Did she want to go to church? She hadn't been but a couple of times in her life. But she did want to spend time with him.
"Yes, I'd like that. I'll ask Brigitte."

"Great." He smiled as if pleased with her answer.

THE NEXT MORNING FLINT and she rode to church services
together, Brigitte having begged off with a headache. She hadn't
made an appearance by the time they left the house.

She dressed in a dark blue Christian Dior suit with a white silk
blouse and navy blue three-inch heels.

He wore his black suit and conservative white shirt with a blue
and white striped tie.

She knew that they made a striking couple as they walked up the
sidewalk and into the auditorium of the small white wooden church
building.

There were about two hundred attendees. She didn't understand
most of the service but followed Flint's lead. It surprised her when
they began to sing, and she heard his strong baritone. He seemed to
know all the songs. She didn't even try to sing, but that didn't keep
her from listening with enjoyment to the congregation of voices raising their praise to God together. She had never heard anything like
it.

He was attentive but not hovering as he focused on the sermon
and the prayers. He left her to participate as she wished. As she
watched his face when the prayers were offered at the podium, she

couldn't help but wonder at his calm but serious countenance. When he opened his eyes at the end of the prayer and caught her staring at him, he only nodded and smiled.

As they drove back to the house, she felt more relaxed than she had for a long time. Exactly why, she couldn't say, but the experience of attending church with him made her feel good.

He drove the BMW slowly through the Sunday traffic. "Did you enjoy the service?"

"I really did, especially the singing. I've never heard anything so beautiful. And I had no idea that you sang like a professional."

"Me? Sing like a professional? I've never had anyone say that before." He glanced at her and then focused on his driving. "I'll admit that I enjoy singing. I've sung all my life. When we were kids, we spent cold winter evenings sitting around the fireplace singing hymns."

"That sounds wonderful. I'd love to have heard that."

"Well, if you come to the ranch when everyone gathers you'll get to." He chuckled. "Mom won't let a visit go by without us singing together. Of course, I like it also."

Did he just invite her for a visit? She wasn't sure, but the idea of traveling to Colorado to his home was enticing.

She smoothed her suit skirt. "After lunch let's go for another ride and just relax. We've covered about everything we can to be ready for the board meeting. George will drive us back to the city about four."

He turned the car into the drive of the Edge of the Pointe and stopped under the portico. "That sounds great. We'll have other times to talk in the next few weeks. You'll be prepared."

He held the car door open, and she stepped out. She placed her hand on his arm. "I do feel so much more prepared than I did last week. Thank you."

"You're welcome. By the way, you do remember that I'm leaving Wednesday to fly home for Thanksgiving?"

"Thanks for reminding me. I had almost forgotten it was the holidays. Then you'll return next Monday as usual?"

"Yes, and we have a week and a half until the board meeting." He opened the door into the house.

She changed out of her suit and into riding clothes. When she came downstairs for lunch, she found Brigitte already at the dining table looking wan and fragile.

"Are you all right?" She peered at her.

Brigitte shaded her eyes. "Yes, I have a migraine. It's eased off some, and I'll do better after I eat. Will you be upset if I beg off this afternoon?"

She sat across from Brigitte. "Not at all. You do what you need to feel better. Flint and I will probably go for a ride on the beach, and then George will be here to collect us."

Brigitte gave a shudder. "The thought of riding a horse makes my head hurt worse. I'll be packed and ready to ride back into the city, but I may be groggy from the migraine medicine."

She laughed. "I may be groggy from so much fun this weekend."

"How was the church service?"

"It was interesting. Did you know that Flint sings like a professional? He said he grew up singing with his family. It was delightful to listen to him."

"That sounds intriguing. I wish I'd felt like going. I'd have enjoyed it." Brigitte reached for the basket of rolls that Maria set on the table.

He came into the dining room dressed in jeans and a western shirt. Brigitte grinned at him. "Here's the cowboy. You ready to chow down?"

"Always. Hope I'm not dressed too casual for such an elegant dining room." He sat at the end of the long table with she and Brigitte on each side.

She passed the rolls to him. "You're dressed fine."

They spent a quiet hour eating and talking. She looked at the two people with her at this table. These were her two best and most loyal friends. What would she do without them? He would be going back to Colorado as soon as the job was completed, which would be within the month if she got voted out of her position as Chairperson of the Board and CEO. She had work for him to do for a few weeks after the Board of Directors meeting, but then he would leave. No matter what happened, she planned to ask Brigitte to stay on as her personal assistant.

Was there a way she could keep him in New York? Not with his daughter in Colorado. She had to face it. It was hopeless. He would soon be gone from her life.

Chapter Eighteen

GUILT OVER HIS ENJOYABLE weekend at the Edge of the Pointe nibbled at his gut. Stephanie and Brigitte were easy to be around. It wasn't just their beauty—which he didn't mind—it was also their intelligence. Although they talked mostly about business, still it had been invigorating to participate in the discussions with them.

The weekend had been infused with fun as well—boating and horseback riding in the surf. How could he have such a good time while his Allie suffered?

With only three days in the office before catching the plane for Colorado, he was too busy to dwell on his dilemma. But once on the flight headed home, his thoughts returned to the dark-haired beauty.

She wasn't a Christian, and he would never consider marrying someone who wasn't. She was the first woman to gain his attention since Valerie's death, and her lack of faith made her unavailable to him. Shifting in his seat and listening to the hum of the airplane, he looked inward. Would he want to marry her if she were a Christian? Physically he had no problem saying yes. She was a beautiful woman. But could she be a mother to a sick child? He didn't know. How would she cope with something like that? Would she even want to? It wasn't really a question since he could never marry her.

Noise, food, outdoor work, and family filled his Thanksgiving holiday. He enjoyed being with his sister Holly and her husband, Benjamin. And on Thanksgiving Day, Stephen, his wife Vicki, and their four children joined them. They lived on a ranch only a two-hour drive from Mom and Dad, but Stephen rarely could get away.

Allie was subdued and seemed content to lie in his lap much of the time. He tried not to let the others know how this scared him as he realized her worsening condition. Stephen's children seemed to understand and would play gently with Allie and then go away when they sensed her tiring. She took two or three naps every day and still seemed tired.

While Allie slept, he worked with Dad around the ranch. There was plenty to do—feed to move for the cattle, salt to put out, fences to check and repair, horses to care for and shoe. On Saturday, he and Dad spent the day crawling all over the roof of the house putting up Christmas lights. They also put up a star on the roof near the chimney and a plastic snowman and reindeer on the lawn. Then Sunday afternoon he helped Dad cut a tree. He helped Mom trim it while Allie lay in her Grandpa's lap and watched.

Allie's smile when they turned on the tree lights was his reward. Although how his folks were going to keep the tree green and alive for three weeks until Christmas, he wasn't sure. The holiday break passed too quickly.

It took everything he had to get on the plane and fly back to New York. His baby was slipping away. How could he leave her? But this job was his one chance to provide what she needed for life. He felt torn as if his mind and heart were pulled in two directions. He longed to see Stephanie and had missed her every minute he'd been gone. But his chest ached from the pain of leaving Allie. If only ... If only Allie could get her transplant and be well. But didn't he believe that heaven was a better place and that Allie would be better off there with her mother? Yes, he believed. He just couldn't stand the thought of being left alone. Was he selfish to try so hard to keep his daughter with him? Still, he had to do whatever he could to help her.

If only she was a Christian and would love him and his little girl. If only he were free to declare his feelings for her. He couldn't. It wasn't fair.

By the time the plane landed in New York, he felt as if he had been at war.

The day of the Board of Directors' meeting passed so quickly that he could barely keep up with what was happening. When the meeting ended, she was no longer on the Board nor CEO of The Wellbourne Group. Thor had won. Flint let out his breath as if he had been holding it all day. Not really surprised at the outcome, his first concern was how she was taking it.

As soon as the meeting adjourned, Brigitte slipped out of the room. He waited by the side of the door until Stephanie made it through the crowd to the hallway.

"Stephanie, no hard feelings I hope. It's just business." Thor had his hand on her arm.

She turned and looked up at him. "Yes, Thor, it's just business. You may want to remember that someday." She turned and walked past Flint.

He strolled behind her as she made her way down the hall. He spoke quietly. "Why don't you go on down to my office? That way you can avoid talking to any of the others."

She nodded. Passing her own office, she walked down to the end of the hall and entered his office.

He looked back and saw that no one had followed. Shutting the door, he guided her to the couch against the wall out of sight of the hallway. "Sit down. Brigitte is getting you some hot tea."

Her eyes had a faraway expression, and she looked at him without seeming to understand what he said. He put his hands on her shoulders and gently pushed her to sit.

Brigitte entered the office carrying a tray with a teapot, cups, cream, and sugar. She set it on the coffee table in front of the couch and poured a cup of tea and added cream and sugar.

"Thanks, Brigitte." He took the cup and placed it in Stephanie's hand. "Now drink your tea." His voice was firm, but also full of concern.

She blinked and looked down at the cup of tea as if she hadn't realized it was there. She slowly lifted it to her mouth and sipped some of the hot liquid.

Brigitte swallowed, and the muscles of her throat moved convulsively as if she struggled not to cry. "Are you all right, Steph?"

She tightened her hold on the cup of tea and glanced up at Brigitte. "Yes, I'm all right. I just needed a minute." She took another sip. "This is a good tea."

He waited, knowing that she was coming out of the shock of what had happened.

She suddenly looked up. "Brigitte, did you follow my instructions?"

"Yes, it's all done." Brigitte glanced at him.

He took Stephanie's hand. "What do you want to do now? Do you want us to call George to come to take you home?" He wanted to gather her in his arms and kiss away any hurt.

She shook her head and looked as if she was just waking from a nap. "No, there is too much to do. I want to pack my things. Thor may be taking over my office in the morning, but I'm not handing it over. I'm not going to do anything illegal, but what is mine, or my father's, is leaving these offices tonight."

He squeezed her hand. "Tell me how I can help."

"Brigitte has already started some things in motion. If I lost the vote today, I wanted to be prepared. George is coming at nine this evening with some men to move all of the art and furniture that belongs to the Wellbourne family. This is a situation where to ask forgiveness rather than permission is the greater virtue." She squeezed his hand as if holding on to a life raft. "Flint, please download all files that you think I might need in the future. I've never signed a confidentiality clause with my own company so I can take what is mine. That includes knowledge about the companies within The Wellbourne Group."

He understood what she was asking and why. He wasn't as clear on the legal side but decided to trust that she knew what she was doing. "Do you have a list of what you want?"

Brigitte pointed to his desk. "It's in the folder there."

She looked around the office. "I'm not really sure where you stand with the company now that Thor is taking over. I'm afraid you're out as far as he's concerned. But to be honest with you, I still need your help. Would you and your firm be willing to work with me personally for a few weeks? I want to divest myself of all of my holdings in The Wellbourne Group within the next few months. Thor and his backers wanted the company, they can have it."

"You do know what that will do to the stock prices?" He was sure she did.

"Yes, it will lower the price of the company stock quite a bit. Even so, I'll still leave the company with more money than I can ever spend. That's why I need you and your firm to continue to work with me. I don't have anyone else I trust."

He nodded. Vacating this office was not a problem for him. All he had here was his laptop and CD player. "Let me call my firm and make sure, but I don't see any reason we can't help you. Where will we work?"

She took a deep breath. "For now we'll work out of my apartment. There's plenty of room. It'll be a temporary solution. We'll have everything moved and set up by tomorrow. It'll mean working late tonight if you're willing."

He shrugged his shoulders. "I have no problem with that."

"Thank you again." For the first time, she looked as if she might cry. "Well, I'll go get busy in my office and check back with you in a few minutes."

Brigitte had stepped out of the office, but she soon returned. "Thor and the others have left the building, and I've sent everyone home early. The three of us are the only ones in the offices. I locked the outer door, and the guard at the front door knows to watch for George and let him in with his helpers."

She let out a deep sigh. "Good. I don't think I could face anyone this evening." She stood and left his office with Brigitte right behind her.

He looked around at the spacious office, probably the grandest office he would ever occupy. He felt not a twinge at leaving it. It had never seemed like his. He plugged in the coffee pot. It was going to be a long night.

Chapter Nineteen

REACHING UNDER THE desk, he removed the electronic bug, broke it open, and tore the heart out of it. Then he grabbed the one under the phone and dismantled it. At last, he could talk freely on the phone with Ben and Tony.

First, he dialed Ben on his cell phone. As he waited for his boss to answer, he opened his personal laptop next to the company laptop.

As he connected them with a cord, Ben answered, "Hello."

"Hey, Ben, it's Flint."

"How did the meeting go?"

He tapped several keys on each computer. "As we predicted, she's out."

Ben's voice held genuine concern. "I'm sorry. She didn't deserve that."

"She's holding together for now. She wants us to continue working for her. As of today, we'll no longer be working for The Wellbourne Group, but for her personally."

"I wondered about that. We received a bank transfer about thirty minutes ago. It is for the full payment, a million and a half dollars." Ben's voice was calm.

"Hmm. So that's what she had Brigitte doing."

"What do you mean?"

He smiled. "At the end of the meeting, Brigitte disappeared, and then a little later Stephanie asked her if it was done. I bet she had a whole list of payments she wanted to be paid out while she was still

CEO. I wouldn't be surprised if she hasn't added year-end bonuses in several of the employees' bank accounts. She knew this was coming."

Ben chuckled. "She's not going to leave anything to chance. Or maybe I should say, to that fella coming in."

"Okay, Ben, here's what we need to do. I'm downloading files right now. I'll send most of them to you. I'm not going to download anything from the company mainframe to our mainframe. It's more tedious to do it this way, but I'm letting it pass through my laptop. That way if there is a problem down the road, our firm will be out of the loop."

"Good idea. Can we destroy the bugs we found in our office here in Cedar Ridge?"

"Absolutely. There's no reason to hide the fact that we know about the bugs now. In fact, we need to get them all cleaned out."

"That's easy as we have known for months where they are. I'm glad not to have to listen to all that jazz anymore."

He laughed. "Tomorrow I'll start working with a staff at Stephanie's apartment until she sets up a new office. I'll call you in the morning for sure. But I may need to call a couple more times tonight. We have to vacate these offices by midnight."

"No problem. I'll stay in the office until you tell me I can go home. Tony is also here. We kind of anticipated it would be like this."

"Thanks, Ben, I'll talk to you later. Get ready for several gigabits to hit our servers."

He disconnected. He checked the computers, connected his computer to the internet, and started the download. Looking at the list of computer files Stephanie had compiled, He nodded. She had chosen precisely what she needed to transfer. After making sure everything functioned as it should, he strolled down the hallway to her office. The usual hubbub from the other offices was eerily absent.

Brigitte and Stephanie were behind the couch removing a painting from the wall.

He offered his strength to take the weight of the large landscape. "I'm not questioning that you know what you're doing, but I'm curious. How can you prove that this painting belongs to the family instead of the firm?"

She chuckled. "Because my father didn't trust anyone. In his will, he listed each, and every piece of art in these offices and left them personally to me. I wonder if he knew this might happen someday. Anyway, he protected me. I can prove beyond any doubt that this painting is mine. The last time I had it appraised for insurance purposes, its value was set at close to eight hundred thousand. The total value of the art in these offices is nearly fifty million dollars, and I intend to take everything that belongs to me."

He grinned. "Do you have an armored car coming to collect it?"

"No, but I do have armed guards coming. They will move the art to a vault where they'll be safe until I decide what to do. I'm sure I won't keep everything, but it'll take a while to decide what to do—sell them, or give some away."

He remembered other paintings in offices and hallways. The ones he thought were copies must be originals, even the Remington in his office. He shook his head. Had he known, he might have spent more time absorbing it.

"I spoke with Ben. Our firm is willing to continue working with you. He said to thank you for the payment. He's standing by as I'm downloading the files you requested."

She nodded. "I'm relieved. I wasn't sure what I'd do if he said no."

"I'll go back and finish. Let me know when the movers get here. Am I to assume that the paintings in my office also need to go?"

"Absolutely. And your chair, also. Brigitte said you really liked it. It's part of your bonus."

He grinned. "Can I have a receipt so I won't be accused of stealing it?"

She managed to smile back. "Sure, I'll get you a receipt."

George arrived with a crew of men who moved everything Stephanie indicated. Receipts were signed, and the truck was driven away with a vehicle in front and one behind as an escort. Her treasures were safely away. A smaller truck had taken furniture, including his chair with a promise to deliver the items to her apartment the next day.

At fifteen minutes before midnight, he took the elevator to the lobby with Stephanie and Brigitte.

On the sidewalk, she stopped to look up at the building and the sign that carried her name.

Brigitte slid into the car, but he waited beside Stephanie. "It seems unreal," she said slowly.

He put his arm around her shoulder. "Give it time."

She leaned into him. "I wish I knew what my father would say if he were here."

"He'd say, well done, daughter. Now, it's time to move on." He tightened his hold on her.

She turned to stare up at him. With a slow nod, she started toward the car.

IN THE MORNING LIGHT, she stared at the confusion of file cabinets, desks, and chairs in what had been her formal dining room. It was a mess. She didn't know where to start. Maybe she should wait for Flint and Brigitte to arrive. With their late night, she had told them not to come before nine. She had thirty minutes yet before she could expect their arrival.

As she wandered around the apartment, the exhaustion from the previous days of stress made her feel as if her thoughts swam through syrup. She hoped Flint and Brigitte were more clearheaded.

Going into the kitchen, she made coffee. Maybe that was the place to start on this morning that seemed so surreal. Just sit down, have coffee, and talk about where and how to begin her new life.

Hearing the elevator doors opening, she went to the hall to find Ivana Zuk taking off her coat. She had forgotten that this was the housekeeper's day to clean.

"Good morning, Ms. Wellbourne. I didn't expect you to be home. Is everything all right?" Ivana hung her coat in the hall closet and stuffed her large handbag on the upper shelf.

"Yes, but I'm making some changes in my work routine that I need to tell you about as it will impact you." She hadn't thought that she needed to let Ivana know what was going on. She looked at the forty-five-year-old woman who had cleaned her apartment two days a week for the last five years. She came and went so quietly and did her work so unobtrusively that Stephanie usually only saw the results and had forgotten that someone had to accomplish the tidiness.

"Yes, ma'am?" Ivana waited for her to speak.

"Let's go into the kitchen for coffee." She led the way, and Ivana followed her.

After they both had poured a mug of coffee and sat at the kitchen table, Stephanie told her that she no longer worked at Wellbourne. For now, she would conduct business out of the apartment.

"After Christmas, I'll locate an office and set up my new company there. Until then the dining room will be a workspace for two of my assistants, and I'll use my home office. This apartment will need more cleaning, and I could use help with meals and shopping. Would you be available a few extra days every week?" She sipped from her mug and waited for Ivana to respond.

"I can work more but not full days. My mother-in-law lives with us, and she's quite feeble. If you're willing for me to come at nine and leave by three, I could probably work four or five days a week." Ivana looked expectantly at her.

She nodded. "That'll be perfect. As long as you can come for a few hours a day and keep things under control."

"So you want everything cleaned, food shopping, and meals prepared?"

"Yes. For example, my assistants will use this downstairs area, and it'll need to be cleaned more often."

Ivana stood and picked up their empty mugs. "Then I better get busy. You tell me if there is anything extra I need to do. We'll keep the same system where you write down anything needed from the shops and I'll either go out for them or have the items delivered."

She gave the woman a hug. "Thank you."

Wandering back into the dining room confusion, she brushed a few tears away. Why was she so weepy this morning?

Again, she heard the elevator and turned to welcome Brigitte and Flint. As she watched Brigitte taking his coat to hang in the hall closet, she realized he had never been in her apartment before.

"Morning, hope you two got some rest after our late night." She took Brigitte's handbag and put it on the shelf beside Ivana's.

Brigitte smoothed back stray strands of hair, which had escaped from her French twist. "Well, I'm still weary from the last few days, but if you have some coffee made that'll help revive me. It's a cold morning, and we'll probably have snow this afternoon."

"I have to agree with Brigitte. Coffee sounds good." He looked around as he stood holding his bag with his laptop. "Where should I put this?"

She waved toward the dining room. "For now set it on the table. We can organize later. Let's go into the kitchen and have some coffee."

They moved into the kitchen where she introduced them to Ivana. After getting coffee for Flint and Brigitte, they sat in the living room and discussed how to get organized.

She sat with her feet tucked up under her as he laid out a plan to reorganize her holdings. Brigitte took notes on her laptop.

He stopped gazed at her. "You all right, Stephanie?"

She didn't feel all right. Nothing was normal this morning, but she didn't know how to explain the strangeness. "Yes, why do you ask?" It was almost as if she didn't know who or what she was anymore. Maybe he would tell her.

He bent toward her. "You're pale—ghostly. Almost as if you're here, but not here. Maybe we should wait to discuss this until you've had time to process what happened." His voice was soft and kind.

She suddenly found tears trickling down her cheeks. She reached for a tissue from the box on the lamp table next to her chair. "I'm sorry. I don't know why I'm crying."

Brigitte leaned forward with a frown. "Maybe Flint is right. We can do this tomorrow."

She shook her head. "No, I'm all right. It's just that my emotions seem all out of whack. You were saying, Flint, that I need to organize a new company under a different name, both for tax purposes and for liability. Did I understand you?"

He gazed at her a moment as if assessing her ability to deal with her new life. "Yes, that's what I'm suggesting. Then as we sell your shares in The Wellbourne Group, we'll reinvest under the umbrella of your new corporation. But I can't start the paperwork until you decide on a new name. I suggest you don't use your own name."

She looked from him to Brigitte. It was hard to think. A new name for her business? "Can you suggest something?"

Brigitte chewed on the end of her pen, then she laid it down on the coffee table. "I know the word Phoenix has been used a lot, but I like the concept of rising out of the ashes into something more wonderful than before. Or, even Firebird."

He smiled and nodded. "I like that concept. Firebird Consortium, or Firebird Consultants."

She liked it too. "What about the Firebird Foundation? I want to help others. That's what foundations do."

"How about two—a charitable foundation and a consultant firm." He rubbed his temple. "The Firebird Foundation and Firebird Consultants."

She liked the sound of that. "We can hire someone to design a logo of a bird rising from the flames. I know it's been done before, but it gives meaning to how I feel."

He stood and waved his hand toward the dining room. "Let's get that room set up so Brigitte and I can get to work. You tell us how you want it arranged and I'll move the furniture."

Brigitte opened her cell phone. "The first thing I'm going to do is call Dwain Chou to come over and run wires to set up a phone system and Internet access. He's a technology wiz. You two get the room organized, and I'll be along in a bit."

She led the way into the dining room, thankful for his and Brigitte's take-charge attitudes. If left to her, she feared she would have hidden in a dark room and cried all day. She couldn't do that with these two ready to help her build a new life.

Chapter Twenty

THE DAYS PASSED SWIFTLY but the nights were brutal. Self-doubt and fear pummeled her brain like bullets in a war zone until she could hardly take any more. Fear of the unknowable future was the worst. She had never experienced anything like it before and couldn't understand what was happening to her. Sleep-deprived, no appetite, achy and ill, she crawled through the days.

Four days before Christmas, Brigitte departed to be with her elderly parents in Boston. At her departure, it was as if light left the apartment in stifling darkness. She found herself crying off and on. She had to get a hold of herself.

The next morning, she waited in the living room for his arrival. In a few hours, he too would be gone for the holidays. She dreaded telling him goodbye.

"You all right?" He stood by the recliner where she lay curled in a fetal knot.

She hadn't realized he had entered the room until he spoke. "I'm not sure. I don't know why I'm so weepy just because Brigitte left yesterday."

He squatted down beside her until he was gazing at eye level. "How long will she be gone?"

"She's taking two full weeks of vacation. Her parents are elderly, and she's way past due for a visit. They need her through Christmas and the New Year. I want her to be there." Tears formed again. Why couldn't she control them? "I just feel so alone."

He frowned. "Do you have anyone to be with over the holidays?"

"I don't have anyone." It sounded pathetic even to her, but it was the truth. "All my friends—and I'm beginning to realize I don't have many—are going to their families."

As she faced the reality that he was her only remaining friend—other than Brigitte—and he was leaving in a few hours, tears that she couldn't control flowed down her cheeks.

He handed her a box of tissues and then placed his hand on her arm. "Why don't you come home with me? We have plenty of space at the house, and everyone would love to meet you."

She stared into his eyes. Did he mean it? Or, was he just being kind to a foolish woman who couldn't stop crying. "Your parents ... what would they think? It's Christmas, not a time for strangers."

He smiled. "It is exactly the time for strangers. After all, the baby Jesus came as a stranger."

She smiled back through her tears. "Are you comparing me to a baby?"

His smile turned into a grin, and he raised one eyebrow. "Aren't we all babies at times? Let's get you packed, and we'll see if we can find a couple of seats together on the plane. You're going to come and experience a Colorado Christmas."

She had no energy to resist his enthusiasm. With Ivana's help, she started packing. Not wanting to arrive without presents for the family, she called a concierge service, described the people she needed gifts for, and had them wrapped and sent over by courier. She didn't tell Flint, but when George loaded her luggage into the trunk of the car, the largest of the four suitcases was full of presents for his family.

He had arranged everything, including the plane ticket, which meant securing the last two seats on the flight. It didn't hurt she paid the full first-class ticket price.

Before leaving the apartment, she hugged Ivana and gave her a gift bag that contained several small gifts including a bottle of bubble bath, a container of special hand cream, a gold necklace, and an envelope with a year-end bonus. "Don't open this until Christmas Day. And please take any food home that will spoil."

"Don't you worry about your place. I'll come by and check on everything. Thank you for my Christmas gift. Your gift will be waiting here when you get back." Ivana hugged her. "Since I didn't know you were going away, I had planned to bring it tomorrow."

"Thank you, but you didn't have to give me anything. All the help you've been this last year is gift enough." She reached for the tissue in her coat pocket as the tears started again. Would she ever stop being so weepy? What was wrong with her?

The ride to the airport was quiet, as she didn't know what to say now that she was on her way to his home. What did he think of her? She could only assume that he saw a frail weepy woman. She had never thought of herself as weak, but her inner strength had vanished since the board meeting. It was as if something that she needed had been stolen away. But how to get it back? She had no idea.

"We're here, ma'am." George's voice startled her, and she glanced out the window to see the curb in front of the airport.

As she and Flint climbed out of the limo, George snapped his finger for a porter to help load the luggage cart. Other than Flint's duffle bag, all the luggage was hers.

They followed the porter toward the check-in counter. She said, "I seem to have brought a lot more luggage than you. I'm afraid I didn't pack very well."

He cocked his head. "Remember I have a twin sister, a mom, and once had a wife. I'm used to women having three suitcases to my one. Also, I didn't give you much time to plan. I'm amazed you packed so quickly."

Relieved he understood, She sighed. She also realized that it was the first time he had ever referred to his dead wife. Did that mean he thought of her as a friend he could speak to about his personal life? She hoped so as she was very grateful for his friendship.

They were soon in their first class seats, and the plane taxied down the runway.

"How long is the flight?" He would know as he's taken this flight back and forth for months.

He shifted in his seat and stretched his legs out. "We should land at Denver International within five hours. I'm concerned about the weather. The forecast calls for a snowstorm to pass through the Denver area."

She looked out the window and saw nothing but clouds. "Does this mean a problem for us?"

"Well, hopefully, the Denver airport will be clear, and then we have an hour and a half drive to the ranch. I told Dad not to meet us and that we would rent a car. It'll cost more, but I don't want him out driving if the weather gets too bad."

"Don't worry about the cost. This trip is on me. You're doing more than your share by inviting me to spend Christmas with your family. I just hope your mother won't mind too much."

He turned in his seat, eyebrows raised. "You don't know my folks, but Mom will take to you as if you're one of the family. In fact, if Mom thought that I didn't invite you because I worried whether you'd be welcome, she would take her wooden spoon to my ears."

She laughed at the image. She looked forward to meeting this woman who bossed her men around and made them like it.

An hour out from Denver the captain spoke over the intercom. "Ladies and Gentlemen, we've just been informed the Denver International Airport is closed due to a snowstorm. We hoped to make it in before that happened, but the storm is moving faster than expected. We've diverted to Cheyenne, Wyoming. Sorry for the inconvenience. Cabin crew, make ready for landing."

He glanced past her trying to see out the window, but only whitish gray clouds filled the sky.

She couldn't decide whether she needed to be afraid or not. "What does this mean?"

He ran his fingers through his hair causing it to spike in places. "It means we're stuck in Cheyenne unless I can find a vehicle to drive to the ranch. I'll need to find something that can make it over the passes, although the highway from Cheyenne to Cedar Ridge isn't bad. I'm more concerned about the road from Cedar Ridge to the ranch."

"Will we try to go tonight?" She couldn't imagine the road conditions he was talking about. Winter in the mountains was something she had never experienced except for a few ski trips when she hadn't been driving.

"No, it's too dangerous. I'll try to get us rooms at a hotel and then see about finding something to drive tomorrow. No matter the road conditions, I must arrive at the ranch by tomorrow night. I promised my little girl I'd be home on Christmas Eve. I intend to keep that promise."

She heard the steel commitment in his voice and never doubted that he'd do as he said. "Then that's what we have to do."

He shook his head. "It may be safer for you to stay in Cheyenne and come on when the storm has passed."

"No way, mister. You're not dumping me in Cheyenne. If you go, I'm going."

He grinned. "Just so I know where you stand."

WITH ALL OF THE STRANDED travelers, the snowstorm made getting a room difficult. She watched him as he stood in a long line at the hotel counter at the Cheyenne airport. She had told him she was okay with them sharing a room, but he shook his head.

She wandered to a seating area. She sat next to a young couple with a baby. The young man wore a U.S. Army uniform.

"Are you stuck here also?" the pretty young girl holding the sleeping baby asked.

She smiled. "Yes, we were on a flight to Denver that had to land here."

The soldier, who didn't look old enough to be out of high school, nodded. "We were on the same flight. We're trying to get to our folks in Fort Collins. We've been traveling for two days now, all the way from Germany."

"I'm Stephanie. My friend over there is Flint. We're trying to get to his parents' ranch outside Cedar Ridge. But we only flew from New York."

"I know where Cedar Ridge is. That's a nice area and not too far from Fort Collins." The young man reached across his wife and offered his hand. "I'm Todd. This is my wife, Tiffany, and our son, Ryan."

She shook his hand. "How old is your baby?" She didn't have any experience with infants.

"He's four months old today," Tiffany said with obvious pride in her voice. "Would you like to hold him?"

Before she knew what was happening, she had a little bundle of humanity cuddled in her arms. "Oh, isn't he beautiful."

Tiffany and Todd both beamed at her for recognizing their special infant.

"Where are you staying tonight? Do you already have a place?" She assumed they did since Todd wasn't in line.

Tiffany shook her head. "We'll manage here. Because of the storm, they won't close the airport terminal."

"You mean to stay here all night with the baby?" She couldn't believe what she'd heard.

"Well ... we hadn't planned on having a layover and don't have money for a hotel room." Todd spoke with hesitancy.

Flint ambled back with a sheet of paper in his hand. "I've got us a place to stay. It's a suite at The Plains Hotel in downtown Cheyenne. They're sending a van to pick us up. The only rooms left in the whole town."

"Flint, this is Todd and Tiffany and their little son Ryan. They're just back from a tour of duty in Germany."

He and Todd shook hands. "You folks stranded also?"

"Yes, sir. We were on the same flight."

"How many rooms are there in the suite?" She handed the sleeping baby back to his mother.

"It's the King Presidential suite and has two bedrooms and a living room. I think they even said it has a Jacuzzi tub. I know it's more than we need and it's pricey, but it's the only rooms available."

She smiled. "I think we do need it. Todd and Tiffany are going to join us if that's all right with you. They don't have a place for the night and have been traveling for two days."

He glanced from her to the two tired young people. "That's a great idea. Let's get our luggage and go meet the van."

"Whoa there, partner. We can't take advantage of you all." A western drawl permeated Todd's objection.

"You're not taking advantage. You're enjoying western hospitality," he said.

She smiled as she stayed with Tiffany and the baby while he and Todd organized their luggage. It felt good to reach out and help someone else. Maybe she was beginning to get that Christmas spirit.

Chapter Twenty-One

AN HOUR LATER, HE HAD his band of travelers settled into the large suite in the old renovated hotel filled with western decor and artwork.

"What do you think, Stephanie? Todd and Tiffany with the baby in the big bedroom, you take the small one, and I'll take the fold-out sofa here in the living room."

She picked up her makeup case. "That's perfect. I'll order dinner from room service."

He scratched his head. "Don't you mean supper? Out here we have dinner at noon and supper in the evenings."

She widened her eyes and raised her eyebrows. "Are you kidding?"

Todd and Tiffany both laughed, and Todd said, "That's the way it is out here. Where did you say you were from?"

She stood as tall as her five foot two inches allowed. "I'm a New Yorker."

He turned to Tiffany. "Do you have everything you need for the baby? Formula, diapers, etcetera."

She blushed and glanced up at Todd. "I'm breastfeeding the baby so we don't need formula, but by tomorrow we're going to run low on diapers."

He stroked the sleeping baby's cheek. "You all get settled and take it easy. I'll find more diapers by morning."

After contacting the concierge and asking that diapers be located, he called his parents.

Dad answered the phone on the first ring. "Flint, is that you?"

"Hi, Dad. Just called to let you know I won't be home this evening. We got diverted to Cheyenne. I'll find something that will make it through the storm and drive in tomorrow."

"Well, I won't say we're not disappointed, because we are. But I'd rather have you safe."

"How bad are the roads?"

"From here to Cedar Ridge they are as good as closed. Samuel got in about three this afternoon just before they closed the airport. He rented a four-wheel drive Jeep. Otherwise, I doubt he would have made it. Abe and his family arrived yesterday ahead of the storm."

"Wish we could have beaten the storm, too, but I'll get there by evening tomorrow. Is Allie asleep?"

"Yes, son. You want I should wake her? She's exhausted with all the people coming and going."

"No, don't. But if she should wake up, tell her I called."

"I'll do that. Your mom wants to talk to you."

He waited while Mom took the phone.

"Hi, son. Where are you staying tonight? Your dad said you were diverted to Cheyenne."

"You know the old Plains Hotel? We have a suite here. We doubled up with a young couple and their baby in a two bedroom and parlor suite."

"That sounds nice. Is Ms. Wellbourne all right?"

"Yes, she's fine. She insists on driving down with me tomorrow. I'm not sure she knows how severe a winter storm can be."

"Well, you take care of her and be safe. I'll have your pecan pie ready when you get here."

He smiled. "Thanks, Mom. Dad said Allie was tired. Is that all?"

"You know how it is. She can't take too much excitement. She loves having her cousins here, but it does tire her out. But she's no worse than when you saw her at Thanksgiving."

"All right Mom. I'll be home tomorrow."

After getting off the phone, He sank onto the bed, his chest tight and a lump the size of the Rocky Mountains caught in his throat. This might be his last Christmas with Allie. Yes, he would definitely be home tomorrow, one way or the other.

He started making phone calls to find some kind of transport for the morning. He finally reached an old high school buddy who put him in touch with Roy Hubbard, the owner of a freight company.

"Do you have any trucks going to Cedar Ridge, Mr. Hubbard? A friend and I desperately need to catch a ride there by Christmas Eve."

"I have a delivery scheduled to go to Cedar Ridge by way of Fort Collins. But my regular driver slipped on the ice and broke his leg. Do you have a license to drive a truck?" Roy Hubbard asked.

"Yes, sir. I have a license to drive eighteen-wheelers. I used to drive feed trucks all over Colorado."

The man sounded doubtful. "It's full of produce, and if I don't get it delivered, I'll lose a lot of money. If you can get it to Cedar Ridge, I'll pay you double."

"You don't need to do that. I'm glad to help you out. It'll solve the problem of how I'm getting there. Do you have chains on the wheels?"

"I'll have them on by the time you pick up the truck in the morning."

HE WAS UP EARLY THE next morning and was soon joined by Todd in the sitting area. They watched the TV weatherman report that only two feet of snow covered the city and the farther into the mountains, the deeper the snow.

He gazed out the window at the overcast sky, which threatened more snow to come. "Let's go down to the coffee shop and eat. I have a proposition for you." He wrote a note telling Stephanie where they were and then led the way to the elevator.

After ordering a full breakfast for both of them, Flint said, "I've got a ride to Cedar Ridge by way of Fort Collins, and you and Tiffany are welcome to come with us." He explained about the truck and that it would have enough room for all of them. "I trust the roads to start out, but there are no guarantees. We might get stuck on the highway."

Todd stirred his coffee. "I want to get home. We've been gone for two years. Eight months of that time, I was in Iraq. Our folks haven't seen the baby. If you're sure enough to start out yourself, I'm willing to take a chance you'll make it."

He cut into the pancakes. "What did you do in Iraq?"

"I drove a tank, a Bradley."

He nodded. "Then you might be able to spell me driving the truck."

"No problem, sir. I also drove trucks."

"Then let's go talk to the ladies and get home."

"You mind if I ask about you and Stephanie? You don't seem to be married."

"No, we're just friends from work. She doesn't have a family, so I invited her to share the holidays with mine. There's no inappropriate behavior going on between us."

"I'm sorry. I shouldn't have asked."

"I'm glad you did. I should have made that clear last night."

"If you'll tell me what our share of the room cost is I'll pay it now."

"You don't owe anything. We would have paid for the rooms whether you all stayed with us or not. Let this be our Christmas gift to you and a bit of appreciation for your service to our country."

"Thank you, sir. That's a help to us."

He took a taxi to the trucking firm. Driving the eighteen-wheeler with more caution than usual because of the snow and ice on the road, he drove the huge truck back to the hotel.

Stephanie and Todd with his family waited on the sidewalk with their luggage. By the time he had everyone settled and luggage loaded, the truck cab was full with Stephanie and Tiffany with the baby in the back seat of the cab and Todd riding passenger in the front.

He started south on Interstate 25, and almost immediately it began to snow. Not only because of the snow on the highway, but also because of the traffic, they were only able to go about twenty miles an hour.

Twice they had to stop and wait because cars sat crossways on the road. It was almost two in the afternoon when he turned the truck into the back parking lot of a local food store in Fort Collins.

Two men from the store came out and began to unload part of the produce.

He convinced Stephanie to return to the cab after a stop in the grocery store restroom.

A big van drove in, and laughing folks spilled out, smothering Todd and Tiffany in hugs and kisses for returning children. He could only imagine what these parents felt to finally have their loved ones safely back home.

Todd introduced an older man. "Dad, I want you to meet Flint Tucker of Cedar Ridge. He and Stephanie rescued us last night and got us here."

"Thank you, young man, for bringing my boy home. And my grandson!"

"I'm glad I could help out." He shook the man's hand.

"Why don't you folks come on out to the house and have a bite to eat?"

"Thank you for the invite, but we need to get on the road as soon as this truck is ready. My folks are also waiting, and I have a little girl who wants her daddy home for Christmas Eve."

"I understand. Well, drive safe."

"Flint, here is my name, address, and phone number. Anything I can ever do for you, just call."

"Thanks, Todd. I appreciate that. Here's my card." He handed it to the young man. "You just take your little family home and enjoy the holidays."

Todd stood tall and saluted. "Yes, sir."

IT WAS ALMOST THREE before the men had unloaded the supplies for the Fort Collins store. The rest of the produce needed to be delivered to a grocery store in Cedar Ridge. Flint was anxious to get back on the road.

The truck roared to life, and he looked at her sitting still and waiting. "You ready?"

"Yes. You say that as if I need to brace myself for something."

He turned the big rig onto the street and drove slowly to the on-ramp of Interstate 25. "It's snowing even more south of here. There's a chance they're going to close the Interstate. We'll do well to make it into Cedar Ridge. I'm not sure if we can make it all the way to the ranch. This rig is lighter now, which is good and bad. I'm going to drive as carefully as I can, but I can't guarantee I'll keep it on the road."

"So you're saying get ready for an adventure." Her smile didn't stay long.

He laughed. "That's one way of looking at it. We have a full tank of gas and a generator for heat separate from the engine. We won't freeze to death, but we may get stuck on the road for a couple of days."

"You really mean it, a couple of days!" The surprise at the thought was in her voice.

"I'll do my best not to let that happen."

The trust in her gaze left him with a warm feeling. She seemed to be handling their traveling difficulties with calm, compared to her reaction after losing control of her company.

He quit talking so he could concentrate on driving. The snow made visibility difficult, and he felt the tires struggling for traction even with the chains. The traffic was almost non-existent now on the snow-covered highway. Only the tire tracks of the vehicles in front of him helped him know where to drive. That and the upright metal posts every few yards along the edge of the roadway.

It took an hour to drive from Fort Collins to the turn off onto Highway 34. No traffic moved in the relentless snow. Struggling to stay on the road he almost couldn't see, required all of his energy.

Although only a little before five, darkness hovered over them as the eighteen-wheeler crept into Cedar Ridge. He couldn't believe it had taken the full day to drive from Cheyenne. Usually, he would have made it in two hours. Being careful not to lose concentration the last quarter mile, he drove onto the snow-covered parking lot of the Big E Grocery Store. He had called ahead, and five men waited to unload the produce.

Climbing down from the big rig, he greeted his old high-school teammate, Sandy Jones, who ran the grocery store.

"Flint, you old dog. When did you take to driving eighteen-wheelers? And who is that with you?"

He finally got free of the bear hug from Sandy who stood three inches taller than he. "Meet Stephanie Wellbourne of New York City. She's spending Christmas with us if I can get out to the ranch."

Sandy glanced up at the open passenger window and gave her a wave. "Glad to meet you, ma'am. A snowy welcome we're giving you." He pulled the collar of his ski jacket up to keep out the snow that still fell. "I tell you, Flint, the only way to get you home tonight is by snowmobile. If we can drive to Shorty's place and get some of the fellows to meet us, we can get you home from there. What do you say?"

"I hate to ask you to do that for me on Christmas Eve. You need to be with your family this evening." He wanted to say, yes please, get me home.

"How's Allie? Don't you think we better get you home for her?" Sandy hooked his thumbs in his belt.

He couldn't respond, he could only nod, and then thumped Sandy's shoulder.

"Ms. Wellbourne, do you have a ski suit?" Sandy shouted up to her.

Chapter Twenty-Two

SHE GIGGLED AT HER image in the mirror over the dresser in the small, crowded bedroom. The borrowed ski suit, several sizes too big, made her look like a red snowman. But at least she'd be warm. He had brought her to Shorty's small home and introduced her to the man and his family. She had lost count of the names of people who appeared to help them get ready for the ride to the ranch.

The little house was so stuffed with people, furniture, toys, and pets that she couldn't tell whether it was even clean. She had never been in the home of someone so poor. Would his home be like this little, crowded place? Maybe it had been a mistake to come.

She wandered into the kitchen where assorted men and women sat around the kitchen table. Children and dogs raced through the house making noise. She shook her head. Pure chaos.

"Sit there across from my mom, Stephanie." Amanda, Shorty's wife, stood at the stove with a baby on her hip. She waved a wooden spoon at a young girl she guessed to be about thirteen. "Wanda, get her a cup of hot chocolate. You want stew and cornbread? The boys are waiting for a couple more fellas to come with their snowmobiles, and then they'll be ready to go."

She complied since she didn't know what else to do. Almost instantly, Wanda set a cup of hot chocolate in front of her followed by a bowl of rich looking stew and a big slab of cornbread.

An older woman sat across from her, with a toddler on her lap. The woman ate stew from a big bowl while the little boy crumbled a piece of cornbread on the table. "Have you ever ridden a snowmobile?"

"No, this will be the first time." She lifted a spoonful of the stew to her lips. A flavor she wasn't familiar with but not bad at all.

"You'll do fine, especially if they put you behind Flint. He's a marvel on them things." She grabbed the bowl of stew and pushed it out of the little boy's reach. "Sammy, you eat your cornbread. Leave Grandma's venison stew alone."

Venison stew? So that was the unfamiliar taste. She didn't know what to say to these people. Why did she feel so uncomfortable? "How far is it to the ranch?" She took another bite of stew.

An older man pushed back an empty bowl. She remembered him being introduced as Grandpa. "From here I suspect it's about twenty miles. I'm not sure how they'll go for sure."

She raised her eyebrows. "Won't they follow the road?"

The man laughed. "Probably not. That's the beauty of a snowmobile. It can go across the country. Here come Flint and Sandy."

He stomped the snow from his boots on the stoop and then entered into the kitchen followed by a couple of other men. He glanced at her and grinned. "You ready?"

She nodded and stood. "Thank you for the stew and for the information." She said to the older couple at the table.

He held up a scarf, a ski mask, and a pair of gloves. "We rounded these up for you and here is a pair of snow boots. See if they fit close enough for you to keep them on. I'll have a helmet waiting for you out at the snowmobile."

She took off her lightweight leather boots and slipped into the heavy fur-lined snow boots. "These will work. Is it going to be that cold?"

He helped her wrap the scarf around her neck and then pulled the ski mask over her head. "Yes, it's cold out there tonight. It'll be close to midnight before we get there. Here, put on these gloves."

While she was getting the rest of the gear on, he was also putting on the same type of cold weather protection.

"Let's go." He picked up her lightweight boots and led the way to a big snowmobile.

She saw five snowmobiles with two people on a couple of them. She couldn't tell if they were men or women. The ones with only a single person had luggage tied behind them. She wished she hadn't brought so much now.

He handed the boots to one of the fellows who put them into Flint's backpack that was secured on the back of one of the snowmobiles. Then he swung his leg over and straddled one of the snowmobiles. "Climb on behind me and hold on to these handles or put your arms around my waist. We should be there in about forty minutes if we don't have any problems. Keep this helmet on and the visor down. The snowmobile in front of us will send up flying chunks of snow and ice."

With care, She climbed on behind him. He lifted her feet and put them on the running board. "Keep your feet up here. Don't let them drag in the snow. They'll catch on rocks and branches."

He checked how her body was positioned on the seat. "Scoot up close to me. We don't want you to bounce off."

"All right." She wrapped her arms around his waist and leaned against his back.

All of a sudden, she couldn't hear anything but the roar of five snowmobile engines revving up and then with a jerk, they were off.

She felt secure as long as she kept her head down. His body blocked some of the cold wind. She tensed her legs and feet to keep them on the running board during the bumpy ride. She had no idea how much time passed before he brought the snowmobile to a stop alongside the others.

"You doing all right?" he shouted.

"I'm doing fine. How much farther?" She didn't tell him that her legs trembled and the cold penetrated where the wind hit them.

"We'll be there in another twenty minutes. We're making good time. I hate that the fellows have to turn around and go back the same distance in the cold. But I'm thankful they insisted on bringing us out."

"Why did so many people need to come?"

"You don't get out in this kind of weather at night by yourself. This way if we have any problems there are others to help us. Ready to go again?"

"I'm ready." She wrapped her arms back around his waist again.

She shivered as the cold permeated layers of clothing. The last part of the ride was misery. She began to question whether she could hold on much longer when he slowed and then came to a stop in front of a large log house ablaze with Christmas lights. Every window in the two-story house was shining with lights as if to welcome them home.

He pulled her arms away from his chest and then jumped off the snowmobile. "Here, let me help."

She couldn't move. Her legs felt frozen in place. She had never been so cold.

He lifted her leg over the seat of the snowmobile. Then he picked her up as he had done so many months before, carried her up the steps to the porch, and then through the opened door. A blast of warmth from inside the house surrounded her.

"Here, son, lay her on the couch." A kindly faced older woman hovered over her.

He laid her on a blanket-covered couch, and the woman positioned a pillow behind her head.

"She, you all right?" He lifted the helmet off and removed the ski mask. "Speak, honey, are you all right?"

She struggled to sit up and pushed her hair back. "I think so. I'm just so cold." Every part of her trembled.

"Here, this will get you warm." An older man who vaguely resembled Flint wrapped a large fur piece around her shoulders. She grasped the edges and pulled the thick fur around her shivering body. Someone placed a mug of hot cider in her hands.

She sipped the hot liquid and looked around the spacious living room. People came from all directions. The snowmobilers stomped in from the cold. Adults and children came from various parts of the house. Everyone seemed to talk at once.

Compared to Shorty's little place in town, this log house was almost luxurious. At one end, a large fireplace with logs blazing dominated the wall. In one corner, a huge Christmas tree glowed with lights.

A pretty woman with long hair the same color as Flint's sandy blond sat next to her. "Hi, I'm Holly. Flint's my twin brother. We're so glad you made it."

"I'm Stephanie."

"I know." Holly laughed. "We've been waiting all evening for you to get here."

Pointing toward the older woman passing out mugs of hot cider to the snowmobilers, she asked, "Is that your mother?"

Holly nodded. "Yes, that's my mom, and the lovely older gentleman in the rocker is my dad. That fellow over by the fireplace is my brother, Abe. His wife, Margo, is upstairs getting their three children bedded down. And the fellow trying to break Flint's ribs in a bear hug is our brother Samuel. Our brother Stephen and my husband, Benjamin, are probably putting gas in the snowmobiles for their return journey. His wife, Vickie, is also upstairs. We have seven children sleeping on pallets in one bedroom. It's hard to get them to sleep with Santa coming tonight."

She glanced around and spotted her luggage by the front door. "I have Christmas presents in that large suitcase for everyone. Should we place them under the tree now?"

"If you feel up to it." Holly stood and led the way to the luggage.

"I'm fine now that I've warmed up." She looked around and saw that all of the snowmobilers and Flint had left the house. She heard the roar of the engines from the front yard. "I can't believe people would leave their families and spend most of the night on a snowmobile to bring us here tonight."

"They didn't do it for you and Flint." Holly looked at her with an intent expression. "They did it for Allie."

"For Allie? Flint's little girl? Why would they do it for a little girl?"

Holly frowned. "Hasn't Flint told you about Allie?"

She rolled the big suitcase over to the Christmas tree surrounded by gifts in the corner of the living room. "Flint told me he has a daughter and that she's three and a half years old." She unzipped the case and handed the colorfully wrapped presents to Holly to add to the ones filling the space around the tree.

Holly shook her head. "That boy. He always keeps things too close to his chest. Let's get your things, and I'll show you to your room."

"All right. Then will you tell me about Allie?" She picked up two of her cases, and Holly took the other two.

"Yes, you need to know." Holly mounted the stairs and led the way to a door off the landing of the second floor. "We've reserved a place for you in here. Actually, it's Flint's room. He's sleeping in Allie's room on a rollaway."

"Oh no, I don't want to take his room." She looked around with interest. So this was where he slept.

"With Allie not feeling well he would probably sleep in there whether you were here or not. Mom has the linens changed. I'm sorry, but you have to share the bath. It's across the hall." Holly pointed toward some towels on the dresser. "If you need more towels just let me know."

"I'll be fine."

Holly sat on the bed and patted the colorful quilt. "Sit, and I'll tell you about Allie."

"Let me climb out of this ski suit. I'm getting too hot." She pulled off the snow boots and then took off the ski suit and placed it folded on the window seat. Then she sat cross-legged on the bed facing Holly.

"I would rather Flint had told you, but he doesn't mention it unless he has to. Allie was born with a serious heart problem. She has already had two surgeries, but the second one didn't go well. Normally the condition can be corrected by the surgeries, but of course, Allie is the special child for whom the surgery didn't work." Holly took a deep breath. "Flint took her to the specialists at Children's Hospital in Denver. They told him she needs a heart transplant within the next few months or she won't last out the year."

She didn't know what to say. So this explained the sense of sadness she always sensed around him. "I'm so sorry." She covered Holly's hand. "Thank you for telling me. It explains a lot."

Holly gave Stephanie a hug. "I'm so glad you came. Tomorrow will be a day for the children, and especially for Allie. We aren't going to grieve until she's gone. For now, we'll laugh, sing, and celebrate her life."

"Now I understand why Flint was determined to get here tonight."

"Yes, he promised his little girl he'd be here when Santa came. It may be his last Christmas with her. He needs to be here for himself, too."

"Is this why all the family is here?"

"Yes. Usually Stephen and Abe alternate holidays with their in-laws. Benjamin lost his parents a couple of years ago, so we always come home to Mom and Dad." Holly stood and plucked a tissue out of the box on the nightstand and wiped her nose. "I'm afraid we'll all be teary-eyed around here. Just ignore us. Well, I'll let you get to bed. It's already midnight." She walked to the door. "Sleep as late as you can, but I'm afraid the children will be noisy running down to see what Santa left."

"May I get up and watch them open their gifts?"

"Of course, it's the best fun of the day, and you'll get to meet my darling husband." Holly winked and left the room.

She unpacked her gown, robe, and slippers. Taking the towels and her makeup case, she found the bathroom across the hall. After taking a quick shower, she snuggled into the bed and turned off the light. She couldn't remember when she had been so tired. A faint scent of something else besides laundry detergent wafted from the pillow. She remembered the masculine smell of aftershave and sweat from the hiker as he carried her down the mountain. She pulled the pillow close and drifted to sleep with the comforting scent of her friend around her.

Chapter Twenty-Three

HE WOKE TO THE FEEL of Allie's little hand patting his cheek. "Wake up, Daddy. Santa's here." From under his arm that cradled her, she wiggled to sit.

"Merry Christmas, sweetheart."

Children's laughter floated from the hall. He glanced at the Mickey Mouse clock on the bedside stand. Six-thirty. Might as well get up as these children wouldn't be going back to sleep.

"Merry Christmas, Daddy. Did you come with Santa?" Allie held up her arms for him to slip her pink housecoat over her head and then slid her feet into furry pink rabbit house shoes. Where did Mom find such cute garments? It was evident that Allie loved them.

"No, honey, I came on an airplane and then a snowmobile. I brought my friend Stephanie with me. She's going to be your friend, too."

"Stephanie? The pretty lady in the computer?" She watched as he dropped a light sweater over his long-sleeved undershirt and then pulled up his Wrangler jeans. He stepped into the comfortable old moccasins that served as his house shoes. Having all his things at the house did lighten his luggage.

Holding Allie's hand, he descended the stairs to find his family gathered around the Christmas tree.

Dad waved him toward the big black leather chair between the fireplace and the Christmas tree. "Sit here, Flint. We want to say a prayer before the kids attack the presents."

As he settled with Allie on his lap, Stephanie slipped into the living room and sat on the couch beside Holly and Benjamin.

Dad stood near the big tree. "Let's pray.

"Father all glorious. We thank you for the safety of all the family and our visitor. Thank you for the gifts you have blessed us with and the joy of these children. Help us to be truly grateful. In the name of Jesus, Amen."

His mother helped organize the children, getting them all to sit in a row on the floor. "Now, remember that we each get a present and wait to open them one by one, so everyone can see what we're getting." She turned to her oldest grandchild, Mark, who was fifteen. "You read the names on the presents. Serena and Angel will hand them out."

Allie's eyes were bright. She watched with eagerness, but he found her content to lean against his chest and wait for a present. Six months ago, she would have been beside her grandmother's side in the middle of it. It told him as much as anything that she didn't feel well.

In the next two hours, laughter, talking, and the rustling of paper torn from presents finally emptied the space under the tree of its treasures. By the time the last one was opened, and the giver thanked, Allie had fallen asleep, snuggled in her daddy's arms.

He made no move but sat holding his daughter. As the women headed toward the kitchen, the men tromped through the snow to the barn to care for the animals. Most of the children sat around playing with their new toys.

She sat in a chair next to the recliner. "She's so beautiful. Is she okay this morning?"

He didn't know how to answer. No, she wasn't all right. "She gets tired too easily. With everyone here, it's hard on her."

"Why didn't you tell me she was so ill?"

"You can't do anything about it. Sometimes it's hard to talk about." He saw concern in her expression.

"I'm glad you made it home for her. And thanks again for bringing me here to see all this. I've never watched children open gifts at Christmas before. It was so much fun. And all of them are so polite. Every child came to thank me for their present."

He nodded. "That's because they all have great parents who teach them."

"You haven't opened your presents." She pointed to the stack of gifts by his chair.

"It was more fun to help Allie open hers. Thank you for the doll." He looked down at his child's sleeping face. He couldn't get enough of watching her, asleep or awake.

She picked up one of the gifts. "Would you like me to unwrap this for you?"

"That would be great." He smiled. "I'd like to see what I got, but not enough to put Allie down." He gently tightened his hold on her and relished the feel of life in his child. If only he could be sure that would continue.

She opened the gift from his brother Samuel, which was a book on mountain climbing in Alaska. She then opened the next one, and the next, until finally, she came to a small oblong box wrapped in silver metallic paper. "This one is from me. I hope you like it." She slid the box out of the paper and opened it, then held up a big watch with several smaller faces within the big one. "It's a watch, especially for mountain climbers. I'm told people who climb Mt. Everest wear them. It shows time, altitude, temperature, and GPS location."

"Wow, this is great." He took the watch from her. "I've seen them in magazines but never up close. Thanks." He knew the watch usually cost a thousand dollars. His present for her had been a leather-bound Bible with notes and a photo of her and Brigitte he had taken at the

Hamptons house. She had seemed pleased with her gifts but hadn't made a comment about the Bible.

"Of course, I think you have to subscribe to a GPS service but that way your family can follow your hikes." She picked up a poorly wrapped gift the size of a children's book. "This says, From Allie. Should I open it?"

"Go ahead. I think she wrapped it herself." He watched as she unwrapped the gift. When she opened it, she found a homemade book of Allie's drawings.

She glanced at the simple drawings of the world from Allie's viewpoint. "Look at this one with you in the computer. These are precious."

He laughed. "Yes, she thinks I live in the computer when I'm in New York. That's how she sees me." The next drawing took his breath away. It depicted the doctors and nurses at the hospital in black and gray while the others had been full of color.

She squinted at it. "What is this?"

"She's showing us how she sees the visits to the doctors and the hospital."

His chest ached as he looked at the next drawing. Even though Allie still drew with only stick figure people, her rendition of her family was apparent. A small figure stood in front of a house with two figures with gray hair on one side and a tall figure holding the child's hand that he assumed must be him. But it was the figure on a cloud in the upper corner that hit like a rock in the pit of his stomach. It could only be Allie's view of where her mother fit into a picture of her family. He had told her that her mother was in heaven with God resting on a fluffy white cloud.

"What Flint? What's wrong with this picture?" She frowned as she glanced from the drawing to his face.

He sighed. "There's nothing wrong with the picture. That's my folks, that's Allie holding my hand, and that's how she sees her mother up in heaven."

"Oh, Flint. That's so sad and yet so beautiful." Her voice had softened almost to a whisper.

He nodded and held his sleeping child closer.

His mother came into the living room. "That child still asleep? When she wakes will you take her up and bathe her? I didn't do it last evening, as she was too tired. I've laid out a new dress for her to wear today."

"Thanks, Mom. I'll take care of her today. You've got your hands full with the food preparation."

She stood. "May I help you in the kitchen?"

"That would be great. We have several still to eat breakfast and more later. Then about two this afternoon, we'll have Christmas Dinner. There are nineteen of us now, and your aunt and uncle will be here in a couple of hours if Fred can get your Aunt Agnes to ride on the snowmobile." Mary patted his shoulder. "I'm so happy you made it home. You ready for breakfast yet?"

"I'll eat later when Allie wakes up. What about you, Steph?"

She smiled. "I'll help your mom and eat later with you and Allie."

"She should wake up in fifteen or twenty minutes. Then it's time for her medicine. Come on, Stephanie. I have just the job for you." Mary led the way toward the kitchen.

SHE GAZED AROUND THE big country kitchen. It was as modern and upscale as her kitchen in New York. Mary even had a Wolf stovetop. The kitchen and eating area ran along the back of the house and were as large as the huge living room. At one end, was a large pine farm table and a spacious kitchen with long granite countertops and hickory cabinets took up the other end. "Wow, what a great kitchen."

Mary laughed. "You're surprised. It didn't used to be this nice. About two years ago Flint and his brothers spent July 4th weekend completely redoing it for me. You would have been amazed at how quickly something can get done with ten men working. It was almost like an old-fashioned barn raising, except it was my kitchen. Friends of the boys came out to help who were plumbers, electricians, tile layers, and then poof it was done."

"How wonderful. I wish I could have been here and watched." She gathered dirty dishes from the kitchen counter and loaded the dishwasher.

"Oh, thanks. I told the girls to go get the kids dressed for going out into the snow. All but Allie and Stephen's youngest are going sledding. Normally, Flint would be in the midst of them, but today I suspect he'll stay with Allie."

"Would you mind telling me how ill she is? Holly told me last night about her heart condition. Flint hasn't said a word about it." She accepted an apron from Mary.

"That boy. He has never learned to share his feelings much, especially since Valerie died." Mary got a pan out of a pull out drawer in the lower cabinet and a bag of sweet potatoes out of the pantry. "Would you mind peeling these and then cut them up into that pan? We'll bake them with butter, cinnamon, nutmeg, and brown sugar on them. You can sit on the stool here at the counter, and we can talk while we work." Mary uncovered a huge bowl filled with yeast dough. She began to form rolls and place them on a couple of large cookie sheets. "I'll get these ready and then let them rise so we can bake them for dinner."

She peeled and cut the sweet potatoes. "I'm surprised that Flint would be willing to work in New York with his daughter so ill."

Mary stopped rolling the ball of dough. "I don't know if Flint would want me to tell you, but I think you need to know. Otherwise, you're not going to understand my boy." She continued rolling out the balls of dough. "Allie needs a heart transplant to have a hope of surviving. Her medical care is paid for by Medicaid. As a child with a serious condition, she qualifies for Medicaid and Flint has used up the insurance coverage on his policy from work. It only covers a million dollars' worth of care and Allie has already gone past that."

"I don't understand. You mean the insurance won't pay for her care?" She had no knowledge of this. The cost of medical care was something she had never thought about.

"No, they won't pay any more. They aren't required to pay beyond the cap of the insurance policy. But Medicaid has stepped in, only they must approve what they will cover and what they deem unnecessary. Somewhere, someone decided Allie would do as well with another heart surgery and have refused to pay for the heart transplant. But her doctors won't do the approved heart surgery as they say it won't help her. Of course, if there's a dispute between Medicaid and the doctors, Medicaid wins as far as payment." Mary covered the small rounded balls of dough with a clean cloth and placed the pan of rolls aside. She then put three sticks of butter in a bowl and lifted it into the microwave.

"You're telling me that Allie can't get a transplant?" She sat with the paring knife as a pointer punctuating her question.

"To get on the transplant lists at the hospital, someone has to be prepared to pay for it. That's why Flint is working in New York and living on nothing. If he can get a hundred-fifty thousand dollars together, he can get her on the list."

"What do you mean, living on nothing?" She waited for Mary to explain.

Taking the bowl of melted butter out of the microwave Mary set it on the counter. She began to put cinnamon, nutmeg, and brown sugar in the bowl with the butter and then mixed it up. "Well, Richard and Nancy are giving him free room, and you're feeding him at noon and supper. Of course, Richard and Nancy will feed him if he asks, but he's trying not to take advantage of their kindness. I don't think the boy is spending money on anything. Everything is going into the fund for Allie. Of course, he has to help pay to keep this place going. Tom and I are both getting Social Security, and all of that goes to pay for things here. Tom and Flint are making some money off the ranch but not much. Cattle prices are down. If Abe and Samuel didn't send us money each month, I don't know what we would do." Mary stopped as if she suddenly realized she had said too much. "I'm sorry, Stephanie. I shouldn't have told you all that."

She shook her head. "Don't be sorry. I'm thankful. I had no idea, and it explains so much." She bowed her head for a moment and tried to sort through what she had just learned. Picking up the last sweet potato, she peeled, cut up, and placed it in the pan. "So Flint is sacrificing possibly his last months with his daughter in hopes of making enough money to save her?"

Mary looked out the big window beyond the kitchen table at the children playing in the snow. "I guess you could say that. It's about killing him, but what else can he do?"

She took the bowl of butter and spices from Mary and poured the ingredients over the sweet potatoes as instructed. "How do you cope with all of this so calmly?"

Mary shook her head. "Who says I'm calm? I sometimes go down by the creek by myself and holler at God."

She raised her eyebrows. "You're kidding. Is that okay? To yell at God?"

Mary smiled. "God the Father understands my heart. I want Allie well, but I also want the will of God. Whatever happens to our precious Allie will work for our good if we but trust God. I learned that when we lost Valerie. And I see my son living out his trust as he deals with having lost his beloved wife and now faces the possible death of his daughter."

She wiped tears and swallowed before she could speak. "You all amaze me. Maybe sometime you could explain to me about this God you trust so much."

Mary gave her a sideways hug and then picked up the pan of sweet potatoes and placed them in the oven to bake. "I would like that very much. You've been such a help to Flint. He's needed a friend."

She hoped that she had been a help. She had come to resenting Flint's frequent trips to Colorado. If only she had understood.

"If Flint had the money, could he get Allie on the transplant list?"

"Oh yes." Mary nodded. "The doctors would already have her on it. It's the hospital and the transplant people who make the final decisions I think. Flint knows all the details."

"Do you think Flint would accept financial help?" She tried to speak casually.

"The way things are now, he'd accept any help he could get. No one wants him to have to bury his little girl." Mary dabbed a dishtowel to her eyes, and her shoulders shook from silent sobs. Then she took a deep breath and put the dishtowel down. "I'm sorry I shouldn't have burdened you with this."

She hugged the older woman. "No, thank you, for telling me."

From the yard, came the sound of revving snowmobile engines mixed with the children's laughter. Mary wiped her eyes. "That's my brother and his wife. Agnes will be in to help with dinner."

Flint entered the kitchen carrying Allie who was wide-awake and dressed in a long-sleeved red taffeta dress with lots of ruffles. He looked from his mom to Stephanie. "You all right, Mom?"

"I'm fine, son. You ready for breakfast now? We won't have dinner for a few hours yet." Mary brushed curls back from her granddaughter's face. "You hungry, baby?"

Allie looked at Stephanie and pointed. "Daddy, pretty lady in the computer."

They all started laughing.

"Yes, Allie, the pretty lady in the computer." He winked at Stephanie and smiled.

"Hi, Allie. My name is Stephanie, but you can call me Steph if you want."

He placed Allie in her chair at the table. "Mom, where's her apron?"

Mary handed him a little white bibbed apron. "Put this on her, or she'll have that dress a mess."

She sat down next to the little girl. "I like your red dress. It's so pretty."

"Christmas dress." Allie patted her dress.

"It sure is a Christmas dress. I wish I had one." She winked at him.

"Grandma can order off the computer. The nice USB man brings it." Allie looked expectantly at her grandmother who nodded.

"That's right, honey, except its UPS man."

He laughed. "Oh no, Mom. You've corrupted my child. She knows how to order off the Internet."

Listening to the laughter, she glanced at him and his daughter. How could he seem so happy in light of his daughter's precarious condition? And he did seem happy.

Chapter Twenty-Four

THE REST OF THE MORNING she helped as best she could and got to know the different members of this large family as they interacted with each other. The Christmas dinner, in the middle of the afternoon, was indeed a feast. Mary had prepared turkey, ham, cornbread dressing, gravy, cranberry sauce, sweet potatoes, creamed potatoes, green beans, carrots, corn, green salad, fruit salad, and hot rolls.

When she thought everyone had eaten all they could hold, Holly and her mother placed desserts on the kitchen counter. Everyone served themselves from the German chocolate cake, fresh apple cake, strawberry cake, blackberry jam cake, various kinds of cookies and dessert bars, pumpkin pie, coconut cream pie, apple pie, lemon meringue pie, and pecan pie.

She had never seen so much food except in a restaurant buffet. Mary placed a pecan pie in front of Flint at the table. "Just as you requested, son."

He grinned. "Thanks, Mom." A big wedge made it to his plate, while he jokingly kept his brothers from stealing his pie.

Tom Tucker, balancing a plate full of desserts, sat next to her. "That all you going to have, Ms. Wellbourne?" He pointed his fork at the small piece of fresh apple cake on her plate.

"Please, call me Stephanie, Mr. Tucker."

"Only if you'll call me Tom."

"I thought I'd start with this piece of cake. Then I can always try something else if I have room for it."

"You strike me as a wise woman." He started on a slice of chocolate pie piled high with whipped cream.

How could he eat so much and remain rail thin? "Do you always have this much food for Christmas dinner?"

Tom surveyed the kitchen full of food, watching his family enjoying the feast. "Sure. Also on July Fourth, birthdays, weddings ... any reason to celebrate. I guess you noticed that Mary is pretty good at putting food on the table."

"Yes, sir. I did notice. She let me help her. I've never cooked for such a large group."

Tom laid down his fork. "Tell me about your family."

She studied the older man whom Flint so resembled. Something about him made her feel comfortable. "My mother died just after I graduated college and my father died about five years ago. I'm an only child. I do have cousins, but that doesn't leave me with much of a family."

"That's one reason Mary and I decided to have several children. We both came from large families and wanted to pass that blessing on to our children. And God granted our desire. Of course, I would have thought all of them would be married by now and giving us more grandchildren." Tom's eyes sparkled with merriment. "But Samuel won't settle down, and Flint's had a lot of tragedy."

"Do you think he'll remarry someday?" She couldn't believe the question popped out, but Tom was so easy to talk to.

Tom briefly glanced across the room to where Flint sat talking to his brother Stephen but looking at Stephanie. "I kinda expect he will."

"And Samuel? Is he dating anyone?"

Tom laughed. "He doesn't tell us. His brothers' teasing can get a little too direct."

She watched as Tom started in on a piece of pumpkin pie. "How long have you lived here on the ranch?"

Tom swallowed and then took a sip of water. "We moved in with Flint when Valerie died. He had to have help with the baby, and we struggled to keep the place we had. So we sold it and partnered with Flint. It's worked out to be a blessing for all of us."

"When did Flint buy the ranch?" She was being nosey, but everything about Flint fascinated her.

Tom didn't seem to mind talking about his son. "Flint and Valerie bought the ranch while they were expecting Allie. They had a place in town, but they didn't want to raise their family there. They both grew up on ranches, and this was their dream."

She placed her hand on the older man's arm. "I can't imagine how hard it was when she died."

Tom laid his rough hand over hers. "It was hard. I thought for a while it would kill Flint. I've never seen anyone so torn up. The worst part was he couldn't cry. As far as I know, he hasn't cried to this day. But you could see the grief on his face. He tries so hard to be cheerful around Allie." Tom patted her hand. "I have to tell you that he seems happier than he has in years since he's been working with you. You're good for him."

She didn't know what to say. "I hope I've been a good friend to him. He's been a lifesaver for me."

Tom pushed away uneaten desserts. "I think I'll finish later. Let's go sit in the living room where the chairs are more comfortable."

"Maybe I should help clear up the dishes?" She looked around, but there didn't seem to be much left to do. Mary, her daughter, and daughters-in-law had already loaded the dishwasher and put the food away.

Tom pulled her chair back. "You're too late. Besides, you're our guest today."

She followed the older man into the living room and settled on the end of a couch near where he sat in a rocker. Flint and Allie had disappeared.

Tom patted his stomach. "I need to rest and let that dinner digest."

She laughed and rubbed her flat stomach. "That's one way of putting it. I don't feel as if I want to eat for another couple of days."

"If you don't mind an old man being nosey, tell me about your plans. Flint doesn't say much, but he did mention you were transitioning into another company."

"That's one way of looking at it. I just lost the control of my father's company. Flint is helping me start another one. I'm in-between right now." It didn't hurt to say it. It didn't even sound as if it had been a bad thing. Maybe she was coping better than she thought.

"How much longer do you think Flint will work out of New York? Or, maybe I shouldn't ask that."

She slid out of her shoes and tucked her feet underneath her on the couch. "No, it's all right to ask. I think we will have everything reorganized in a month or two and then whatever work Flint does for me could be done from here by computer."

"Of course, his mother and I miss him being here, but Allie needs him home."

She nodded. "Before I met Allie I didn't understand. We need to get her daddy home as soon as possible."

Abe entered the living room and plopped in a recliner. "I have made myself sick eating so much. As a physician, I should know better."

She looked toward the kitchen, but none of the others had drifted into the living room. "Abe, could I ask a favor?"

"Sure, what can I do for you?" He lifted the footrest.

"Can you explain Allie's heart condition in terms I can understand? Why won't the third surgery help her?"

Tom stopped rocking. "I'd like to hear your take on it, too, son. I just know bits and pieces."

With a deep breath, Abe steepled his fingertips and looked at the floor. "Allie was born with a congenital cardiac defect known as Hypoplastic Left Heart Syndrome or HLHS. In HLHS, all of the structures on the left side of the heart—which receives oxygen-rich blood from the lungs and pumps it out to the body—are severely underdeveloped. Staged reconstruction, in a series of three operations, is usually performed to reconfigure the child's cardiovascular system." Abe glanced from his father. "You remember, Dad, Allie had the first one, the Norwood operation, the week she was born, even before we had Valerie's funeral. Then she had the Glenn procedure when she was six months. But we hit a snag due to complications. The third operation is not advisable now. Instead, the doctors recommended a heart transplant."

The explanation mesmerized her. Complex and technical, yet it made perfect sense.

Abe met her intense gaze. "Allie's heart can't keep up with her growing body. It's wearing itself out. Within a few months, it'll give out. When it does, we'll lose her unless she gets a transplant."

She leaned forward. "But if she does get the transplant she'll be all right?"

"If she stays on her meds and keeps ahead of the rejection process she could live a fairly normal life. Then again, she might only have five or ten years. There's no way to tell." Abe looked at his father. "Is this what you've been told, Dad?"

Tom nodded. "You've helped with some of the medical stuff that wasn't really clear to me. I always hesitate to ask Flint or Mary. They have enough on their plates." He turned to her. "I'm glad you asked Abe."

"What does it take to get a child on the transplant list?"

"For Allie, it's simply a matter of money. Flint has filled out all the paperwork. The doctors have given their statement of need. Once the funds are guaranteed, then she'll move onto the active list.

Then we start praying for a heart to become available." Abe ran a hand over his face. "Of course, that'll be the hardest part."

She looked from Tom to Abe. "Why is that?"

Tom sat with his hands together as if praying. "For Allie to get a heart a child has to die. It won't be anything within our control, but still, we're concerned about the donor, and the parents who'll lose their child."

She felt as if she had been punched in the stomach. She had never thought of organ transplants from this angle. "Is that something that distresses Flint?"

"Yes, it affects all of us. That doesn't mean we'll refuse a heart for Allie." Abe blinked away tears that didn't fall.

Flint and his whole family must be burdened with this scenario. What a Catch-22. She shook her head. "I wish it could be some other way."

Abe's small laugh sounded mirthless. "Don't we all? There's research into artificial organs, but so far nothing comes close to functioning as well as a live organ."

"I feel foolish for being so concerned about losing money and control of a company. Compared to life and death, my problems are simple."

Tom shook his head. "But that's not true. The burdens we each bear are important to our lives. Your problems affect your life, and you must live with them and with the stress those problems cause."

"How do you deal with the constant stress? Always knowing that death may be just around the corner?" She couldn't imagine how they remained so calm and even seemed to enjoy life.

Abe leaned forward. "We do what we can, and then we give it to God."

"You pray?" She couldn't see how that would help.

"God will be with us, whether Allie makes it or not. It'll be hard, but we won't go through it alone." Tom asserted. "We'll support each other and lift each other up to the Lord."

"You really believe, even in this situation, there is a supreme being who cares?"

Both men nodded. Tom managed a small smile. "I believe that with all my heart."

She rubbed her temple. These two men apparently shared Flint's sincere confidence in God's sovereignty and goodness. How could they when their whole world could collapse in a matter of months? "It would be comforting to have such a belief."

Chapter Twenty-Five

TWO DAYS AFTER CHRISTMAS, he stood on the porch with Mom and Dad. They watched Abe and family drive away in their rented four-wheel drive vehicle on their way to the airport.

"I know Abe has to get back to his medical practice, but I wish they could have stayed longer." Mom let out a heavy sigh and wiped a tear from the corner of her eye.

He hugged her. "You still have Holly and me for a few days."

Dad winked. "And we're thankful for that." He patted his arm. "I'm going to work in the barn."

"I need to start some bread to rising." Mom turned toward the door, then stopped and looked back. "Flint, why don't you see what Stephanie might want to do this morning."

He found her in the living room sitting on the couch with Allie. Her two new favorite dolls sat between them. Although Allie had many other stuffed animals and dolls, for now, her new Christmas dolls were her favorites. No doubt she'd still sleep with New York Teddy, the bear from Brigitte.

Everyone had responded to Stephanie's charm, and she had fit in easily with his family. Of course, his brothers teased him about her beauty. But none of the family encouraged him to get more involved with her knowing she wasn't a Christian. Over the last few days, the family talked of Scripture and spiritual things just as they always did. Each evening they met around the fireplace and sang hymns together. She seemed to enjoy the singing and even tried to join in with the aid of a songbook. He couldn't imagine a life without hymns.

With everyone gone except Holly and Benjamin, he intended to enjoy the quiet of the next five days with Allie and Stephanie.

She called to him. "Hey, big fellow, what you doing there, just staring?"

"Yeah, big fellow." Allie giggled. "That's you, Daddy."

He strolled to the couch, picked up the dolls, and wiggled between Stephanie and Allie. "I was watching two of the prettiest girls in this room."

Allie looked around. "But Daddy, no other pretty girls are here."

He tickled her. "I know." He placed the two dolls in Allie's lap. Turning to Stephanie, he said, "It's a beautiful, cold day out. After this little one goes down for her nap, how about going on a hike in the snow with me?"

"Oh, that would be fun. But won't it be cold?"

"I expect it will." He nodded. "That's why you have to dress for the weather. But the walking will keep you warm."

She laid her hand on his arm. "I'm having so much fun. Thank you for inviting me."

He gazed into her violet eyes and let his eyes drop to her perfect lips. He could easily kiss her, and he didn't think she would pull away. Instead, he shook his head—more to clear his thoughts than anything else. "We should thank you for gracing this home with your presence. I've never seen Allie take after someone so easily." He stood and headed for the kitchen, more to protect himself from his thoughts than want. "Would you like a cup of coffee?"

She gazed up at him. "No thanks."

When he returned in a few minutes, he found Allie asleep on her lap. He smiled. "I'll carry her to bed."

She stroked the child's hair. "She sleeps a lot."

He sat at Allie's feet. "The doctors say it's because her heart works so hard it doesn't take much to wear her out."

"Ready for that walk now?"

"Let me put Allie to bed and tell Mom what we're doing." He drained the last of the coffee and set the cup on the end table. He carried his child to bed. Pulling the covers to her chin, he planted a kiss on Allie's forehead. He turned to find Stephanie watching him. "I know Amanda's ski suit is too big for you, but it'll keep you warm."

She nodded. "I'll go get ready and meet you at the back door."

NOW DRESSED FOR THE trek, he led the way through the snow with her following in his footprints. Sunglasses were necessary with the glare bouncing off the snow. He wanted to climb the trail up the ridge back of the house, but it was too icy for someone as inexperienced as she was. Therefore, he stayed on the trail along the flowing creek. The tall, distant peaks shimmered in the clear blue sky. His Colorado Rockies couldn't have been more beautiful to present to her. He came to a granite outcropping where he stopped and dusted off the snow.

"Let's take a breather."

She seemed to be gulping air. "I need one. There's no oxygen here."

He could have kicked himself for not thinking. She wasn't used to the altitude, nor the cold. "Why didn't you say something? We didn't have to walk so fast."

A smile played her lips. "I couldn't get enough breath to say anything."

"Do we need to go back to the house?" He must remember she wasn't a country girl.

"No." She took a deep breath. "But could we walk a little slower?"

He chuckled. "I can manage that. But first, we'll rest a bit."

"Are we following a trail? It seems awfully flat."

He looked along the path they had made in the snow. "Mostly. In the summer, this is a path across the pasture and along the creek. It goes for miles down the valley and isn't a bad place to run."

"But in the snow, how do you know where it is?"

He unhooked the water bottle snapped on his belt and offered it to her. "I just know."

She gulped a long drink, then wiped her mouth. "Where to now?"

He gave her a close look. She seemed to be breathing normally again. "You sure?"

"Lead on." She flashed him a full smile that ignited something deep within him. Time to get moving.

He enjoyed showing her his home and the spots on the ranch that were especially meaningful to him. He loved his place. A warm feeling filled him seeing her start to fall in love with it, too. As they returned to the house, he took her through the barn and introduced her to his horses.

"If this weather holds maybe we can take a horseback ride tomorrow." He rubbed the horse's nose. "Old Winston here is an easy ride, and he's surefooted in the snow."

She patted the horse's neck. "Where did you get a name like Winston?"

"He came with it. I bought him off a fella a few years ago and never changed his name." He walked to another stall where a tall palomino stallion eyed them. "This big fellow is Charger. I ride him more than the other horses. Holly usually rides Winston."

The next morning, he spent time in Allie's room playing with her and her dolls. Stephanie came into the bedroom and joined them.

"You be the mommy." Allie handed Stephanie the little mother doll from the playhouse. "You be the daddy." She also placed a doll in his hand.

He winked at Stephanie as they both sat on the floor beside the three-story dollhouse that was taller than Allie. "And who are you?"

"I'm the little girl."

"What are we doing?" He sat crossed legged and leaned forward to peer into the rooms of the dollhouse that he had built the year before.

"Mommy and Daddy are taking the little girl to the doctor."

They played for the next thirty minutes following Allie's lead as she made up the story. Teddy bear played the part of the doctor. He shook his head at how accurately Allie portrayed the doctor's visit, even using correct medical terms. His child had learned way too much, way too early.

She didn't seem to mind playing, in fact, she got into the imaginary story a lot easier than he did. While he watched them interacting, a wistfulness tugged at his heart. His child needed a mother.

After Allie fell asleep, he saddled Winston and Charger. He and Stephanie rode west toward the high mountains. Climbing higher and higher, after an hour he stopped near some boulders.

"Let's walk to the top of that trail. We'll have to be careful of the ice and snow, but I think we can make it." He dismounted.

She slid off her horse and handed the reins to him who tied the two animals to a tree branch. "It looks steep. You sure we can climb it in the snow?"

"I've been up this trail in worse conditions than these. Don't worry, I'll help you."

She pulled her gloves on tighter and eyed the trail with a frown. "You may have to. Remember I'm a city girl."

He led the way up the snow-covered trail. He didn't intend to go far but wasn't telling her, as he wanted to surprise her. He heard her slipping slightly and turned to offer his hand.

She grabbed his hand, and he struggled to keep his own balance as they staggered up the trail together. With no warning, they stood on a shelf of rock gazing out over a panorama of valleys and mountains. It was one of those rare crystal-clear days, and the snow-covered scene was at its best.

"Oh, Flint!" Hands clasped over her chest, she stared at the grandeur. Looking up as he wrapped his arms around her to keep her steady, she said, "Wow and double wow. Thank you for bringing me up here."

He tightened his arms around her waist, as the edge of the ledge was only a few feet in front of them. But he also relished the feel of holding her close. If only ...

"You're welcome. This is my favorite place. We're really on government land but my ranch edges up to the national forest land, and so it feels like my place." He looked over her head at the distant mountain peaks, some of which he had climbed. "This view is why I bought the ranch. It's one of those magical places where you can feel close to God. When I need to think or pray, I come here."

"If I weren't here, is that what you would be doing? Praying?"

He nodded.

"What would you be praying for?"

He took a deep breath and let it out in a slow sigh. "What I always pray for, Allie's healing if it is God's will. That I'll be strong enough to take whatever comes. That I'll let it push me toward God, rather than drag me away from Him. I also pray that I can be there for my family as they are for me. And then, I pray that I can do good work for my firm and for you."

Her eyes opened wide, and her eyebrows shot up. "You pray for me?"

He gazed into her violet eyes that Mom called Elizabeth Taylor eyes. "Of course, I pray for you." Why was he sharing so much with her? He wanted to tell her everything—to let her into his innermost being. Was he falling in love with her? He'd tried so hard not to.

"Thank you. I don't understand prayer, but I appreciate your concern."

"It's easy to have concern for you." He let his eyes drink in the beauty that was Stephanie. He lowered his head, but a horse neighing in the distance returned some sanity to his brain. He stepped back and said, "We better start down the trail if we want to make it home by supper."

The weather held clear during the rest of their stay. They went hiking or horseback riding every day. He found himself more and more at ease with her even while he reminded himself that she was simply a friend from work and could never be more. His heart ached to hold her in his arms. As he knelt by Allie's bed watching his child sleep, he spoke to the Father of his desire.

"Dear God, please give me the strength to resist my longings or else work in Stephanie's heart that she will become one of your children. In Jesus' name, Amen."

Chapter Twenty-Six

SHE GAZED OUT THE KITCHEN window waiting for the coffee to brew. The grayness of Central Park's naked trees in the cold Monday morning light matched her spirits. To be surrounded by familiar places and things at home was a relief. But the week and a half in Colorado with his family had been the most fun in her life. It was so different from anything she had ever experienced before.

He and Brigitte would arrive within the hour. She sighed and glanced at the wall clock. The return to New York meant he would finish his work within a few months and return to Colorado for good, without her.

The bell signaled the arrival of the elevator.

"Hello, anyone home?" Flint. Her heart flip-flopped.

She took a deep breath and called back. "I have coffee made. Care for a cup?" She glanced toward the foyer.

He removed his overcoat and then finger-combed his hair. "Yes, I want coffee. It's fourteen degrees out there."

With the coffeepot, cups, cream, and sugar clinking on the tray, she balanced her load into the living room and deposited it on the table with a flourish. "Let's sit in here."

She indicated a wingback chair.

With a nod, he took a cup of coffee and settled in the chair. "We should decide what we need to accomplish in the next few months and then break it down into weekly tasks."

Sinking into the chair across from him, she slipped off her shoes and curled her feet underneath her. "Why don't you give me your ideas."

He wrapped his fingers around the cup as if to warm them. "We have to start with organizing your new companies. With the sale of your Wellbourne Group stocks, you have a fair amount of liquidity to dispose of. You need to decide where you want to invest next and how much you want to put toward the Foundation. You also have a fortune in the art in the vault. What are you going to do with that?"

With the tips of her fingers, she massaged her temple. Another one of those headaches she had come to recognize as tension threatened to explode at any moment. "I'll give you the broad outlines of what I want to be done and then let you make the detailed decisions."

"But that's a job for a CFO."

She nodded. "Would you and your firm do this for me on a continuing basis?"

He squinted and frowned. "You want us to manage your portfolio on a fulltime basis?"

It sounded different when he rephrased it. She paused to sip coffee. Is that what she was asking? She trusted him, and after meeting Ben Booker and Tony Williams while she was in Colorado, she felt she could trust them, too. Why not give the day-to-day tasks of managing her money over to them?

"Yes, that's what I'm saying." The best part of it was that it would keep him in her life. Was that her primary motive? She wasn't sure, and maybe it didn't matter. She did need help.

He quietly drank his coffee before he answered. "I can talk to Ben and Tony. But I'll have to work from Colorado. I won't stay in New York."

"I don't expect you to stay here. There's no reason the work can't be done from Colorado." Now that she had met Allie, she understood his need to be home. What rule said her new company had to be located in New York?

He shifted in his seat. "Let me talk to Ben and Tony, but whether we become your financial management team or not, there's work to do now. What attorney do you want to use?"

"That's a difficult question. All the attorneys I've worked with up to now are employed by The Wellbourne Group. I don't want to use any of them. What attorney does your firm use?"

"We have several." He set his cup on the table. "It depends on the need. I know one attorney I think could do the work. Let me make a couple of calls and get back to you." He glanced at his watch. "It's too early to call Colorado. Let me look at the market and work some first, and then about eleven, I'll get the information for you."

She turned as the elevator doors opened and Brigitte breezed into the apartment.

Rising to greet her, she slipped her shoes on.

"Welcome back." Brigitte hugged her. "Did you have a good time in Colorado?"

"I had a wonderful time. Wish you could have been there. I rode an eighteen-wheeler, a snowmobile, and I enjoyed Flint's mother's pecan pie." That summarized a smidgen of the new experiences she had in Colorado.

He took Brigitte's coat and hung it in the closet. "How was your Christmas?"

"It was good, but quiet compared to yours. Mother and Father were happy that I could be there for a few days. My brother and his wife with their little girls came for part of the time." Brigitte poured herself a cup of coffee and sat on the couch. "After they left I just rested and visited with my parents."

"I'm glad you got to spend time with them. Did they beg you to move back to Boston?" She slid out of her shoes and curled her feet underneath her again.

Brigitte laughed. "You know I can always count on that discussion. They're just lonely."

"That's one thing I didn't feel in Flint's home. How many people were there for Christmas dinner?" She turned to him with eyebrows raised.

He smiled. "There were only twenty-one of us. Just the usual."

She wanted to stare at his smile, but they needed to get to work. "Where do we begin?"

THE NEXT TWO WEEKS evaporated before she realized they had passed. When she rode with Flint to the airport for his flight to Colorado for the weekend, she fought the urge to tag along. But He didn't ask her. Watching his broad back as he entered the airport terminal and disappeared, a sense of cut off settled over her. He apparently enjoyed her company, but she felt the invisible line between them that he seemed unwilling to cross. If only she knew what that line was.

ON HIS RETURN TRIP to New York after his weekend home, He stared out the plane window at the gray clouds. Several times his sighs ended in shudders as if he had been crying. His chest ached. His little girl was dying. Allie's decline in just two weeks had shocked him. They could no longer play. She was too weak, so he sat in the recliner and held her. It took all the willpower he could muster to leave and get back on the plane. Each time it was harder.

The pilot began the descent into Kennedy International, and he raised his seatback. He would work with Stephanie for another two weeks and get as much done as he could, then he must go home. Relieved to have made a decision, he still felt a sense of loss. Leaving New York meant the end of his relationship with her. He would be working for her but not seeing her in the day-to-day way that had become so comfortable.

When he stepped out of the elevator at the apartment, she met him.

"Is your cell phone turned on?" she asked without a greeting.

He put his computer bag down and pulled his cell phone out of his overcoat pocket. "No, I turned it off on the plane and forgot to turn it on again. Why?"

She took his coat from him. "Your mom called. You need to call her immediately."

He turned his phone on and punched the speed dial. "Mom? What's wrong?"

"Flint, Dr. Edwards has tried to reach you. He said something about a heart for Allie. But how could that be? She's not even on the list." Mom sounded as if she was crying.

"I see I've had several calls from the same number in Colorado. That must be the doctor. I'll call you back and let you know what this is about." He clicked off, tapped his phone, and waited for the next call to go through.

She hung his coat in the hall closet and then disappeared into the kitchen while he walked into the living room, listening to the phone ringing Dr. Edwards' number. He was tempted to bite his fingernails, which he hadn't done in years.

"Dr. Edwards speaking. Is that you, Flint?" The voice sounded breathless.

"Sorry you couldn't reach me. I was on a flight to New York."

"Are you in New York now?"

"Yes, sir."

"Flint, we have a donor heart for Allie if we can get her to it."

Tightening his hand around the phone until his knuckles threatened to burst through the skin, he asked, "What do you mean, a donor heart for Allie? She's not on the donor list."

"She was put on the list two weeks ago when the fee was paid. It's a miracle, but there's a child on life support that's a near perfect match. The parents are going to remove life support within the next few days. They've agreed to donate the child's organs."

His vision blurred and he rubbed his temple. "I don't understand. How did the fee get paid? I didn't pay for it."

"It came as a cashier's check. I thought you knew. We have to move fast to take advantage of this donor's heart."

"What do we do?" He took a deep breath and forced every other thought out of his mind.

"The child is in the hospital in New York City. We need to get Allie there as soon as possible. I think she can travel all right and it will be easier to do the surgery there. I have talked to the doctors there, and I have confidence she will have a better chance with them."

He closed his eyes and tried to think. "I'll call my parents. They'll get her on a flight right away. How much time do we have?"

"If we can have Allie at the hospital ready to go when the organ is harvested, she'll have a much better chance."

He shuddered at the way the doctor so casually expressed the donor process. He hated that term. "I'll make arrangements and be in touch. Is this the best number to reach you?" How would he get Allie to the airport in Denver? The roads were still covered with snow. He had barely made it to the airport.

"Call me at this number as soon as you can." The phone click echoed in his ear.

A frown marring her beautiful face, Stephanie entered the living room with a tray of coffee and donuts. "Is it Allie?"

He nodded. "Someone sent the money and got her on the donor's list. They have a heart for her." His legs suddenly wouldn't hold him, and he abruptly sank onto the couch and buried his face in his hands. *They have a heart for Allie.* Taking a deep shuddering breath, he looked up and stared at her. She must have sent the check.

She placed her hand on his shoulder. "Do you need to fly back to Colorado?"

"I've got to get Allie to New York. The donor child is here." His body trembled. "I'll call the airlines and see how soon I can get her on a flight."

She shook her head. "My corporate jet is available. I'll contact the pilot and have it readied. You call your parents and have them prepare Allie for the flight. Is the airfield in Cedar Ridge capable of handling a Gulfstream?"

"Yes. I'll pay you —"

"You will not pay me. I'm doing this for Allie. Now, call your parents, and I'll get the plane prepared. By the time we get to the airport, it should be ready."

He punched speed dial for Mom's cell. His hands shook so he could hardly hold the phone. "Mom, it's true. They have a heart for Allie, but we have to get her to New York."

"How can that be? She isn't on the list."

"Someone donated the money two weeks ago. I think we both can guess who." He rubbed his eyes, trying to calm down.

"Oh, Flint." He heard a thread of hope in Mom's voice.

"Stephanie is arranging for her jet to fly me there. You and Dad need to be at the airport in Cedar Ridge with Allie. We'll fly back and have her here by this evening." He looked at Stephanie across the room speaking into her phone. How did he repay such a gift?

"Your father is out in the barn. We'll get ready and be at the airport by the time you arrive. Will it be okay for Holly and Benjamin to come?"

"Let me ask Stephanie." She had just completed her call. "How many can your plane carry?"

"It's a fourteen passenger. The pilot and copilot will have it ready in an hour." She pushed a strand of hair behind her ear. "I'll call

George to take us to the airport." Phone in hand, she scurried from the room.

"Mom, have Holly and Benjamin come. There's room. I'll call you in an hour and tell you what time to be at the airport. How's Allie?"

"She was sad this morning when she woke, and you were gone, but when I tell her she's coming to see you, I'm sure she'll perk up." Then she echoed the question he had been turning over in his mind. "Oh, son. Can this miracle really be happening at last?"

Chapter Twenty-Seven

HE USED THE DRIVE TO the airport to place several phone calls. He asked his three brothers to pray. Next, he called Richard Anderson to ask the church for prayers for their journey, for the surgery, and most of all for the couple losing their child as his was given hope.

Gripping the arms of his seat, He was unable to relax during the five-hour flight to Colorado. This was a very different plane than he usually took. He'd been surprised to meet Judith, the flight attendant when they'd boarded. The luxury that Stephanie lived with all her life continued to amaze him.

"Sir?" Judith approached his seat. He looked up.

"The pilot asked me to inform you that we'll be on the ground in Cedar Ridge for about forty-five minutes for refueling. It's not necessary as we could probably make it back to Kennedy International with the fuel we have, but he would rather start with a full tank in case we have to detour around bad weather. He hopes to be back in New York by midnight."

He glanced at Stephanie across the aisle asleep in her reclined seat. "How long until we land?"

Judith consulted her watch. "In the next thirty minutes. The medivac helicopter landed about ten minutes ago with our passengers."

"Thanks for the update. We're picking up my daughter who is ill. We'll need to keep the cabin warm for her. Can we take her on board as soon as we land or do we need to wait until the plane is fueled?"

He wished he knew more about private jets, but since this was his first experience, he just didn't know.

Judith smiled. "I look forward to meeting your little girl. I'll have to ask the pilot as I'm unfamiliar with this airport." She turned toward the cockpit.

Stephanie stirred and raised her seat slightly. "I hope you don't mind that I dozed off."

He smiled at her. She could do anything she wanted. Just look at what she was doing for him. "I hope you feel more rested now. We should land in about thirty minutes."

She looked out the window. "I can't see anything but clouds." She turned back to him. "Did you relax any?"

"Not really. This seems surreal. I can't believe we're flying to pick up Allie so she can receive her new heart. It happened so quickly. But I prayed a word of thanks for the generous heart that is making this happen." He gave her arm a gentle squeeze. "Stephanie, how can I ever repay you?"

She shifted in her seat. "I thought it was supposed to be anonymous. How did you know?"

He smiled. "You're the only one with the funds and the heart."

"Well, I did it for Allie. She deserves a chance. You don't need to repay me because it wasn't done for you."

He took her hand. "You're right, it wasn't for me, but I'll ask God to bless you every day of my life. Thank you for Allie."

She squeezed his hand. "My repayment will be seeing that little girl running and playing like other children. It's little enough when you've helped me so much."

Judith returned from the cockpit. "The captain asked us to prepare for landing. He's not worried about it, but he'll have to apply the brakes rather sharply because of the shortness of the runway. So buckle up and make sure everything is secured."

Stephanie snapped her seatback upright. "Thank you, Judith. We're all set. I brought several extra blankets on board. Do you think we'll be able to make a bed for the child and buckle her in safely?"

Judith grabbed the seat arm to balance as the plane wobbled through a patch of turbulence. "I know exactly how to make a bed for her and make sure she's safely buckled in. Now, I better get myself seated as we're about to land. By the way, the pilot said we've been cleared to land on the runway next to the terminal, and the fuel truck will meet us there. Our passengers should be able to board immediately. It seems everyone is cooperating to make this flight as easy as possible for your little girl."

As soon as the plane had come to a complete halt, he unbuckled, stood, and tugged on his overcoat and gloves. He saw Stephanie grab her coat, wool hat, and gloves. "It's ten degrees and snowing. You don't have to get out of the plane."

"True, but I want to make sure that your parents and Allie are okay. A little snow and cold won't hurt me."

Judith released the door and looked out. "The steps are down."

He climbed down the narrow steps and led the way across the tarmac to the terminal. A big tanker truck drove up, and men began the refueling process. He noticed the pilot was supervising the procedure.

Through the glass terminal door, he spotted Dad just inside. The cold penetrated his outer garments, and his boots crunched salt like cereal on the tarmac. Snowflakes drifted gently with a promise of more to come. He liked the feel of the cold crisp air, but it wasn't good for Allie. He glanced back at the plane. Would they have to de-ice before they could take off?

Dad pushed open the door. "Well, son, when I dropped you off this morning, I sure didn't expect to see you again so soon."

He hugged Dad. "Me either. Only the Lord knew this was going to happen. Where's Allie?"

"In the seats over by the wall with your mother. We've only been here a short while. There comes Holly and Benjamin now."

For the next few minutes, he greeted everyone and then bustled them on board. He left the luggage to the other men and carried Allie on board.

Judith stood by a seat. "Here's a place for the little one. What's your name, sweetheart?"

Allie's eyes were big and round as she stared around the plane. "Allie and this is Teddy. He's a big New York bear." She clung to her stuffed bear.

He sat her on the blanket spread over the seat and settled next to her. Judith buckled her in. "There, you're all set. Your daddy doesn't have his seatbelt on yet. You make sure he puts it on before the plane starts." She spread a couple of blankets over the little girl.

Allie glanced at him and then back to Judith. "Like in the truck?"

Judith smiled. "Just like in the truck. We all have to wear our seatbelts."

"Let me check that everyone is okay and then I'll put mine on." He stood and strode toward the back of the little plane where Holly and Benjamin were buckling in.

"I've been crying all afternoon. I can't believe it." Holly leaned forward and embraced him as he knelt on the floor in front of her. "Thanks for letting us come with you."

He hugged his sister, also thankful they could come to share this time with him. "We have to thank Stephanie for making it possible. Are you all right?"

"I'm fine. Benjamin is the one you need to worry about."

Benjamin grinned. "Yeah, I'm the one petrified of flying."

"Why are you afraid of flying?" This was something new he just learned about his brother-in-law.

"Because I've never flown before and in this little a plane, it's a bit scary." Benjamin's mischievous grin belied his words.

"If you have any problems let me know. We're about to take off, so I better get to my seat." He walked the aisle to where his parents sat holding hands. "You two doing all right?"

Dad nodded. "We're fine. How are you doing?"

Rubbing the back of his neck, he said, "When I first got the call I was pretty shaken up, but the ride here helped me settle down. I'm still in shock. Within the next two days, Allie will receive a new heart. Just saying it sounds amazing after months of hoping and all our prayers."

Judith appeared at his elbow. "Sir, you need to sit down and buckle your seatbelt. We're about ready to take off."

He quickly kissed Mom and Dad each on the cheek and then returned to his seat next to Allie.

She sat across from him. "Allie told me about riding in the helicopter. It sure sounds like fun."

He looked at Allie who nodded vigorously. "It was, Daddy, it was. You would like it. Except it was noisy and Grandma frowned a lot."

All of a sudden, the engines roared to life, and the plane began to vibrate. Allie looked at him with panic. He held her fragile hand in his and gave it a little pat. "It's okay, honey. It's just the plane starting. We're flying to New York."

After the plane was in the air, Judith took everyone's meal order. He hadn't even thought of food since early morning. It was now six in the evening. They had a choice between chicken or beef. The first scent of the hot food started his saliva flowing, and his stomach demanded to be fed.

He asked Dad to say a blessing, and then he dived into the food. "You eat something, Allie."

"Okay, Daddy." She took a single green bean and started chewing on it.

After eating, the drone of the plane lulled him to sleep as he held Allie's hand.

"Flint, wake up." Stephanie's voice penetrated his sleep, and he sat up trying to figure out where he was. Then he saw Allie's sleeping form.

He squinted at Stephanie as he rubbed the top of his head. "Where are we?" How could she look so beautiful after the day they had been through? She looked as if she had just stepped out of her apartment ready for the day.

"The pilot said we're a hundred miles out and should be landing within the next thirty to forty-five minutes, less if we don't have to circle."

"Son, what's the plan when we land? I don't even know where we're going." Dad held on to the back of Flint's seat.

"Stephanie has invited us to her place. The doctor suggested that since we're getting in so late, we should go there. If they need us, they'll call. We'll be fifteen minutes from the hospital."

Dad moved over by Stephanie's seat and put his hand on her shoulder. "You're turning out to be our guardian angel. Bless you."

"Thank you, Tom. I don't know about being an angel, but I'm happy to do what I can for Allie. She has become so precious to me."

He shifted in his seat. His muscles ached from prolonged sitting. "I expect they'll admit Allie to the hospital tomorrow and keep her there until the heart is available."

Dad stretched his back while rubbing it with his arm behind him. "Don't know how you all have done it today. Just this short ride and I'm bushed. You've been at it for fifteen hours now."

"When Allie is better, I'll rest up." Although ready to drop, he had to keep pushing for now.

She patted Dad's hand. "Hopefully we can all get some rest tonight. Will someone need to stay up and watch Allie?"

"I'll stay up with her." He knew that sleep might not be easy to come by.

Dad shook his head. "We'll take turns. You got to get some rest if you're going to make it through this."

Judith came up the aisle just then. "Sir, would you please be seated? We're making our approach into Kennedy."

After they landed, He descended the steps from the Gulfstream carrying Allie wrapped in a blanket against the cold. He was relieved to see the long black stretch limo just a few feet away. "George, good of you to come out this late."

"It's my pleasure, sir. How is the little one?" George opened the back door.

"She's tired, but Lord willing, in the next couple of days she'll get the medical treatment she needs." He carefully slid into the limo.

Allie stirred in the blanket, her voice weak with fatigue. "We at the big New York, Daddy?"

"Yes, honey. We're going to Stephanie's apartment to stay tonight." He smiled at her as she settled in beside him. His parents, Holly, and Benjamin climbed to the other side and sat in the side seats.

"How are you doing, sweetheart?" She reached over and pulled the blanket up closer to Allie's chin.

"We go to your house?"

"Yes, you're coming to visit me. I'm so glad, especially that you brought Teddy with you." She clasped the hand that Allie offered.

The drive to the apartment seemed longer than only an hour. Once there, he carried Allie to the bedroom Stephanie indicated for their use. Mom trailed into the room, and they soon had Allie in a gown and bedded down in the single bed. He hoped he would get some sleep in the other one. He unpacked the oxygen pump, plugged it into the electric socket, and placed the tube on Allie's nose.

"Go on, Mom. You and Dad get what rest you can. I'll let you know if the hospital calls." He hugged Mom and pushed her gently toward the door. "Allie will be okay till morning."

Alone with Allie, he turned the lights out except for a small lamp. Kneeling by her bed, he told her a story until she went to sleep. Then he stayed on his knees and prayed for strength to get through the coming days. He poured out his gratitude for God's gracious provision for the donor's heart.

And he prayed for the parents who would lose their child in the process.

Chapter Twenty-Eight

HE WOKE TO SEE HOLLY sitting in a chair by Allie's bed. "Been there long?"

"Not long. I just wanted to spend some time with Allie and pray. How are you?" She moved over and sat on the edge of his bed.

He sat up, leaned against the headboard, and took her hand. "I'm not sure ... just need to get through this. Thanks for being here."

"I needed to be here. Allie's precious to me. I hate you both have to suffer this. After Valerie, it has been so hard."

"Yes, I've been thinking a lot about Valerie and what she would say about the decisions I've made recently, being away from Allie these last few months and even the decision to have the heart transplant." He rubbed his stubble-covered jaw. Valerie would always be with him as he looked at the face of his child that so resembled her mother's.

"What answer did you get?"

"Just trust God to take care of Allie and be with me. You know how Valerie was. Her first thought always was what does God want? I try to follow that example. It's hard sometimes." He trusted his twin to understand. They might not look alike, but they often seemed to think the same thoughts.

"I know." She stood and glanced at Allie. "She's sleeping a lot these days."

"Maybe it's for the best. She needs all the rest she can get to be ready for what's to come." He hoped he could find the strength. Having already been through two heart surgeries with Allie he knew how

bad it could be, only this time his little girl was old enough to remember the pain. Could he stand to see her go through it again, this
time even worse? Only with God's help would he make it through
this.

"I'm going to shower and then breakfast will be ready.
Stephanie's friend Brigitte arrived, and a lady named Ivana is in the
kitchen." Holly reached up and ruffled his hair. "Mom said she
would sit with Allie while you showered and shaved."

"Leave my hair alone." He grinned and batted her hand away.
"I'm sure it looks just fine."

After Holly left, he watched Allie sleep. She wore the oxygen
tube and the small unit pumped away. He got up and fitted the pulse
oximeter over her little finger trying not to wake her. It registered
barely ninety. Maybe she did need to be in the hospital. Anything less
than ninety was dangerously low for her.

"What's the number?" Mom peeked around his elbow.

"It's just up to ninety. I'll call our contact doctor at the hospital."

"Go get showered and dressed then make the call. You need to
be ready for a long day." Mom kissed his cheek. "We're going to make
it through this with God's help."

"I'm so glad you and Dad are here." He hugged her tight.

Mom smiled as she pushed him toward the bathroom door.
"Where else would we be? Now go."

With Mom watching Allie, after his shower, He felt free to go
downstairs hunting for coffee. He found everyone around the
kitchen table except for Ivana and Stephanie who were cooking
breakfast. It seemed natural to give her a sideways hug as he greeted
everyone else. The first sip of coffee from the mug she handed him
tasted good.

"Breakfast will be ready in about five minutes." She poured herself a mug of coffee.

"I need to make a phone call then I'll eat." He carried the mug into the dining room and sat at the table still cluttered with the papers and equipment. He pulled out his phone and punched in the doctor's number.

"Hello, Dr. Jefferson here."

"This is Flint Tucker calling about my daughter Allie, Allison Tucker."

"Oh, yes, I've been expecting your call. Where are you and how is the child?"

"We arrived in New York after midnight. We're staying with a friend across from Central Park East. Allie is asleep. I just checked her oxygen, and it barely hit ninety, and we have the oxygen pumping."

"I'm not surprised, but that's too low. Bring her in this morning with the expectation of her staying for a possible evening surgery."

Even though He expected it, the news still jolted like a fist hitting his gut. Fighting for breath, he asked, "When we get to the hospital where do we go?"

"Enter through the front door. Someone at the information desk will escort you to the transplant floor. There's a waiting room for family members."

"Thanks. How quickly do I need to get Allie there? She's still sleeping."

"Well, it's seven-thirty now. Why don't you check her oxygen absorption levels every fifteen minutes and have her here by eleven. If her level goes below 85, you need to come in at once. Be sure she doesn't ingest anything but a few sips of water. She needs to fast for the surgery. When you get here, we'll start an I.V. to replenish her nutrients." The doctor's voice had a calm, kind sound to it.

"Thanks, Dr. Jefferson, we'll definitely be there by eleven."

He hurried back into the kitchen. "They want Allie at the hospital by eleven if her oxygen absorption doesn't drop. Dr. Jefferson expects to do the surgery this evening." He stopped as he looked at the concerned faces surrounding him.

Dad got up from the table where he had just finished his breakfast. "Sit here, son. You eat, and I'll go tell your mother. No argument. You have to keep your strength up today."

"All right, Dad." He slumped into the chair not sure he had the energy to lift a fork.

She placed a plate of eggs, ham, and toast in front of him. "While you eat I'll call George. He'll be on standby until we need him." She took his coffee mug and handed it to Ivana. "Please refill this."

Everyone was so considerate. He wished he didn't need it, but he did. He ate without tasting the food, doing it for Allie. He would be strong for his little girl.

Allie's pulse and oxygen absorption levels fluctuated like a barometer in a hurricane. He couldn't wait. The family entered the hospital at ten with him carrying a bewildered Allie snuggled in a blanket in her daddy's arms.

She looked around, frowned, and shook her head at him. "Not my hospital, Daddy. We go to my hospital."

"This is the big New York hospital, honey. Remember we rode on the airplane to the big New York?" How could he explain this to his little girl?

Dad had gone ahead to the information desk and now walked back to meet them with an older woman following him. "Flint, you have to fill out papers. They said you could meet up with Allie later and that one person could go with her now. Mary, that should be you."

He tightened his hold on Allie and then made himself relax. He mustn't share his anxiety with her. "Okay, little bunny. You go with Grandma, and I'll see you in a few minutes." He handed her off to Mom.

As quick as he could, he read and signed the necessary papers. She stayed with him while the others went upstairs to the waiting room. With his mind reeling from the legal and medical jargon, his hand shook as he punched the elevator button for the pediatric transplant floor.

"Let me have your coat. I doubt you'll need it while sitting with Allie." She took his coat and then kissed his cheek. "She's going to be fine. I just feel it."

"Thanks for everything." He had said it before but how could he really convey his gratitude for what she had done for Allie and for him?

Exiting the elevator, he followed the directions to a room where Mom sat with Allie. Stephanie stepped toward the family waiting room.

"Daddy, I want to go home." Allie turned accusing eyes on him as soon as he stepped into the room. "I don't like it here." When he sat on the side of the bed, she began to cry and climbed onto his lap.

"Shh, little one. It's going to be okay. I'm here, and I won't leave you." He held her frail body close and rocked.

A nurse entered the room pushing a metal cart containing a variety of medical paraphernalia. "Hi, Allie, I'm Sonia. Mr. Tucker, we need to start an I.V. Will you hold her for us?"

He nodded and swallowed over the rock in his throat. He whispered into Allie's ear. "We have to be brave now. Let's sing a song." He cupped her little face so she had to watch his, instead of what the nurse was doing to Allie's right arm. "Mom, you sing too." He began to sing *Ole McDonald had a Farm*. Mom joined in, but Allie just blinked into his eyes with her huge round eyes.

When the nurse inserted the needle for the I.V., the prick registered and Allie tried to jerk away, but he held her tight.

"Ouch, Daddy, Ouch. Bad lady hurt Allie." Frowning with her lips tight, she appeared more angry than hurt.

"It's okay. Just a little bit and it won't hurt. See, the nice lady is smiling at you." He continued to hold Allie while the nurse attached the I.V. tube and positioned it to the pole.

"There, Allie, I'm all done." She attached a small stiff pad to Allie's arm. "Sir, she mustn't pull on the tube. The I.V. is secured. With the pad, it should be all right. They called down a few minutes ago and said they might be ready for her within the hour. You can stay with her for another few minutes and then we need to take her up to the surgery floor."

"Can't I go up with her?" He wasn't going to let go until the very last second.

"No, sir. Only patients and medical personnel can go to the transplant surgery floor. It's a safety precaution because of contamination. Staff will provide updates every fifteen minutes in the waiting room."

Mom put her hand on his shoulder. "Son, just hold her until you have to leave her and then we'll pray together in the waiting room. I'll tell the others." She leaned over and kissed Allie on the cheek. "Grandma loves you very much, Allie. I have to go see Granddad."

Allie nodded and hugged Mom. "Love you, Grandma. You got any cookies? I'm hungry."

Mom smiled through the shine of tears in her eyes. "I'll have to bake some cookies at Stephanie's house just for you." She patted his cheek and quickly left the room.

Sonia put an oximeter on Allie's finger. She adjusted the cord and made sure the reading registered on the instrument cart. "There's a sedative in the I.V. Allie will start to get drowsy soon, not completely under but enough that she won't remember anything. She won't realize you're not upstairs with her."

"Thanks for explaining. I'll just rock her for now, and when you tell me, I'll lay her down." When he laid her down, they would soon take her upstairs, and he would have to let go of his little girl. He didn't know how he could be able to do that. He'd done it twice already, for other surgeries, but that didn't seem to make it any easier. He held Allie in his arms as he had done when she was a baby, gently swaying back and forth, as he felt her relax.

An African American man who looked to be in his fifties entered the hospital room. "Hi, I'm Dr. Jefferson, the head of the transplant team."

He didn't try to shake the man's hand, as he didn't want to disturb Allie who was drifting in and out of drugged sleep. He simply inclined his head. "I'm Flint Tucker, Allie's father."

The doctor checked the instrument readout. "We're running ahead of schedule. The donor heart will be available within the hour. We need to take Allie upstairs now." He looked at Flint and then at Allie asleep in his arms. "Do you have family here with you?"

He swallowed before he could speak. The hard knot of fear in the middle of his chest grew with every passing second. "My parents, sister and her husband, and some friends are all in the waiting room."

"Good, you don't need to be waiting alone. We'll keep you updated. The surgery takes hours, and then Allie will be in the ICU for several days. She'll stay in the hospital for a couple of weeks." He glanced at his watch. "I'll give you another ten minutes and then we need to take her upstairs. I know this is hard. We'll do the best we can." He gently touched Allie's cheek and then looked up at Flint. "I have two daughters."

"Thanks, Dr. Jefferson." He watched the doctor's back as he left the room.

"Please, God, make this man a great surgeon today. Bless Allie and let her be all right. And Father, please be with the parents of the child who is giving mine a chance to live and care for their child in your heaven. Overall, may your will be done in the name of Jesus the Christ, Amen."

He hugged Allie, kissed her right cheek for himself and then her left cheek for her mother. "I love you, little one and now I release you to God's care." Gently, he laid her sleeping form on the bed and watched as Sonia covered her with a white blanket. With Allie's dark hair spread out on the white sheets, she looked as close to what he thought an angel would look like as he could imagine. The fist in the middle of his chest expanded until he didn't know if he could stand it.

Two more nurses entered the room and helped Sonia roll the bed to the elevator.

He held Allie's hand as he walked alongside the gurney until they reached the elevator.

Sonia put her hand on his arm. "I'm sorry, but this is as far as you can go."

"I know." He sighed. "Take care of my baby." The elevator door closed. He stood and stared at it as he imagined the journey ahead for his little girl.

Chapter Twenty-Nine

"SON, COME TO THE WAITING room and let's pray together." Dad put his arm around his shoulder and guided him down the hall. "There's a surprise for you."

The first thing he saw as he entered the room was his three older brothers. Abe, Samuel, and Stephen all surrounded him in a massive hug.

When they finally broke apart, he looked from one to the other. "I can't believe you all came. How? When? Thank the Lord, I'm glad you're here."

Abe flung his arm around his shoulder. "We had to come. I can only stay a few days, but Stephanie has offered her plane to fly me home."

He hugged Abe and glanced at Stephen. "You could have come on the plane last night."

Stephen shook his head. "I couldn't get to the airport in time and didn't want to hold you up. I caught an early flight this morning."

Samuel punched him on the arm. "I've never been to New York. You gave me an excuse to take a month off work. Can't do much this time of year in my part of Alaska anyway."

"Let's gather the chairs and pray awhile." Dad tugged a couple of the upholstered chairs from where they sat around the wall of the room and arranged them into a circle. The brothers followed his lead.

He sat with his brother, Abe, on one side and Stephanie on the other. He bowed his head. What did she think of their prayers? Did she even know how to pray or believe the prayers would have an effect? Maybe being with the family and hearing the prayers would be a witness to her. If so, it would be because of Allie.

They took turns praying and leading songs for an hour. After the time of prayer, the waiting began. He paced up and down the hallway outside the waiting room for a couple of hours. Different people took turns walking with him. Later in the morning, Richard and Nancy Anderson arrived, as did Antonio and several others from the congregation.

The movement around him floated in and out of his consciousness in waves. Mostly his thoughts concentrated on the floor above where his child lay.

Brigitte pulled a sizeable wheeled cooler filled with sandwiches and bottled drinks into the waiting room. Later he saw her seated beside Samuel with their heads together in close conversation.

Stephanie seemed to be quietly talking with one and then another off and on, but not demanding his attention, for which he felt grateful. He had nothing left to give her as his whole focus was on what was happening on the floor above.

Whenever the desk phone just outside the waiting room rang, everyone stopped talking and waited for the attendant to give an update on the surgery. Often Abe would translate, giving them a layman's explanation.

"Allie is on the bypass machine," the attendant announced. "The doctors are getting ready to implant the new heart."

He pulled a straight-back chair to the window and got on his knees, resting his arms on the seat of the chair, and buried his head in his hands as he prayed.

Please, dear Father God, let my child survive and not reject the new heart. You know my heart. You bring me comfort in this time of fear. Be with me, my Savior and let the words of my heart be spoken on my behalf by the Holy Spirit. All I can do is beg for my baby's life. Your will be done in all things. Just hear the cry of my heart, my Father.

He repeated the same prayer over and over. The sweat poured from his body as he beseeched the Father for Allie's life.

Hours later, he heard the desk attendant announce, "The heart is in place and beating. They've taken Allie off the bypass machine." He thanked the Father in heaven, took several shuttering breaths, and stood on shaky legs.

"Now we wait for the healing." Dad put his arm around his shoulder. "Go to the men's room, wash your face, and come on back to wait for the doctor. Hopefully, they'll let you see her in the next couple of hours. The family has worked out a schedule. One of us will always be praying nonstop for as long as we need."

He wished he could let out the cry building in his heart, but the lump in his throat seemed to block it. He wrapped his arms around Dad's neck and felt strong arms holding him. "I'll do what you say. When I get back, maybe I'll drink some juice or coffee."

Abe stood. "Let me walk to the men's room with you. I could use a break."

He grunted. "I can go by myself, you know."

"Sure you can, little brother. Maybe I have to go, too." Abe led the way out of the waiting room and down the hall.

After refreshing himself by splashing cold water on his face, he did feel revived. On the way back to the waiting room, he stopped at a window in the hallway where he could see the city. Night had fallen.

"Getting the new heart going again and taking Allie off the bypass machine is major. Allie's chances for a full recovery just jumped up by several digits." Abe smiled.

He nodded. "It's hard to imagine that another child's heart is beating in her chest."

"Are you prepared for how sick she is? Even worse than the other two surgeries?"

"I know it in my head, but am I prepared to see it? How do you prepare for that?"

Abe scratched the end of his nose. "I have no idea. I keep asking myself how would I feel if it was one of my children. God has blessed us with three healthy children. Maybe that's why Allie means so much to me. She's been through more than most people ever have to deal with and you've witnessed it all. You've been a wonderful example to me, little brother. You've helped my faith grow."

He didn't know what to say. Abe had never expressed anything like this before. "I just get through it. I don't know what else to do." He looked at his big brother. "I'm glad your children are healthy. I wouldn't want anyone to go through this."

Abe nodded. "I know. Today I got more of a chance to talk with Stephanie. We owe her a lot."

"Yes, I tried to think of ways to thank her, but all I've figured out to do is say it."

"That's all you need to do. And keep praying she will come to faith. We talked about the existence of God today. She wanted to know exactly whom you thought you were praying to. It was one of those moments when I could tell someone about my faith."

"Maybe that's why the surgery needed to be in New York, as a witness to her." He thought that over as it was a new thought.

Abe shrugged. "Only time will tell but let's hope so. I really like her, and she seems to have a sweet spirit, besides being beautiful." He glanced down the hallway. "There comes Dr. Jefferson. Let's go get the results of the surgery."

He stepped into the waiting room. "Dr. Jefferson is coming." Everyone stopped their conversation and watched the door expectantly. Dr. Jefferson was still in his scrubs. "Well, Flint, your little girl is doing just fine."

Grabbing a chair, he sunk into it. His legs no longer wanted to hold him.

Pulling up a chair, Dr. Jefferson sat knee to knee with him. "The new heart is pumping like crazy. Her blood pressure is stable, her blood absorption is at normal, and she's responding well in all aspects."

"Thank God." His response got an amen from several other family members. "When can I see her?"

Dr. Jefferson rested his hand on his shoulder. "Whenever you want. We have an observation window you can look through into the ICU. The question is when will we let you touch her? Probably later tonight or early in the morning. We'll keep her sedated for a few days, very lightly. By tomorrow, we can bring her out of the sedation if all is going well. She'll need familiar faces and voices around her." He glanced around at the faces and then back to Flint. "I understand you're a widower. Who is Allie used to being with?"

"My parents and my sister Holly have taken care of her all her life. My parents live with us." He nodded at Mom and Dad.

"Then the four of you should be there to go into the pediatric ICU for the next few days. When we move her to a room of her own, she can have other visitors but only for short periods. Of course, if anyone develops any kind of respiratory infection, please don't come to the hospital at all. As her father, we want you to be with her as much as possible. When she gets her own room, we'll have a bed in there for you."

He breathed a sigh of relief. At least he didn't have to fight the hospital personnel to see his daughter. "Thank you. I appreciate that."

Dr. Jefferson looked around. "Anyone have questions?" He paused and then said, "Good, I'll go check on our girl again and then send an attendant to come to take you to Pedi ICU. I know you won't do it, but you should try to sleep tonight. We are in for a long haul, and you need to be rested for Allie's sake."

After the doctor left, he stood to look at everyone in the waiting room. "I want to thank all you for your time and prayers today. I know you'll keep praying. It's already almost eight, and most of you have been here all day. Please go get something to eat and a good night of sleep. If you prefer to stay or come back tomorrow, I appreciate it. The Lord knew I couldn't go through this by myself and He didn't let me down."

"May I lead a prayer of thanksgiving? Then Nancy and I will go on to the church where the rest of the congregation has met to pray for you and Allie." Richard stood and took his wife's hand. One by one, everyone joined hands.

He could barely swallow. The muscles around his Adam's apple seemed to be convulsing up and down. The sense that he wanted to weep was overwhelming, but no tears came. No one had told him that the whole congregation was conducting a prayer vigil for his child. He could only nod his head at Richard.

"Let's pray. Our Father, we thank you for bringing our sweet Allie through this ordeal so far. Be with her the rest of the journey. Be with the family of the child who died and made possible this gift. Bless Flint and all the family and help them prepare to raise this child to be your servant instead of preparing to bury her. We can only humbly thank you. In the name of Jesus the Christ, Amen."

He stumbled over to hug Richard. "Thank you for that prayer. It says what is in my heart."

"You're welcome. If we can do anything let us know. We'll be back tomorrow."

A patient assistant entered the room. "Flint Tucker?"

"That's me."

"Follow me, and I'll take you to Pedi ICU."

When he saw Allie through the glass looking so tiny, he almost didn't recognize her. Tubes wound around her little body connecting to machinery everywhere. He could only stand and stare at his child.

"Oh, Flint, she looks so small and hurt." Mom quietly cried into her handkerchief. "But the doctor seemed so sure she was doing fine."

He put his arm around her shoulder and pulled her near. She had spent almost four years caring for his child. Their child. "She's going to be fine. We have to believe that. It's just so hard to see her lying there hurt. But we'll be like Joshua after the Lord told him to be of good courage for his God would be with him." He prayed he could keep his courage through whatever lay ahead.

"I'm going to buy her a bike with training wheels when we get home." Dad pulled out his handkerchief and loudly blew his nose.

He smiled. "Where did that come from?"

"Well, I thought about it at Christmas, but she was too weak to ride. Now I know Allie is going to get strong like any other kid and she'll want a bike."

"You're right. We can now start thinking in terms of our future with Allie and not be afraid of what we're going to do. Thanks, Dad. I needed that. We still have to help her get over this surgery, but we can also rejoice that we have this new chance for life." He felt the fist in his chest relax a notch—still not completely gone, but one day he hoped he could relax and enjoy his child.

Chapter Thirty

SHE FINALLY CRAWLED into bed at midnight. Her body ached from the day's stress and tension, but her eyes refused to close. She stared into the darkness. The apartment was quiet with everyone finally down for the night occupying every bed. When had that ever happened before? Although the day had been hard, at the same time it had been fascinating to watch Flint's family and friends interact. She flopped to her back trying to relax. Images of him hovered behind her eyelids. How he had suffered. She had so wanted to wrap her arms around him in comfort. But the best she could offer was housing and transportation and then stay out of his way. The sight of that big strong man kneeling in prayer loomed large in her mind, sending shivers shimmying up her spine.

She had never seen anything like it before. They really believed that God would hear their pleas and answer. She shook her head and turned to her side. One day she must ask Flint to explain.

Heaving a huge sigh, she squeezed her eyes tight, but the image of him on his knees with his face in his hands continued to swirl through her mind. They all acted as if seeing him in prayer was normal. The brothers hadn't seemed as emotional as he had, but she guessed that was partly because they were men. Besides, Allie wasn't their only child. It had been intriguing to watch Brigitte and Samuel huddle together. Was there a romance budding there?

Maybe she could grab another opportunity to talk with Abe. He wasn't afraid to answer her questions and seemed so knowledgeable.

Feeling sleep creeping up, at last, she let out the breath she'd been holding in. Would he be able to sleep at all tonight?

SIPPING HER FIRST CUP of coffee, she sat in her crowded apartment office trying to sort out the events of the last two weeks. She had never spent so many hours with this many people around. It surprised her that she had come to care for them so deeply in such a short time. She gazed out at the beautiful park view. She loved Flint's family, and they seemed to care for her. She had done what she could to ease his worries. She pictured him keeping vigil at Allie's bedside.

A sigh of satisfaction escaped her lips. It felt good that she had been able to facilitate Abe and Stephen's return home, as well as Holly and Benjamin's. Usually, her giving took the form of an impersonal check. Sending them off in a limo ride to the airport and then flying them in her corporate jet gave her a sense of giving back that was more personal than anything she'd ever done before.

The elevator dinged announcing someone's arrival. She expected Brigitte, but as she walked down the hall, she heard a male voice and then Brigitte's laugh. Samuel stood next to Brigitte helping her out of her coat.

"Morning, Brigitte. Is it still as cold as it was yesterday?"

Brigitte tugged off her snow boots and slipped into shoes. "It feels even colder because the wind is up. February is going to be colder than January, you mark my word."

Samuel grinned. "So among your many talents, you're a meteorologist too?"

"Well, no, but I have a feeling." Brigitte's cheeks reddened.

"I think he's teasing you." She really liked Samuel, especially because he made Brigitte laugh. "Are you going to the hospital soon?"

He nodded. "I want to be there when the doctors do rounds, which is usually about eleven. I'm expecting them to discuss Allie's release."

"Let's sit in the living room and talk a minute." She led the way. "I want to ask your opinion about something."

Brigitte moved toward the kitchen. "I need a cup of tea. Anyone else want coffee or tea?"

Samuel settled in one of the recliners. "I'll take a coffee."

"Nothing for me." She sat on the couch, slipped out of her slippers, and curled her bare feet under her. "I wanted to ask what you thought would be best for Allie after she leaves the hospital. I hope you know my apartment is available for as long as she needs to stay in New York."

Samuel leaned forward, mixed expressions playing on his face. "You can't imagine how much we appreciate what you're doing for us."

She brushed her hair back. "I'm doing it for Allie. For all of you too, of course, but that little girl has simply captured my heart."

Samuel nodded. "The first week or so she'll need to be close to the hospital in case she has problems. Then it might take another three to six weeks before she can fly home, at least that's what I know at this time." Samuel watched Brigitte carry a tray with a cup of fragrant tea and a mug of aromatic coffee. The pleasant smells mixed as she approached.

She smiled at the adoring look that passed between them. Yes, romance was definitely in the air.

After delivering the coffee, Brigitte sat at the end of the couch next to Samuel's chair and sipped her tea.

She cleared her throat. Best to keep her comments about their relationship to herself for now. Instead, she said, "I want to offer my house in the Hamptons for Flint and Allie to use during this time. There's plenty of room for the family to come to visit for as long as

Allie needs to be near the hospital. What do you think Flint will say to that?"

"I can't speak for Flint, but my guess is he'd be grateful."

"I want to talk to him this morning, so he'll know his options." She lowered her legs and slipped into her shoes.

THE HOSPITAL FELT FAMILIAR after two weeks of visits. Bustling with energy, the constant sounds imparted a notion of efficiency and importance. She shrugged off her coat and gloves as she strolled next to Samuel on the way to the waiting room. Only one person at a time was allowed to visit Allie and Flint.

They found Tom and Mary seated in the waiting room. Samuel kissed his mother's cheek. "Hi, has Flint left Allie's room this morning?"

"No, he hasn't left her room since yesterday. He's barely sleeping at all and only nibbling at food." Mary shook her head.

"Well, I'm going to suggest that he take Stephanie down to the cafeteria. Then I'll sit with Allie myself," Samuel said. "She has something she needs to talk to him about."

Tom punched Samuel's arm. "Just tell him to go and good luck. We've tried to relieve him, but except to take a shower and sleep for a couple of hours, I don't think he's left Allie's side for ten days."

"Come on Stephanie, I'll shove Flint out the door, and you grab his arm and drag him to the cafeteria." Samuel grinned at her as she followed him down the hall toward Allie's room.

She waited in the hallway while Samuel entered the room.

After a few minutes, Flint came out. "Samuel said you needed to ask me a question."

Words caught in her throat when she saw him. He appeared gaunt and pale. In these few days, he'd lost weight, making the bones of his face more prominent. Linking her arm through his arm, she started toward the elevators. "Yes. We're going to talk over a hot cafeteria lunch. No argument. Samuel wants to visit Allie."

He raised his eyebrows and pulled back slightly. "Am I being kidnapped?"

She laughed and tightened her hold on his arm. "You might say that. It's a conspiracy to get you out of Allie's room for an hour." She punched the down button, and they waited for the elevator. "How is she this morning?"

"She's doing great, although she'll be angry at me this afternoon. They're taking the last of the staples out. For some reason, when they do something that hurts she turns those big eyes on me as if I've betrayed her." The elevator doors opened, he waved her into the elevator and pushed the button for the first level.

She watched the floor numbers pass on their way down. "I understand that. You're her protector, and you're supposed to keep all the hurt away." She met his gaze. "Except you can't do that. But she's too young to understand."

"I just hope it doesn't erode her trust in me." His voice carried a note of worry.

"I don't think you have to be concerned about that. Who does she see sitting beside her bed every day but her daddy? She may get mad at you for the needle pricks, but distrust you? No way."

"Thanks. I worry what all this is doing to her." When the elevator doors slid open, he guided her into the cafeteria and perused the menu board. "All of a sudden I'm hungry for hot food."

After getting their meal and sitting at a corner table, he bowed his head and asked a blessing on the food. Being used to this behavior by now, she closed her eyes.

When she looked up, she found him scrutinizing her face.

"Did you really have a question or was that just a pretext to get me out of Allie's room for a while?"

In that moment, she lost herself in his deep blue eyes and had to shake herself back to the present. "I do have a question. But also we needed to get you out of that hospital room for an hour so you could eat something."

He seemed to have forgotten his need for food as he continued to hold her gaze. "What's the question?"

She took a deep breath and stared at her salad. "Allie seems to be doing so well. I expect you'll be allowed to take her out of the hospital in a few days. What do you think of taking her to my place in the Hamptons? We can have the helicopter on standby if she needs to return to the hospital quickly. It wouldn't take any more time than driving from my apartment."

His face went blank. Was he just thinking or was he upset by her suggestion? She blinked and bit her lower lip. Should she give him time to think it over?

After a long pause, he drew in a long breath and slowly exhaled. "That would be wonderful. It would be the best thing for Allie. How can I thank—"

She shook her head. "You have thanked me, your family has thanked me. No more. Let me have the joy of giving to Allie."

He nodded slowly as if processing her answer. "You've done so much. I don't know how to properly express my gratitude to you."

"Raise that child with love and kindness and always pay attention to her. That's what I ask in return. Now, when do you think we can take Allie to the Hamptons?" She forked a bite of salad and watched with approval as he began to attack his roast beef.

"I'll ask the doctor when he removes the staples from Allie's chest and let you know." He stopped chewing, his fork suspended in midair. "I haven't forgotten the work I need to do for you. Ben and Tony have already gotten a

lot done, and Farley Terrago, the attorney, has been working on the incorporation papers."

She gasped. "Flint Tucker, don't you dare worry about my business while you're taking care of Allie."

"I didn't mean to upset you. After she's past the crisis, I'll get back to work. I wanted you to know I hadn't forgotten there's work to do."

"All right then. Just remember Allie takes first priority. Always."

"I don't want to assume, so I'll ask. Is it all right for Mom, Dad, and Samuel to come out to the house?"

She smiled. "Go ahead and assume. Any of your family is welcome. The house is yours for however long you need it."

He rubbed his temple. "What if you and Brigitte came too? Then we could work a few hours every day? Allie will need to nap so we'll have time."

"Only if you're sure." She put down her fork and dabbed her lips with her napkin. "We can use the third-floor salon for the office and turn the rest of the house over to your family. Your mom will love it. I'm not sure about your dad. He seems anxious to get back home."

He grinned. "Yeah, he's worried about the ranch and the animals. Of course, he knows the ranch is being cared for, but he's used to staying active. Too much sitting around gets on his nerves."

"Does your mom need him here? Maybe he should go home."

He pushed his empty plate away, leaned on his elbows, and folded his hands. "She did need him. But with Allie getting better each day, maybe not so much now. I know she won't leave Allie, but she might be ready to send Dad home. I'll talk to them." He tilted his head, eyebrows cocked. "What about you? How are you doing? Really. All of this must be completely foreign to your lifestyle."

Her knife and fork clinked on her empty plate when she arranged them across it. How could she explain what this time had meant to her? "I have felt more useful and engaged in the last two weeks than I ever felt before. To be involved in giving someone life has been an amazing experience." She leaned forward. "To watch you and your family deal with something so stressful has been a true learning experience. Not to mention the joy of seeing Allie bright-eyed and smiling so quickly after such a horrendous surgery. Well, words fail me. Thank you so much for letting me be part of it."

He stared at her intently. "I guess you know my family has come to love you. We consider you one of us now."

A sudden lump formed in her throat. His family, but not him? Is that what he meant? Did she want that? "You have a great family, and I've fallen in love with them, too. Holly even asked if she could consider me as the sister she never had. I was so honored."

"Well, we're a normal bunch of folks with the usual problems and faults. If you're going to be part of the family, you have to take part in the squabbles too."

"That's part of what fascinates me, you're a normal family. My life has been different from most people, I guess. Too much wealth, too much privilege, and too little family."

"You came through it all right. You're a well-adjusted young woman."

"Thanks. I want to be well-adjusted."

He looked at his watch. "I'm glad you kidnapped me. I needed to get out of that room. But the doctor will be coming in soon."

"Then we need to head back." She gathered her purse. Many other words she wanted to say to him almost spilled from her lips, but she'd have to save them for another time.

Chapter Thirty-One

THREE DAYS LATER, SHE accompanied Tom, Mary, Samuel, and Brigitte to her home in the Hamptons. With good traffic conditions, they planned to be there several hours before Flint and Allie arrived by helicopter.

"Stephanie, Flint told me you have a large house, but I hope all of us being there won't be a burden." Mary pulled her coat tighter. Even though it was toasty warm in the car, the snow-covered ground hinted at the chilly outside temperature.

Patting Mary's hand, she gave a reassuring smile. "Don't worry about being a burden. It's a gift to have you there. The house is plenty big for everyone. My caretakers, Enzio and Maria, have organized everything for us. I told them to put you in the west wing on the second floor. That way you'll only be a few feet from Allie's room. I'll offer Flint his own room, but I'm not sure whether he'll use it or not. He may want to stay in Allie's room."

Mary took her hand and held it. "I'm going to see that he does use it. That boy is worn out. Unfortunately, this is exactly what he did after Allie's first two heart surgeries. He wanted to be with her every second. He's afraid he'll lose Allie just as he did Valerie. But now it's time to start getting back to normal."

Tom stretched his legs as if relishing the space in the limo. "You're right, Mary. Maybe we can all work together to get Flint eating and sleeping regularly."

"I know we mustn't leave her alone just yet. Would it help if I hired a nurse to stay with Allie at night?" Hiring nurses to stay

with Allie was a minor expense, but she knew her wealth was something Flint's family difficulty comprehending. She must tread lightly
around this subject.

"What do you think, Mary? Would Flint go for that?" Tom
leaned forward.

Samuel spoke from his seat beside Brigitte. "I think you should
do it without asking Flint. Just say it's already in place."

Mary frowned. "He might not like us deciding without his okay."

"Let him get mad, and then we'll deal with him. It's for his own
good." Samuel's authoritative voice made it sound like the logical approach.

She raised her eyebrows. "Would this be one of the family squabbles Flint said you have from time to time?"

They all laughed.

Tom laughed so hard he had to wipe his eyes. "I guess you could
say that. We sometimes get into arguments, but never fights. Of
course, Flint would have to give in on this one because it would be
for Allie."

She decided to be assertive. Round-the-clock nursing would be
in place by the time Flint and Allie arrived.

HE HEAVED A CONTENTED sigh. George met them at the
small airport and now eased the limo to a stop in the circular driveway. Bringing Allie to Stephanie's place in the Hamptons was the
next best thing to going home. The beauty of the setting had not di-
minished since his last visit. Snow covered the estate like a dusting of
powdered sugar. He stopped a moment to admire the view. Then he
lifted Allie out of the car and carried her through the marble foyer.
He didn't stop until he got to the huge windows in the spacious living room. "Look, sweetheart, that's the ocean."

Allie leaned away from his arms trying to see everything at once. "Where're the mountains, Daddy?"

He chuckled. That was all she had ever known. "They're all back in Colorado on the ranch. We'll stay here and visit Stephanie for a few weeks and then we'll go home to the mountains."

"Do fishies live in that ocean?"

"That's right. Big fishies and little fishies. Now let's go find your bedroom." He mounted the stairs to the second floor to find Stephanie waiting for them, a big smile gracing her face.

"We've brought her things up. You'll stay in the corner room like last time, and Allie will be next door to you. Your folks are across the hall." She led the way into a sunny bedroom painted in shades of blue. A large double bed and a sitting room alcove faced the sea. She pointed. "The bath is through there."

"Thanks. This will be great, but I really don't need a room. I'll probably be spending most of my time in here with Allie." He settled Allie on the bed and proceeded to remove her coat and boots.

Mary entered the room. "You will not be spending all of your time in here. You'll start sleeping in your own room and get some rest."

"Mom—"

"Don't argue with me, young man. We're all going to take care of Allie. And you're going to start getting back into a normal routine. Just how much weight have you lost in the last two weeks? And look at your eyes, all dark and sunk in. Have you checked a mirror lately?"

He knew better than to argue with Mom when she was in this sort of mood. To tell the truth, he was tired, more so than he'd ever been in his life. Tired to the core. "All right, Mom."

"Grandma? You mad at Daddy?" Allie looked from Grandma to him.

"No, honey, I'm not mad at your daddy." Mom reached up to kiss his cheek. "See?"

Just then, Brigitte arrived, followed by a woman who appeared to be in her fifties. The room was fast getting crowded. "Stephanie, this is Helen Morgan. The agency sent her over."

"Hi, Helen, nice to meet you." She stepped aside. "This is Allie, your patient, and this is her father, Flint Tucker."

The woman stepped to the bed and smiled at Allie. "Hello, Allie. My but you're a pretty little girl."

"What's this?" He frowned glancing at the women in his life.

Mom laid a hand on his arm. "Stephanie hired Helen to sit with Allie. She's a nurse." She shook her head as Flint started to speak. "Just say thank you and be grateful. We're all tired. You spend the daytime with Allie, but at night you're going to get some proper rest."

He wanted to protest and take back control of his life, but he was too tired to argue. "It seems every time I turn around I'm thanking you for something, Stephanie. Thanks again."

"You're welcome. Do you have the discharge instructions from the hospital for Helen to see?"

He nodded and handed the folder to the nurse. "Here's all the information we have about Allie's aftercare. For a few days, we're to take it easy and then gradually let her do what she wants. Just make sure she takes her anti-rejection medicines. She has to return to the hospital once a week for a checkup."

"No problem, Mr. Tucker. I've cared for children following transplant surgery. Allie and I will do fine. My co-workers are also experienced."

She edged toward the bedroom door. "Brigitte and I will leave so you can get Allie settled. If you need anything else just let me know."

Mom pushed him toward the door. "You go with them and let me help Helen get Allie settled. Go for a walk or take a nap. If you're needed, I'll come to get you."

He looked at his daughter. Allie showed the nurse her Teddy bear and dolls as they took them out of the suitcase. He knew she would be all right, but it was hard to let go of his hyper-vigilance. Mom was right, though. He needed to get back to normal for Allie. "All right." He followed Stephanie and Brigitte into the hallway.

"I told Samuel I'd give him a tour of the grounds." Brigitte headed downstairs.

"We'll see you at dinner, or supper, as this family calls it." She smiled at him. "What do you want to do with our few hours of free time?"

"I want to walk along the beach in the snow. I've never done that before. It'll be a new experience. Want to come?" He watched her eyes light up. "Okay, then. I'll meet you downstairs in ten minutes."

He went to his room and changed into heavy socks and boots. Before leaving the room, he grabbed his cell phone and checked that the battery was charged. If needed, Mom could call him. With lighter steps than he had taken in many weeks, he ran downstairs to meet Stephanie.

The next two hours of walking at the water's edge with the cold wind off the ocean helped clear his head. They didn't talk much, but he felt comfortable being with Stephanie and enjoyed the winter day. Thoughts of moving forward and returning to Colorado with Allie on the mend gave him hope for the future such as he hadn't known since Valerie's death. The only cloud was that Stephanie wouldn't be there to complete the picture.

He glanced at the beautiful woman striding so confidently by his side. What would it take for her to believe in God? Even if that barrier between them disappeared, there was the difference in their lifestyles to consider. He could never provide for her as she was accustomed. She did seem comfortable around Allie, and it was apparent that the child adored her. But the day-to-day routine of caring for a sick child, would she be able to handle that? Maybe he didn't have to think of Allie as a sick child anymore once she recovered from the surgery.

She met his gaze as they stopped to look out over the ocean. "You keep looking at me with such a serious expression. Have I upset you or do something to offend you?"

He stepped back. "Of course not. Just the opposite. You've been thoroughly kind and generous. I just have a lot to think through. You know, Allie loves you and she doesn't even understand how much you've done for her. She just adores you because you're you."

Her eyes widened. "You really think so? I love that little girl and want the best for her."

"I was also thinking that I've got to start looking at Allie differently. All her life she has been so ill, but when she gets her strength back, she'll be more like other children. I'm not used to that." He wanted to say much more to her, but he must be fair to her and to himself. Better not start something he couldn't finish. So he turned and led the way toward the house.

At the house, he left her downstairs and went to check on Allie. As he looked into her bedroom, he found Helen, the nurse, sitting in a chair reading a book and Allie asleep on the big bed. He decided not to disturb them.

Mom came out of one of the bedrooms. "Did you have a nice walk, son?"

"I did. There's something magical about walking in the snow beside the ocean. I love to smell the salt air in the chilly breeze." He led the way into his bedroom. "I checked in on Allie. Do you know how long she's been napping?"

"Oh, what a bright sunny room. Stephanie said you stayed in this room before?"

"Yes, one long weekend when we came out here to work in November."

"To answer your question, Allie's been asleep about thirty minutes. I'm going to wake her for supper and try to get her on a more normal schedule. She seems to like the nurse. If Stephanie doesn't mind, I'm going to ask Helen to eat with us. That way Allie will think she's a new friend visiting."

"That's a good idea. I doubt Stephanie will mind."

"I talked to your dad. He wants to go home if you're okay with that. He's worried about the stock even though he knows the neighbors are watching out for us."

"He could fly home, check on things, and come back in a couple of weeks. I'll use the money I saved to pay for Allie's heart surgery to pay for the airline tickets."

Mom fingered the Italian silk draperies. "Stephanie is awfully rich, isn't she? I knew she was well off, but this house is something else. Paying for the surgery, the plane, and now the nurses, she's done a lot."

He nodded. "Yes. She's extremely well off."

"Does that bother you? Would that keep you from showing her how you feel?" Mom peeked at him quickly before looking back at the exquisite drapes.

How much should he share? "Her wealth is a consideration, but it's not the only factor. I'll be honest with you, Mom. I could easily fall in love with her, but she's not a Christian. I'm praying for words to say to her but I never seem to find the right ones. I'm afraid if she does care for me she'll want to become a Christian because I want her to and not because of true conviction." He ran his fingers through his hair. "How can I know for sure? I've talked to Richard and David about it. They both suggested that I hold back and see whether she searches out Christ for herself, without my urging."

Mom laid her hand on his arm. "I've been praying too. She's such a lovely woman."

He covered her hand and squeezed. "Have you noticed how well she gets along with Allie? I almost think Allie prefers her to me."

"I wouldn't say that, but they do get along. We must be patient and keep praying. Have you told her how you feel and why you can't act on your feelings?"

He looked at the floor and shook his head. "No. Like I said, I don't want her to seek Christ as a way for us to be together."

"Son, I'm proud of you for being so wise. It's hard, but you're right. We must let God work in His own way." She kissed his forehead. "I'm going to check on Allie and your dad. Stephanie said we would eat by six. I think that's early for her, but she's accommodating us for Allie's sake."

"I'll carry Allie down to supper. I don't want her climbing the stairs, and I don't want her to know there's an elevator just yet. I don't trust her not to try to use it by herself. You do realize that as she feels better, we may have a little tyrant on our hands."

Mom laughed as she walked out of the room. "I've thought of that. Won't that be fun?"

He could only shake his head at the thought. It was still hard to imagine his child well.

Chapter Thirty-Two

THE THIRD-FLOOR SALON was now an office. Sitting in her favorite chair, she gazed out at the winter sea that was slate gray with little caps of white foam dancing on top drifting with the stiff March wind. Her cup of tea soothed her spirits as she considered the enjoyment of playing hostess to Flint and his family in the Hamptons. A month had already flown by—a busy month with Flint, Allie, and Mary. Tom left for Colorado but was due back in New York in a couple of days.

Samuel had stayed an extra two weeks before returning to Alaska a week ago. She smiled at the mental image of Brigitte's long face and slumped shoulders after his leaving. Every time she turned around, Brigitte was on the phone talking to Samuel.

Allie had become a little whirlwind. Her constant request was, "Want to play?" She was definitely feeling better.

Their major chore had become keeping her from overexerting herself. Previously they had to be vigilant because she was so ill, and now they had to keep an eye on her because she was just as likely to race out the door to the beach, looking for the horsies.

She watched him struggle to find the balance between indulging Allie and setting boundaries. It often made her smile to see his conflicted expression. Thankfully, it was his responsibility and not hers, as seeing those wide eyes made her want to give the child anything she asked for. For the first time, she understood how easy it would be to spoil a child.

The work they accomplished toward getting her money and investments in order paid off. Ben and Tony had set up her corporation and foundation with the help of the young attorney Flint recommended.

With the looming prospect that Allie would be released by her doctors to return to Colorado within the next couple of weeks and management of her businesses being fully transferred to Booker and Williams, she faced the reality that her houseguests would soon be leaving. Her day-to-day working relationship with Flint would end when he took Allie home to Colorado.

At times she felt that he wanted to say something, even to reach out and touch her, but he didn't. With all her heart, she wanted to know what was on his mind. She had grown to love the tall westerner. He respected and liked her, she could tell. But did he love her? She wasn't sure and didn't know how to find out unless she asked. Something always held her back. Perhaps fear of the answer.

"Have you seen Allie?" Breathless, he ran in and glanced around the third-floor salon.

She smiled. No telling where the child had gotten to now. "Where did you see her last?"

He ran his fingers through his hair. "One second she was coloring at the kitchen table, and Mom turned her back. Poof, she was gone."

The teaspoon clinked against the teacup as she set the half-empty cup on the side table and rose to her feet. "Well, let's go look for her."

"You don't think she could have gotten into the indoor pool?" Worry oozed from his question.

She shook her head as she followed down the stairs. "No way. That door is locked, but we'll check it anyway."

"I shouldn't have taken her swimming. Now all she wants to do is swim, visit the horses, and go to the beach."

"Isn't that a good thing? I would think you'd be pleased that she's feeling well enough to do all those things."

He gave the laundry room a once over before moving toward the door to the swimming pool. "Of course I'm glad she feels so much better. But I haven't adjusted to keeping up with her new burst of energy. Before, I wasn't as concerned because she didn't have the strength to get into mischief."

"Well, she's not in this part of the house and as you can see the door to the pool is locked. Where else should we look?" She couldn't guess where a little girl would explore.

"I'll search the ground floor and then start looking outside." He took the stairs from the basement floor to the first floor three at a time.

Almost running to keep up, she tried to think of something Allie had said that might give a clue as to her whereabouts.

As they walked through the foyer and entered the long living room across the back of the house, she spotted a little black shoe peeking out from behind a chair next to the floor-to-ceiling windows. She grabbed his arm and guided him to the chair.

Allie sat on the floor gazing out at the sea.

"Sweetheart, what are you doing?" His voice was suddenly soft and kind.

She looked up at them with wide, round eyes. "It's so big, Daddy. How did God make it so big?"

"What's so big?" He squatted down and gazed into his daughter's eyes.

"The whole world." She pointed toward the ocean. "I can't see the other side."

He sat cross-legged next to his daughter and patted the floor. "Have a seat, while we figure this out."

She sat on the floor, feet flat and knees bent. Just able to see over the dunes, she looked at the ocean from Allie's level, stretching out in all directions with no end.

"What do you think about the big world?" He asked his daughter.

Allie turned a serious glance toward him. "God works hard to make so much. But he did a good job. I like the world."

Curious that a child would believe God made everything. "How do you know God made the earth?"

Allie twirled a hair curl near her ear. "'Cause someone had to make it and only God is big enough."

He hugged her. "That's right, sweetheart, someone had to make it."

"Tell me about God, Allie. Where does he live?" Stephanie asked.

Allie looked at her. "Don't you know where God lives?"

"I'm not sure. Tell me. Where does God live?"

Allie cut her gaze to her father and then back to her. "God lives everywhere, but when he's not busy, he lives way up in heaven." She pointed out the window at the gray sky. "My mommy lives with him. With all the other people who died. They have parties and stay up late. You can tell because the stars are really lights from God's house in heaven. God has a lot of work in heaven making babies and thunderstorms. So he sent his Son, Jesus, to come and visit us. But Jesus has gone back home now."

He raised his eyebrows and glanced from Allie to Stephanie. She winked at him. "How do you know all this, Allie?"

Allie pointed at her daddy. "Because Daddy told me and Granddad and Grandma and Aunt Holly. Everyone knows." She frowned and then her frown cleared. "Daddy, why don't you tell Stephanie the stories about Baby Jesus and the animals and the ark, okay?"

He nodded. "Yes, I can tell her all the stories."

Mary came into the room, stopped, and put her hands on her hips. "What is going on in here? I've been looking all over for you, Miss Allie."

Allie ran to her grandma. "I've been telling Stephanie about God and Jesus. She didn't know."

"I'm still not sure about a lot of things, but who can argue with a little girl about God?" She was surprised by the serious look on his face. But there must be a God if a child could see it. Maybe she would ask him to tell her the story of baby Jesus.

Allie grabbed her hand. "Come play with me, please."

She laughed at how good it felt to have the attention of a child. "What do you want to play?"

Allie didn't hesitate. "Candy Land! You play, too, Daddy."

He picked her up and held her high on his chest. "All right. If Stephanie is willing, let's play Candy Land. You want to play, Mom?"

"No, thank you. I've played my share of Candy Land. It's your turn. I better go help Maria get supper ready." Mary headed back toward the kitchen.

"Is this a hard game?" She asked as they climbed the stairs to Allie's bedroom.

He chuckled. "I think you can manage it."

ON THEIR LAST DAY IN the Hamptons, she sat on the pew next to him in the small church near her home. Allie sat between them. Although the doctors had released Allie to mingle in large crowds and to travel home to Colorado. Allie wore a little mask over her nose and mouth for extra protection against other peoples' germs.

Richard Anderson was the guest speaker. He and Nancy were coming back to the house for lunch. She tried to listen to his lesson, but all she could think about was that Flint and Allie were leaving the Hamptons for her apartment in the city that evening. And then tomorrow they would fly to Colorado, without her. Tom had come for a visit and taken Mary to Colorado to get things ready for Allie's return.

"When we love someone with the agape love of Christ, we can let them go. From a distance, we can shower them with our love through our prayers." Richard's words got her attention. What was agape love? Was that what she felt for Flint? It must not be because she didn't want to let him go. Ever.

She glanced over Allie's head at him and caught him looking at her. He smiled and then turned to give Richard his attention. She was sure she saw love in that look but still not a word from the man on that subject. Maybe she would get a chance to ask Richard what agape love meant.

Allie climbed into her lap and leaned against her. Not knowing what else to do, she wrapped her arms around the little girl. In just a few minutes, Allie was asleep. When the service concluded, he reached down and gathered Allie to carry her to the car. Allie laid her head on her daddy's shoulder and went back to sleep.

"She's tired out from her first outing, but I'll wake her for lunch." He settled his daughter into her car seat and then held the door for Stephanie. "Richard and Nancy will follow us with Harold and Edna."

She had recently met the preacher of the local congregation and his wife so she had included them in the invitation for Sunday lunch.

When he started the fifteen-minute drive to the house, she looked back at Allie. Her tiny body was slumped against the arm of the car seat as she slept. "Is she all right?"

He kept his eyes on the road. "I think so. She'll probably be a little livewire as soon as we hit the house."

"I must tell you that I enjoy attending services on Sunday mornings. I've attended church more since I met you than ever before in my entire life."

He nodded but didn't look at her. "I'm glad you enjoy it. I like going with you. Harold is a good preacher."

"Yes, but I have to say I like Richard better. He's more lively and tells stories that help me understand what he's talking about."

He cleared his throat. "I'll grant you that Richard is a more dynamic speaker, but Harold goes deeper into the text, which appeals to me."

She shook her head. "You have to remember that I don't know the text, as you call it. When he goes deeper, I'm lost and don't have a clue what he's talking about."

"Do you want to know?" His voice sounded casual.

She snapped her gloves on tighter as she considered how to respond. "Yes, I think I do."

"What would you say to discussing the Bible through email and phone calls after I go home tomorrow?" He glanced at her and then quickly back at the road.

"I'd like that. Maybe I can send questions, and you can answer them."

"I can do that. It'll be fun." He smiled at her after he pulled to a stop under the portico.

"Daddy, I'm hungry." A little voice squeaked from the back seat. She laughed with him. "She seems to be awake."

The afternoon passed quickly as they sat around the dining table enjoying the meal Maria had prepared. She listened to the three men talk about biblical topics. She couldn't follow all they talked about, but she understood enough to be amazed at their knowledge.

Nancy and Edna discussed their children and grandchildren at the other end of the table. Allie quickly tired of the grownup talk, brought her dolls downstairs and played on the floor.

"This has been great, but if we're going to get home before dark we better start," Richard said.

She looked at her watch. They had talked for three hours.

Everyone headed toward the foyer and the coat closet in preparation for leaving.

"Richard, we'll see you in a few months when we bring Allie back for her checkup." He shook his hand. "I'm going to hold you and Nancy to your promise to come to visit us in Colorado."

Nancy gave him a hug and kissed Allie. "We're planning on it. I've already bought a book on Colorado to plan what I want to see."

Harold shook Stephanie's hand. "You don't have to wait for Flint to come to visit again before coming to church services. You're personally invited to come anytime you want."

She promised she would. "But I'm going back to my apartment in New York with Flint and Allie tonight. I won't be back out to the Hamptons for a few weeks."

After their guests departed, Flint and she finished packing and got all of Allie's different medicines and toys boxed for the trip. By the time George arrived with the limo, they were ready.

"I appreciate you putting us up for the night at the apartment. And of course, for the corporate jet to take us home tomorrow." He held the book Allie was looking at on the ride into the city.

"It's my pleasure. It'll be easier for Allie than having to take the helicopter to the airport. George will be at the apartment by nine to drive you to the airport if that's not too early."

He grinned. "That's one of the great things about going by private jet. You get to pick what time to fly. I'm afraid you've spoiled me for economy flying."

"Daddy read to me, please." Allie patted his arm to get his attention.

"I'll read to you when you're going to bed. For now, I'm talking to Stephanie. You just look at the book." He turned the picture book back to the first page.

"You're such a good father. I'm amazed at how you handle all kinds of situations. How do you know so much about parenting?"

He scratched his temple. "I'm not sure. I guess from watching my family. Even Stephen, who is so quiet most of the time, is just great with his kids." He tilted his head and gazed at her. "You're not bad with Allie yourself. Where did you learn how?"

At his praise, she felt a warm glow spread across her chest. "Thanks for saying that. I just follow your lead." She patted Allie's head. "She's such an easy child. I'm going to miss her."

"We're going to miss you too. Aren't we, Allie?"

"Why? Where is Steph going?" Allie looked up with a frown.

He rubbed his face. "Remember I told you that we are going back to Colorado, but Stephanie is staying here."

"Why?"

He didn't seem to know what to say so Stephanie jumped in. "I have to stay here and work. Also, Brigitte will be coming back from Boston, and I need to be here with her."

"You do your work and then come to my house to stay." Allie nodded, and the curls around her face bounced as she figured out the solution.

"I'll see you when you come to visit the doctors in a couple of months." She didn't know what else to say to this child. With all her heart, she wanted to come live with her and her daddy. Why wouldn't he say something?

ON THE RIDE TO THE airport the next morning, she felt sick at her stomach. She hadn't slept well, and tears fought to escape. When she looked at Allie smiling and healthy, she was glad to send her home to live a full life, but that joy warred against a deep well of sadness at Flint and Allie leaving. She glanced at him in the other corner of the car with Allie between them in her car seat. She was surprised to catch him staring out the window with sadness on his face. Was he regretting this separation, too? What other reason would make him look so sad?

At the airport, he carried Allie up the ten steps into the Gulfstream jet with her following. Judith was again on duty and set about buckling Allie in the seat.

She knelt in front of this child she had come to love more than her own life. "Goodbye, Allie."

Allie wrapped her arms around her neck and hugged as tight as her three-and-a-half-year-old arms could. "Bye, Stephanie. You will come soon?" Big tears started to form and then slid down her cheeks.

"Yes, honey. I'll come to see you. Take care of your daddy for me. I love you, sweetheart."

She turned and left the aircraft in a hurry so Allie wouldn't see her tears.

He followed. "You all right, Stephanie?"

She let him wrap his arms around her. She buried her face in his chest and hugged him. "You take care of that child."

"You know I will. I'll call you when we get home." He swallowed. "God bless you and thanks for everything." He kissed her cheek and then her forehead. She longed to feel his kiss on her lips.

Before she was ready, he released her, turned, and disappeared up the stairs to the airplane. Catching a sob while trying to maintain control, she climbed into the empty back seat of the limo. "George, please drive slowly so we can watch them take off."

"Yes, ma'am." George pulled the limo forward where she could sit and watch the small jet taxi down the runway and blast off in a burst of sound.

Her stomach hurt, and her breath came with difficulty. As the plane became a small dark dot in the sky, she couldn't hold back the tears any longer. She put her face in her hands and sobbed.

Chapter Thirty-Three

HE WAS TOO BUSY MAKING sure Allie chewed her gum as the jet took off to do what he really wanted which was to watch out the plane window as the limo became smaller and smaller until finally, it disappeared. His chest ached as he remembered the feel of Stephanie's arms around his neck when he said goodbye to her.

"Daddy sad?" Allie patted his face.

"Yes, little bunny, I'm sad to leave Stephanie." Why he told her the truth, he didn't know, but it seemed to help.

"Allie sad, too." She glanced up at him with dark eyes so like her mother's. Tiny tears flowed down her cheeks. How he wished he could cry with her.

"We'll see Stephanie again. Remember, she said she would come for a visit." He wanted her to do more than visit. He wanted her to live with them. "We'll pray that one day Stephanie can come, okay? Until then let's think about seeing the mountains and horses. Don't forget Grandpa and Grandma will meet us at the airport." He needed to distract her, just as much as he needed to divert his own thoughts.

HOME AT LAST, HE STOOD on the front porch and looked toward the high peaks. After a night of sleep in his own bed for the first time in six weeks, he wanted to be outdoors. Snow still covered the ground although in another few weeks they could expect warmer weather. What was Stephanie doing this morning? He trudged back inside and opened his computer. Maybe he should just call her. Was he calling because of work, or because he missed her so much? Did it matter?

HIS FIRST DAY BACK in the offices of Booker and Williams felt strange. He sat at the conference table across from Ben and Tony with Farley next to him. Was it only seven months ago he had started the journey with The Wellbourne Group and Stephanie? In some ways, it seemed like years. In others, it was only yesterday.

"Flint, you still with us?" Ben's voice penetrated his thoughts.

"Sure. What were you saying?" He rubbed his face and straightened in his chair to help focus.

Ben leaned forward. "I was saying that we have Stephanie Wellbourne's new corporation organized and her investments in pretty good shape. But we still don't have instructions about her foundation. There's too much money sitting around. Can you talk to her or would you rather one of us did?"

"I'll talk to her. There's been so much going on it's been hard to get to everything. To tell you the truth, I don't think she really knows what her plans are for the Firebird Foundation." He knew he had to talk about it soon, but when he called her, they always seemed to end up talking about other things.

"Well, see what you can do. I'll say she is more than generous to pay for our services. We'll keep new business coming in, but for now, she's our biggest client. It was a real blessing the day you met her." Ben spread his hands out flat on the table.

Tony nodded. "Ben's right. We want to keep her happy. That's your job, Flint, as she seems to like you." He exchanged a knowing look with Ben.

"All right, fellows. I'll continue as the go-between. I appreciate the job you have done over the last seven months. It hasn't been easy to disentangle from a company as large as hers and get another corporation set up."

Farley asked, "When do you think she'll come out for a visit?"

"She spoke of coming, but no date was set."

On his drive back to the ranch, he admitted that was probably his fault. He hadn't asked her to set a date. How could he without revealing how deeply he cared? The temptation to declare his love to her in spite of her not being a Christian was strong. Every time he talked to her on the phone, he wanted to beg her to come. Surely God would understand his need for her. Then he looked at Allie. He must give her a Christian mother. There was no other choice.

Allie was the same but not the same. She had the same perky personality and intense curiosity about everything as she had before the surgery. The difference was that now she had the energy to carry out her interest. Each night he went to bed exhausted from trying to keep up with her.

SHE WAITED FOR BRIGITTE to come downstairs. She had spent the night, and they were going to Flint's church together. While she slipped into her coat, she thought of Flint and Allie. With the time difference in Colorado, they would be leaving for church about the time she and Brigitte got back.

"You ready?" Brigitte wore a navy blue suit with a white silk blouse. Her blonde hair was up in a French twist, which suited her.

She smoothed her deep purple dress coat and grabbed her purse. "George is waiting at the curb."

As George expertly maneuvered the car through the New York streets, she asked Brigitte, "Why are you attending church so much now? You didn't used to go this often."

Brigitte smoothed her hair back. "Over the last couple of months since I met Samuel we've talked a lot about God. He helped me understand God wants me to do more than believe. He wants me to participate in the family of God."

"Are you doing it to please Samuel?"

"I've asked myself that and I don't think so. I'm doing it for me. Samuel got me thinking about where I wanted to be spiritually, but I would still be going even if I weren't involved with him."

She raised her eyebrows. *Involved*? That was the first time Brigitte admitted that it was more than a friendship. "Just how involved are you with Samuel?"

Brigitte smiled. "I wondered how long it would be before you asked. We're taking our time and getting to know each other. He invited me to visit him in Alaska when the weather gets warmer. I'm planning to go."

She laid her hand on Brigitte's. "I'm so glad. You deserve someone like Samuel. He seems like a fine man. Isn't he a little older than you?"

"Yes, he's ten years older. It doesn't seem to matter to either of us. Neither one of us has been married. He told me he has been waiting for the best." She grinned. "He says he's found it."

"I wish..." She didn't finish her sentence.

"I know, Steph, I wish it too. Don't give up hope."

She enjoyed the service. She was becoming acquainted with some of the people. Having Brigitte there helped her feel comfortable, but she also missed attending the services with Flint and hearing his deep voice as he sang the hymns.

Richard and Nancy stood at the back greeting everyone after the service. "Stephanie and Brigitte, welcome ladies."

"It was an interesting sermon, but it raised a lot of questions for me. Would it be possible to make an appointment with you to discuss the Bible?" She hoped she wasn't being too forward.

Richard's expression broke into a broad smile. "I'd be glad to set a time to talk. When would be good for you?"

Nancy spoke up. "Why don't you two girls come to dinner tomorrow evening and then you can talk with Richard?"

Richard nodded. "That's a wonderful idea. How about six?"

She hadn't planned to make an appointment so soon but saw no reason not to accept the invitation. "Brigitte, will that work for you?"

"Sure. What can we bring?"

Nancy shook her head. "You just come and let me prepare dinner."

Richard smiled. "Bring your Bibles."

MONDAY EVENING, SHE took the Bible Flint had given her for Christmas. She had been reading different sections, but usually had more questions than answers. She also brought a bouquet of fresh flowers for Nancy.

After the meal, they gathered around the table in the small dining room and spread out their Bibles. She hadn't brought anything to take notes with, but Brigitte carried her ever-present laptop.

Richard led a prayer asking God to open their hearts and minds to His will and words. "Since I don't know what you already know, I suggest we start at the beginning and study the story of the Bible."

She opened her Bible to the first page. "That's a good idea. I only know snippets of the Bible story. Brigitte knows much more than I do."

Brigitte raised her eyebrows. "I may know more of the stories, but I'm not sure I know a lot more about God. I think the beginning is a great place to start. You do mean the beginning of Genesis, don't you?"

Richard laughed. "That's the first beginning I know."

For the next three hours, they read the Scriptures, and Richard gave explanations and then told them the Bible stories in his own words. They had progressed through several chapters into Genesis when Richard yawned and leaned back in his chair. "We need to halt our study for this evening. When do you want to meet again?"

She hesitated. "Well, I'd like to continue tomorrow. Would that be possible?"

"You say when and I'll be ready," Richard said.

She didn't have words to explain what the Bible study meant to her. She couldn't get enough. Richard gave her books to read and DVDs to watch. They met for two to three hours every day except for Saturdays when Richard had to prepare his sermons for Sunday.

Except for her calls with Flint, she spent most of her time studying. She began to understand some of the things he had said to her and what she had seen of his faith.

She was in the middle of reading the book of John when her cell phone rang. It was him.

"Hello."

"Hey, Steph, how are you doing?" His deep, mellow voice rolled out of the phone like a soothing balm.

"Hey, yourself. How's Allie?" She was in the habit of asking about the child first because that always seemed most important.

He chuckled. "She's fine. She tried to climb the tree out front. Scared me. But then I guess I scared my folks when I climbed it at that age."

"What was she doing outside? Isn't it cold there?"

"We've had a Chinook come through, and it's warm today, in the low sixties."

"A what come through?"

"A Chinook is a warm wind that blows over the Rockies and warms things up. It'll get cold again and even snow, but we may be through with the worst blast of winter."

They talked awhile about her business. He was getting the Firebird Foundation organized. She needed to give him directions about what she wanted to do with her money. She just didn't know. Giving it away was too general. She must make decisions soon, but all she wanted to do was study her Bible.

"Richard told me that you are studying with him," He mentioned.

"He did, did he? What did he say exactly?"

"Only that you were coming over to study."

She decided to leave it at that. "Brigitte and I go to their place sometimes. Nancy has prepared some meals for us also. She's a great cook."

He wasn't deterred. "What are you studying?"

"I'm reading the book of John."

"That's great. I love the book of John."

"What do you love about it?"

"I love what it reveals about the teaching and thoughts of Jesus. I feel as if I know Jesus better each time I read it."

"The thoughts of Jesus, I'll have to look for that." What kept her from telling him how much she had been studying and learning? She was sure he would be happy.

"I'll call tomorrow. I need to go see what Allie's doing. Mom is out with Dad measuring the garden. Dad says it's too early to plow and plant, but Mom is anxious to get her garden going."

"Give Allie a big hug from me." She smiled at the image of the little girl hugging her daddy. If only she could have had as close a relationship with her own father. He had never been her daddy, only her Father.

"I will. You're in my prayers."

"Thanks, I'm praying for you." It was the first time she'd told him she prayed.

"Bye, Steph."

She put down the phone thankful she had at least that much contact with him. Did he miss her? Did he spend hours thinking about her? She thought way too much about the tall westerner. Every night she went to bed thinking of him and woke every morning with him on her mind. But she wouldn't tell him of her feelings until he spoke first.

Chapter Thirty-Four

HE LOOKED AT ALLIE'S animated face. She resembled Valerie more every day. "Daddy, let me explain you. I'm a big girl. My birthday I four. So now I can ride the horsey. I not a baby."

He tried to keep a straight face as Allie sat in his lap facing him. "I said no horseback riding yet."

"But Daddy, you ride Charger and not get hurt." Allie placed her hands on his cheeks. "Please, Daddy."

He grabbed her hands and pressed them tighter against his face. "You can ask all you want, and the answer is still no. It's too windy, too cool, and too soon according to the doctors. You'll get to ride later this summer. But not now." He wanted to say yes, but the doctors had said she shouldn't ride yet. Allie knew how to whittle away at his resolve.

She twisted her face into what he had come to recognize as a pretense of crying when she didn't get her way. He cupped her chin in his hand and lifted her grumpy face. "Allie, you need to respect your daddy. No means no. If you keep asking, I'll have to give you a consequence. I know you want to go riding with me, and I want you to come, but only when the doctors say it's okay. I love you too much to risk hurting you." She didn't understand how serious a fall could be so soon after a heart transplant. He had to protect her from that.

Staring at him, she seemed to consider his words. How much did an almost four-year-old comprehend? "Okay, Daddy. You promise when the doctors say okay, you let me?"

"I promise." He hugged her and set her feet on the floor. "Now go play because Daddy has to get to work." This meant he walked from the living room down the hall to his office.

He sat at his desk staring out the window. As usual, his first thoughts were of the dark-haired woman in New York. He tried to control his thinking about her, yet her face was before him constantly.

"You all right, son?" Mom stood in the office doorway. She wandered in and sat in the wingback chair next to his desk. "You look so unhappy. What's the matter?"

Should he tell her the truth? "I guess I miss Stephanie." He picked up a pencil and tapped the top of the desk. "I know it's foolish, but she's on my mind a lot."

"Well, I miss her too. She's so easy to love and has done so much for us."

He looked out the window toward the mountains. He hadn't said anything about his feelings to Mom, but he did love her, otherwise why couldn't he get her out of his mind?

"Do you talk to her much? I know you call back and forth about business, but do you talk about other things?"

He let a small grin loose. "Yes, Mom, we talk about other things. Maybe that's part of the problem. I talk to her too much. I should forget her and start looking for a Christian wife and mother for Allie."

"That's the first time you've mentioned the need for a wife since Valerie died. You know it'll four years next week. Perhaps you just need to be patient a little while longer and see what the Lord does."

"That's the only sad part about Allie's birthday. It's also the anniversary of her mother's death." He remembered how Val had looked as she laughed with joy at discovering she was expecting a child. When Allie laughed, he saw the same joy.

"Flint?"

"Sorry, Mom. Just a lot of memories today. What did you say?"

"I was asking if you're okay with having a party for Allie. I could tell people not to come, and they'd understand, but everyone wants to celebrate her birthday this year. Even Abe called a while ago. The family can't come, but he's decided to fly in."

"That's great! Sure, let's have a party. We definitely have something to celebrate."

Mom gazed at him with a frown until he asked, "What?"

She patted his arm. "Nothing. I was just thinking about the party."

After Mom left his office, he continued to stare out the window at the snow-capped mountains. If only...

SHE LISTENED TO BRIGITTE talk to her mother on the phone. "Yes, Mom, I know Dad's unhappy in the assisted living, but you can't bring him home."

Brigitte glanced at Stephanie and rolled her eyes. "I know it's hard. I'll come up for a couple of days this week. Love you. Bye." She closed the cell phone and sat staring at it.

She couldn't imagine what it was like for Brigitte's mother, seeing her husband of forty years deteriorating from Alzheimer's. "Is your mom all right?"

Brigitte gave a deep sigh. "Not really. She's so worried about Dad. Hope you don't mind, but I need to go to Boston for a couple of days. I'll go tomorrow and be back by Thursday. Samuel is flying in on Friday or Saturday."

"It'll be good to see him. You do what you need to do to care for your mom and dad."

"I hate to miss the Bible studies, but maybe Richard will give me some lessons to work on while I'm gone."

"I would offer to postpone the lessons, but I don't want to miss them either. Maybe I can take notes and share them with you." She learned so much each time they sat down and spent a couple of hours with Richard. They had started a study of Acts that morning. So much was being explained.

Somewhere along the journey through the Old Testament and the four gospels, as Richard called them, She realized she not only believed in the God of the Bible but also believed that Jesus was the son of God. Did she believe that Jesus himself was God? She wasn't sure. But she loved his message of love and hope.

The cell phone rang. She saw his number on the caller ID. "Hello."

"Hey, Steph. How are you?" As always, his bass voice surrounded her with warmth.

"I'm doing well. How are things in Colorado?" She was much more interested in what was going on there than at her place in New York.

"We took Allie to the Children's Heart Institute in Denver. This was her official three-month checkup. Of course, we've seen the doctors in Cedar Ridge every week, but this was a big one."

"Don't keep me in suspense. What did they say? Is she doing all right? Are there any signs of rejection?"

"Whoa there, partner. Give me a chance to tell you." She could hear the smile in his voice. "They said everything was fine. There are no signs of rejection. They adjusted the meds and said to keep her contained for another three months. They sure don't understand how hard that is. She's all over the place. Dad found her in the barn the other day."

"By contained, you mean to keep her from exerting herself too much?"

"Yeah, we shouldn't let her do anything that would cause pressure around the incision or the heart area. Like falling out of a tree. I caught her trying to climb the one out front again. I had to put her in an extended time out."

She smiled imagining Allie's face. "I bet that was harder on you than her. How are you doing?"

"Fine, just trying to keep up with everything. It's almost a relief to stop and talk on the phone."

"Flint, may I ask you something personal?"

"Sure. Ask anything you want."

"Tell me about when you became a Christian. How old were you? How did you know what to do?" She hoped he wouldn't think she was too forward, but she really wanted to know if what he had done matched what she was reading in the Bible.

"I'll be happy to share that with you. Let's see, how old was I? Holly was baptized at camp that summer. I thought about it too, but I didn't want it to be because of Holly. I must have been fourteen because it was just after our birthday in September. I had heard the story of Jesus and how he died on the cross for our sins." He was silent for a moment. "I'll just be truthful with you. I'd gone through puberty, and a lot of things were different. My thinking was different, and I realized that things I was doing and thinking just weren't right."

She couldn't imagine him doing things that were bad or evil. "What did that mean for you?"

His voice was deep and serious. "I realized I was a sinner and separated from God. I couldn't stand that, being outside of the grace and favor of God. Even then, I loved God. I knew what I had to do: repent of my sins, believe that Jesus was the Christ, and be immersed in water to re-enact the death, burial, and resurrection. When I came out of that creek water forgiven of my sins, I knew I was a child of God, a Christian. Dad had talked

to me about it several times because he was determined I understood what I was doing. He asked me to read the New Testament through in a week, which was an effort at fourteen. But it helped me clarify and understand what God wanted of me. It helped me make a choice for my life to follow Jesus."

She took a deep breath. She had never heard him talk so openly about his faith before. This was from his heart and revealed much about his relationship with his God. "But how do you stay sinless? How can you be perfect? I read that verse last night where it said to be perfect as God is perfect. How do you do that?"

He chuckled. "That's a great question and one I asked Dad not long after my baptism. I had lied to Abe. I don't even remember now what it was about, except that as soon as I lied, I thought I had blown my chance at heaven. Fortunately, I felt free to tell Dad about it. He put his arm around my shoulder, and we walked down to the creek. There he explained to me about the blood of Jesus covering my sins as long as I tried to do right and was truly repentant. Dad admitted to me that he sinned, not as much as when he was a young man, but still it happened. But that he depended on the blood of Christ to offer a protective covering, and God would still see him as sinless. I didn't understand it all, but it gave me hope."

"It gives me hope, too. I know I couldn't be perfect, but you're saying that God provided a way for me even if I'm not perfect." She hoped she understood but wasn't sure.

"Yes, you keep reading the Bible and studying with Richard. You'll understand it one of these days."

"Thanks for sharing how you became a Christian. You've given me things to think about."

"Don't ever hesitate to ask questions about spiritual matters. I'll always be willing to try to answer your questions. If I can't answer them, I'll go study until I can."

"I'm going to hold you to that."

SHE SPENT THE NEXT two days reading the New Testament through from beginning to end. Then she went to Richard with her list of questions. So much was becoming clearer while at the same time she began to question just how good a person she was. She had always considered herself a good person, but in the Scriptures she read about being a righteous person.

Brigitte returned on Thursday evening and arrived at the apartment at nine on Friday morning.

"How are your parents?" She could tell it had been a hard visit from the tired look around Brigitte's eyes.

Brigitte brushed her loose hair back from her face. "We're losing Dad bit by bit. The doctors warned us that this would happen, but he's fading so fast. Mom has lost weight and is so tired. I tried to get her to go to the doctor while I was there but she refused. She promised to go next week."

"I'm sorry, Brig. I can't imagine how much that must hurt to see your parents suffering but not be able to stop it."

"Thanks, it helps to have someone to talk to about it. I feel so helpless to stop their decline and aging." Brigitte began to cry. "I feel like I've already lost Dad. He barely recognizes me now."

She had known it was bad, but not this bad. She moved to the couch and put her arm around Brigitte. "I'm so sorry." She didn't know what else to say.

After a while, Brigitte grabbed a tissue and blew her nose. "I'll be all right. It's just that it hit me all of a sudden this week that I may lose them both soon. I'm so glad Samuel is coming. He's such a comfort to me."

She smiled. "I'm glad the two of you are getting along so well."

"I want to share something with you. You're my best friend, and I want you to know."

"What is it, Brigitte?"

"From our studying and the time I've had to think the last few days, I've decided to become a Christian."

Her eyebrows shot up. "I thought you already were a Christian."

"I've always believed in God and accepted Jesus as the Son of God. But I've never been obedient the way God wants me to be to become a Christian. I've never truly admitted my sins and repented." Brigitte rubbed her temple and closed her eyes. "I've never died to my sins through being immersed into the name of Jesus to have my sins forgiven and to receive the Holy Spirit." She opened her eyes and reached for the Bible that was on the table. "The Scriptures show me that this is what God is calling me to do to be His child."

She recognized what Brigitte was describing from her own reading of the Scripture, especially the book of Acts. "So what do you do now?"

Brigitte looked out the window for a moment and then back to her. "I'm going to talk to Richard and Samuel. Then I'm going to pray about it. I trust that God will guide me toward the decisions I need to make to be right before Him."

"I'm not sure I'm as far along in my thinking as you are, but what you're saying makes sense to me. May I go with you when you talk to Richard and Samuel? I have questions that may be the same as yours."

"Sure, Steph, I'd like that. We've traveled many roads together. We might as well travel this one together."

Chapter Thirty-Five

SHE HADN'T BEEN ABLE to sleep well for the last three nights, but she found herself listening closely to Richard on Sunday morning in spite of her fatigue. So many questions. She had talked several times with Flint, asked him how he thought and felt around the time of his baptism and becoming a Christian.

She and Brigitte had spent time on Saturday quizzing Richard and Samuel about spiritual matters. She was impressed with how knowledgeable both men were about the Scriptures.

Sunday in church services, Brigitte and Samuel sat on the pew to her right and Nancy sat on her left. Richard's sermon gave examples of conversions from the book of Acts. Every time he told of one of the people from so long ago being baptized and being saved from their sins, she knew that those verses were talking about her. She was a sinner. Hadn't she lied, been envious, knew to do good and turned aside, and been disobedient to God? Yes, she was a sinner. Even her years of unbelief had been sinful. Did she fully believe now? Could she accept that Jesus was the Christ, God himself? How she regretted the many years wasted in unbelief. She hadn't known what God wanted from her. But now she did. She wanted to be clean, to be forgiven, to be loved and comforted by God. At last, she understood the way to get there.

When the congregation stood to sing at the end of the sermon, she turned to Brigitte and whispered, "I'm going to ask Richard to baptize me. I don't want to wait another hour to be right before God."

Brigitte took her hand. "May I go with you?"

"Are you sure?"

"Yes."

Holding hands, they walked together down the aisle to where Richard waited.

He greeted them with a hug. "Let's sit here on the front pew and talk while the congregation continues to sing." He waved them to the empty front pew. Samuel and Nancy joined them. After everyone was seated, he turned to her and Brigitte. "Ladies, why have you come down to the front today?"

She looked at him with puzzlement. "Don't you know why?"

He smiled. "I can guess, but I need to hear you say it. I don't want to put words into your mouths."

She glanced at Brigitte. Her palms were sweaty, and she couldn't seem to get a deep breath. "I came to a realization that I need to get right with God. I want to be baptized for the forgiveness of my sins and receive God's Holy Spirit as it's written in Acts 2:38. I want to be washed clean by the blood of Jesus through being baptized. I want to be a Christian."

Richard wiped tears from his eyes. "And you, Brigitte?"

Brigitte squeezed Stephanie's hand. "I also have become aware of my sins before God and want to be washed clean. I don't want to wait another minute."

Richard placed a hand on each of their shoulders. "God bless you both for your faith and tender hearts. I'm going to ask you to stand before these witnesses and tell them why you've come forward. Then you'll go with Nancy and prepare for the baptism." He looked from Brigitte to Samuel. "Do you want me to baptize you or would you like for Samuel to do it?"

Brigitte turned to Samuel. "Doesn't it have to be a preacher who does it?"

Richard shook his head. "He can or I can. The person doing the baptism doesn't matter. It's the condition of your heart before God that matters."

Brigitte smiled. "Then I want you to baptize me, Samuel."

Samuel's eyes filled with tears and he hugged Brigitte.

"I'd be honored."

She looked at Richard's kind face. "I want you to baptize me."

"Then let's stand, and you tell the congregation why you came forward."

They stood, and Richard had one arm around Stephanie's shoulder and the other around Brigitte.

They each, in turn, told briefly why they had come forward. When they finished, the congregation said, "Amen."

She had a sense of peace that the battle to make a decision was finally won. They followed Nancy to a small room behind the front platform where they were shown garments to change into for the baptism.

She stepped into the warm water with Richard. It came to her waist. Richard explained that all she had to do was hold her nose shut with her fingers and lean back on his arm and he would lower her into the water and then lift her back up.

Richard placed an arm behind her back and then raised his right hand. "Stephanie, I now baptize you into the name of the Father, the Son, and the Holy Spirit for the forgiveness of your sins so you may receive the gift of the Holy Spirit and live eternally with God."

He lowered her into the water until she was completely covered, and then raised her out of the water. She pictured her old sinful self being buried with Christ. When she came up out of the water, a sense of cleanness and freedom overwhelmed her. Such a sensation of joy burst forth that she began to cry from the sheer emotion.

Richard hugged her and kissed her on the forehead. "Welcome to the family of God, my sister."

She could only say, "Thank you."

She climbed out of the water to Nancy who stood waiting with a large towel.

Brigitte stood beside Nancy and gave her a hug before descending the steps toward Samuel who waited in the water.

She watched as Samuel repeated the same words, lowered Brigitte into the water, and then lifted her out. Reminded of what the Scriptures had said about the baptism of Jesus, she realized that she and Brigitte had both gone down into and up out of the water just as Jesus had done so many years before.

She wasn't sure Samuel would let Brigitte go from the hug he gave her as she came up from the water. He cried and smiled at the same time. Something deep within her was moved to see this strong man so affected by what Brigitte had done. Even with her abounding joy, wistfulness for Flint's presence kept the event from utter perfection.

THE NEXT WEEK WAS FULL of wonderment to her. She felt like a new person as if she had lost a weight she had carried for years without realizing it. She and Brigitte sat at the dining room table going over some papers that Flint had sent. The documents only required her signature, but he insisted that she understand what she signed.

"Brig, how do you feel now that you know you're a Christian?"

Brigitte put down the document she had been reading. "It's strange. It's as if everything is the same, but not the same. I live in the same apartment, wear the same clothes, eat the same food, but I know that I'm different in a fundamental way—as if my eyes have been opened to see things in a whole new way. Does that make sense?"

She nodded. "It makes complete sense. I couldn't have described it any better. I asked Samuel if he thought I should call Flint and tell him, but he suggested I do it in person when we go to Allie's party. I'm so thankful Mary called to invite us."

"I am, too. Did I tell you that I'm going on to Alaska with Samuel when we leave the ranch? He's invited me to come and see where he lives and works." Brigitte reached out and placed her hand over Stephanie's. "I might as well tell you. Samuel and I talked about getting married. But before he asks me, he wants me to see his home and where he works. He wants me to be sure I can cope with it. Except for how far it is from my parents, if I'm with Samuel, I really don't care where I live."

"Oh, Brigitte. I'm so glad. Samuel couldn't find a better wife."

"He has always told me he was waiting for the best. He's sure the best I've ever found."

"I know God will bless the two of you with a wonderful marriage." She hugged her best friend who was now also her sister in Christ. "Will you let me give you the wedding as my gift?"

"That would be wonderful but don't you think we better wait until Samuel actually asks me before we start planning a wedding?" Brigitte's face glowed, and her eyes sparkled.

"No, we know he's going to ask, so we need to get started."

Chapter Thirty-Six

HE OPENED HIS EYES, fully awake. As he stretched his long legs, he remembered that today was his daughter's birthday. How the year had flown by and with so many events. While he dressed, his thoughts tumbled through the day she was born, which was also the day he lost Valerie, his sweet wife. What would she think about how he was raising their daughter? He tried his best to be a good father. Had it been enough? He ambled into Allie's room. He would spend the whole day doing whatever his little girl wanted on her birthday. Well, everything within reason.

He knelt beside her bed and watched her sleep.

"Lord, bless this child today and help me be the father she needs. Give me wisdom. If it is your will, give her a Christian mother. In the name of Jesus the Christ, Amen."

Had he really prayed that? Give her a Christian mother meant he had to start looking for a Christian wife. He sighed. How did he go about that? All he wanted was to have Stephanie by his side.

He tickled Allie under the chin and smiled as she woke, stretching and yawning. "Good morning, sweetheart. Happy birthday."

Still half-asleep, she managed to smile as she rubbed her eyes. "My birthday."

"Yes, your birthday. What do you want to wear? How about your new jeans and Wrangler shirt?" She had new boots among her birthday presents. He hoped they fit.

She nodded and pushed the covers back so she could wiggle her legs into her jeans. "I'm four years old now. I'm a big girl."

He pulled her shirt over her head. "Yes, you're a big girl. Are you too big for your daddy to carry downstairs to breakfast?"

"No, Daddy, not too big to carry." She held out her arms.

Part of him hoped she'd never get too big to carry, but he knew that was impossible. For now, he lifted her into his arms and carried her down the stairs to breakfast.

They planned the party as a noon meal with games for the children. Since the weather was unusually warm, he helped Dad set up tables in the backyard.

He was glad Allie's birthday was on a Saturday as it made it easier for everyone to come. Friends from church and town started arriving by eleven. Abe came with Stephen and his family just behind Benjamin and Holly. There were at least twenty children, including Stephen's four. The noise soon cranked up to crowd level.

Allie maintained a constant run trying to see everything and everyone at once.

Dad rang the bell that hung just outside the back door. "All right, everyone take a seat. We'll have a prayer, eat a big meal, watch Allie open presents, and then go find a spot to take a nap." Everyone laughed knowing he was serious about the nap.

The adults and children settled into chairs on each side of the long tables. He noted with satisfaction that there were about fifty people there for his baby's birthday.

As he sat, several people around him looked toward the driveway, and he turned to see why. A vision floated across the lawn. He stood so suddenly he knocked his chair over. Before he thought about it, he sprinted across the lawn toward Stephanie, Brigitte, and Samuel.

Allie spotted them about the same time and ran past him with her arms flung wide. "Stephanie. Brigitte. Uncle Samuel."

She set down the gifts she carried and knelt to receive a bear hug from Allie. In a flash, Allie turned to Brigitte and Samuel to get her hugs from them as well.

He stood in front of Stephanie and gave her his hand to help her stand. "Hello, Steph."

"Hello yourself." She smiled. "Your Mom wanted to surprise you and called to invite us."

For a moment, he was speechless. He couldn't take his gaze off her. When words came, they came out husky. "I'm glad she did." He grabbed her up into his arms, swinging her off the ground. "I've missed you."

Dad and Mom, along with the rest of the family, greeted the newcomers.

"Let's sit down. Folks are waiting to eat." Mom walked over and ushered them to the table where space had been made for them.

Dad stood again. "We welcome all of you here today. Most of you know each other except for Brigitte and Stephanie who have flown in from New York for Allie's birthday. Be sure and get to know them. But for now, let's pray.

"Father, we thank you for the blessing of this occasion and ask that we might celebrate many more. Thank you for each one who came. Bless Allie and help us raise her to be your faithful child. Thank you for the bounty of this food and bless the hands that pre- pared it. In the name of Jesus the Christ, Amen."

He took a plate of food, but he didn't eat. He couldn't stop look- ing at Stephanie seated so close next to him. "I can't believe you're here. Mom didn't say a word."

"She called to ask if I would like to come to the birthday party and then she suggested I keep it a surprise. I hope you don't mind."

Her beauty struck him anew. He wanted to take her into his arms and show her how much he didn't mind. "I'm glad you came. I'm thrilled you came." His voice trembled.

"Hey, little brother. Swim out of those eyes." Samuel sat across from him grinning.

He reached over and punched Samuel on the arm. "Why didn't you warn me you all were coming?"

"And miss the look on your face when you first saw Stephanie? Can't a guy get a little fun now and then?"

"How come you arrived together?" He wanted to turn the conversation onto Samuel to leave him free to drink in the sight of her. He still couldn't believe she was sitting in his backyard eating his mother's fried chicken.

"We flew down together. I've been in New York for the last week." Samuel took Brigitte's hand and held it. "I couldn't stay away from this beautiful creature."

He smiled at the radiant Brigitte. "I can understand that." He looked around. "Where'd Allie get to?" He spotted her curled up in Abe's lap. He couldn't hear what she was telling him, but Abe seemed mesmerized.

He turned to Stephanie. "After Allie opens her presents, Mom is going to put her to bed for a nap. We're trying hard not to let her get overly tired today. Let's go for a horseback ride then and catch up."

She smiled. "I would like that."

He sat next to Allie as she opened the present from her grandmother. He wanted to reach over and tear the box open to speed things along so he and Stephanie could be alone to talk. Biting the inside of his cheek, he made himself sit quietly while his daughter took her time opening the box that revealed a miniature tea set.

"Daddy, look, a teapot and cups and everything." Allie started to pull the whole set out.

He reached to stop her. "Thank Grandma and then open your next gift. You can play with this later."

"Okay." Allie jumped up, ran to her grandma, and gave her a hug. "Thank you, Grandma. I love my tea set."

"You're welcome, precious." Mom beamed at Allie.

He waved Allie back. "Here, open this pretty present."

Allie started carefully tearing the paper from the box. "Look at the bunnies, Daddy."

He took a deep breath. "Yes, bunnies on the wrapping paper." Patience, he had to be patient and let Allie open all of the presents at her own pace.

When all the presents were finally unwrapped, he could see that Allie was almost wiped out with fatigue by all the toys, the clothes, and the final gift from her granddad, a little pink bicycle with training wheels.

Mom picked Allie up. "Wave goodbye to everyone."

Allie waved and smiled. "Bye-bye. Thank you for my party."

He pressed a kiss on Allie's cheek. "Go with Grandma and later we'll play with your new toys." He watched as Mom carried her into the house.

Catching his breath, He turned to find Stephanie talking to Abe, Samuel, Stephen, and Dad.

He strolled over to the group, trying to keep his anticipation from showing, and pulled up a chair. When he sat down, the conversation stopped abruptly. "What were you talking about that you stopped when I came over?"

Abe slapped him on the back. "We're talking about you of course. I heard a rumor that you and Stephanie were going horseback riding. If you're going, you better get started."

"You still want to go, Stephanie?" He wanted to get her away from his older brothers. No telling what they were talking about. Suddenly he felt every bit the youngest brother he was.

"Yes, I'm ready to go."

"We'll go saddle the horses. You two better get jackets. It may get chilly toward late afternoon." Samuel and Stephen stood and started toward the barn.

"I'll get you a jacket. Be back in a minute." He dashed to the mudroom and grabbed his jacket and one of Mom's for her.

By the time he met her beside the barn, his brothers had Winston and Charger saddled. He placed his hands around her slim waist and lifted her so she could get her foot into the stirrup. Mounting Charger, he led the way west down the valley toward the high mountain peaks.

Chapter Thirty-Seven

SHE GUIDED HER HORSE behind his mount tingling with excitement at the chance to be alone with him for a few hours.

They rode to the trail that led up to the lookout over the mountain panorama. On their last visit, snow and ice had been everywhere. Today the warm air caressed her face, little wildflowers carpeted the meadows, and birds were chirping. Spring had arrived.

He tied the horses to a tree branch and offered his hand as they climbed the path. Although still wet in spots from the melting snow, it was an easier climb than before.

She gazed out over the far-reaching mountains. They looked like a lady clothed in a green and brown dress with a snow-white hat. Aware of the heat of his body just behind her, she sighed. How should she share her new faith in God with him? She wanted to tell him so badly. Her life had changed, and she desperately wanted to share that with him. She felt him standing just behind her and then his arms circled her waist.

"There's a pretty deep drop here." His voice was gruff and muffled by her hair.

She placed her hands over his. She didn't care what excuse he used to hold her.

"I need to tell you something, but I'm not sure how to say it." His voice sounded hesitant, even sad.

What was it he wanted to say? "Just say it."

"You know that I admire and respect you very much. You're a wonderful person and beautiful inside and outside. You're great with Allie." He turned her to face him.

She started to respond, but he placed his finger on her lips. "Please hear me out. I need to get this said." Then he paused and gazed into her eyes. "As much as I care for you, I can't go any further in a relationship with you. I need a Christian wife and a Christian mother for Allie." He looked as if he might be close to tears.

A small smile crept over her lips. She could hardly contain her news, but she waited. What else did he want to say?

"Please don't hate me for this decision. I don't want to make it, but I have no choice. God's way comes first, and I have to do what is right for Allie."

She took a deep breath. "Do you mind if I stay friends with Allie?"

"Of course. I want you as a friend, too. It's just that anything more than that is not possible, no matter how much I want it."

She saw the torment in his face and heard it in his voice. In a strange way, his rejection was as much a declaration of his love for her as any words he could have said.

HE COULD HARDLY BREATHE. A fist expanded in his chest. He had felt the same explosion pressure during Allie's surgery and when he buried Valerie. Why was she smiling? Did she understand? He had told her he couldn't move forward with any kind of relationship, but her response wasn't what he expected at all. A little regret would have been nice. Instead, she gazed at him with softness and even tenderness.

She placed her palm on his cheek. "Now I have something to tell you."

He didn't want to hear her accept his rejection, but it was inevitable. "Okay."

"Thank you for saying that you admire and respect me. I feel the same about you and much more." He started to respond, but she placed her finger on his lips, mimicking his gesture. "It's my turn to speak."

He nodded slowly.

"I made a decision that you had a major part in bringing about, but I didn't make it for you. I made it because I needed to for me and because it was the right thing to do." She placed both arms around his neck. "I became a Christian. Richard baptized me last Sunday. I'm free from my sins and now a daughter of God."

He stared, not believing his ears. "Oh, Stephanie." A feeling of such joy gushed up from his soul that he couldn't contain it. He gathered her in his arms, buried his face in her hair, and began to sob. To his great surprise, tears of joy poured forth—tears locked inside him for four long years, tears he hadn't been able to cry at Valerie's death or Allie's surgeries—now they ran out of him in great cleansing rivers.

She tightened her hold. "I thought you'd be happy?"

He lifted his head and swiped at his wet cheeks. "I am happy." Another sob forced its way from his throat. "That's why . . . I'm crying." He swung her up in his arms and held her close. He wanted to dance his joy with her in his arms, but the cliff edge was too close. At last, he had a little control of himself and could speak clearly. "Why didn't you tell me? Why did you let me go on and on when you knew what I so desperately wanted to hear?"

She laughed and squeezed her arms more tightly around his neck. "Well, you told me to be quiet."

"Does everyone else already know?" He couldn't believe they had kept such an important secret from him.

"Samuel and Brigitte are telling them now. He baptized Brigitte last Sunday, also. We became sisters in Christ together."

He picked her up in his arms as he had those many months ago on the trail at their first meeting and searched her face. "Stephanie, can I tell you what I really wanted to say instead of what I thought I had to say?"

"Of course." She ran her fingers through his hair.

"I love you with all my heart. I can't stop thinking about you. You fill my waking, and you fill my dreams. I want you to be my wife. I want you to be the mother Allie has never had. I want to spend the rest of my life with you walking together toward God." He ran out of breath.

She pulled his face toward hers and just before their lips touched, she whispered, "I love you, too."

He pressed his lips to hers with a feeling of love and rightness that cascaded throughout his entire being. The black hole in the depths of his heart filled with the knowledge that she returned his love.

When he finally let her lips separate from his, she said, "I love you, Flint, but not as much as I love God. Is that okay?"

"Yes, that's perfect. I want you to love God more than me, but me second always."

"I do love you and have for a long time. It's only been in the last few weeks I began to understand why you never said anything. I'm glad you didn't tell me why before. I probably wouldn't have understood. Now I do, and I respect you for such strength."

He wanted to stand there holding the love of his life and gaze out over the mountains, but they needed to get down the path and back to the barn before dark. "I love you, and I'm asking you to marry me. But you know I'll never be as wealthy as you. I'm just an ordinary fella who loves a beautiful, rich woman."

"There's nothing ordinary about you, Cowboy. My wealth will be your wealth. I need help with it. I want to use it for God's glory, but I'm not sure how to go about that. I know you can help me."

He thought of all the good works that wealth could do. What an adventure God was placing in front of him. "We need to talk about a lot of things. But you haven't said whether you will marry me or not." He held his breath waiting for her answer.

She kissed him. "I will marry you as soon as possible."

He had one more question. "Are you willing to leave New York and live at the ranch with Mom, Dad, and Allie? I can't turn them away. They've given too much to Allie and me these last few years."

She rubbed the back of his head and neck in a slow caress. "I love your parents. Of course, I'm willing to live at the ranch with them. Although could we consider building a wing onto the house just for us? At least another bathroom?"

He grinned. "I don't know. My room has always been big enough, and padding across the hall to the bath isn't so bad."

"Oh."

He shook his head. "I'm kidding. Of course, we can build an addition to the house. We've always needed more bathrooms. I could use a bigger office, and you'll want your own office. I can use the money I saved for Allie's surgery and didn't have to use."

She smiled. "We'll talk later about how to pay for things. For now, would you please kiss me again?"

He had no problem responding to her request. When he could breathe again, he said, "We really do have to get going. Can we tell the folks and Allie we're getting married?"

He put her down but held onto her shoulders as she settled on her feet. She looked at him. "We can tell the whole world as far as I'm concerned. Flint and Stephanie are getting married!"

When they got back to the house, he, with her help, took care of the horses and then they walked across the backyard to the house holding hands. At the back door, he took her into his arms and kissed her long and hard. "That will have to last a while. It's also something we need to talk about later. Until we get married, we're going to have to watch how much we kiss if I'm to keep my thoughts right before God."

She stepped back. "I hadn't thought about that. Yes, we need to talk about it as I'm not sure I understand what God wants."

He removed his arms from around her soft body. "That's part of my responsibility as the more mature Christian." He cupped her chin in his palm and barely brushed her lips with his. "After all you're just a week-old baby Christian."

She grinned. "But I plan to grow up as fast as I can."

He opened the back door. "Let's tell the folks our news." With a lighter step than he had trod in years, he followed his love into the house.

The sweet melody of *Amazing Grace* filled their ears. They found the family in the living room with songbooks out, singing hymns.

As he stood in the doorway next to her, he glanced at his family scattered around the room. He was so blessed. Allie and Stephen's two youngest sat on the floor playing. His heart almost burst with the joy and the hard fist he'd carried in his chest for so long wholly disappeared.

At the end of the song, he cleared his throat and said, "Folks, Stephanie and I have news. I asked, and she's agreed to marry me." Everyone rose and crowded around them, hugging first Stephanie and then him. Words of congratulations on the upcoming marriage were given, but also words of joy as she told them about becoming a Christian.

Allie sat on the floor frowning at the turmoil. He lifted her into his arms. "Come here, little one. Daddy has something to tell you." He sat on a couch with Allie in his lap. "You know Daddy loves you with all his heart?"

"Yes, Daddy. Allie loves you this much." She swung her arms wide.

"Well, Daddy also loves Stephanie and wants her to be his wife and a mother for you. Would that be okay? She will come and live with us always."

Allie glanced from his face to Stephanie's, who was talking to her grandma and Brigitte. "She could sleep in my room. Let's ask Stephanie to stay always with us."

He smiled. He had some explaining to do to his little girl.

Chapter Thirty-Eight

SHE GAZED AT HIM AS he drove the truck back toward the ranch. They had just left Abe, Samuel, and Brigitte at the airport in Cedar Ridge. The joy that bubbled up at using her wealth to make life easier for everyone in the Tucker family added to the contentment of the day. The Gulfstream would fly to Los Angeles, drop Abe off, and then take Samuel and Brigitte to Alaska.

What a miracle that this strong Christian man seated next to her loved her and wanted to marry her. She watched how his eyebrows tapered and admired his long, thick eyelashes.

He glanced at her and then back to the county road that led to the ranch. "What?"

She smiled and traced from his eyebrow to his jaw with her finger. Even though he had shaved that morning, she felt the beginning of stubble. "Do you know what a handsome man you are?"

"I've always thought I was kind of ordinary." He glanced at himself in the rearview mirror. "Yep, still ordinary in spite of a beautiful woman loving me."

"Well, I think you are extraordinarily handsome. I only wish I had eyelashes as long and thick as yours. Why do guys always get them and we girls don't?"

"My eyelashes?" He chanced another quick glance in the rearview mirror before looking back at the road. "What are you talking about?"

She laughed. He really had no clue how handsome he was. It just added to his charm. "Have you thought about when you want to get married?"

He reached for her hand. "There's a justice of the peace in Cedar Ridge. How about today?"

She saw laughter in his eyes. "Be serious. We need to decide on a date so I can begin to plan."

He squeezed her hand. "I'm teasing. Well, sort of. I want you to have the wedding you've always dreamed about. I'll try to be patient, but I personally see no reason to delay."

She thought about it. "What about the second Saturday in June? That'll give us about a month."

"Where do you want to have the wedding? All those details I'm willing to leave up to you."

She laughed. Such a typical man. "I'll decide where to have the wedding if you'll plan the flowers."

"Uh ... you're not serious are you?" The confused look added to his charm.

"No, I'm not. We'll plan together, but anything you're not concerned about, I'll plan. I'd like to get married at the ranch. We could rent a tent and have the ceremony on the front lawn."

"Mom and Holly would love that. You sure? I don't mind going to New York."

She shook her head. "No, I don't have many people who would attend other than business acquaintances. Brigitte will be my maid of honor, of course. I'd like to ask Richard and Nancy to come because I want both Richard and your preacher, Dave, to officiate."

"I'd like that too. Okay. We'll have the wedding on the front lawn at the ranch. If we're getting married in a month, we better send out invitations. Can you handle picking out wedding invitations?"

"What if I get a few samples, and then we decide together?"

"That'll work." Although whatever she wanted he would be will-ing to agree with.

As soon as she got to a computer, she would begin her lists of what would need to be done. She would be glad when Brigitte re-turned from Alaska, as she would be a big help. "I want to have a big, family wedding with your family and friends there. But don't let me get so involved in the planning that we neglect what we need to do to prepare to be a married couple. I want our marriage to be based on God."

He pulled over and stopped the truck on the shoulder of the road. He took her hand. "Let's pray about it right now."

"Thank you. That's what we need to do." She closed her eyes and listened to his deep mellow bass voice as he prayed for wisdom and common sense while they prepared their wedding and for God to be the center of their union.

THAT EVENING AFTER supper she helped Mary clear the dishes and clean the kitchen. She heard Flint upstairs arguing with Allie as he bathed her and got her ready for bed. Allie exerted her opinions more frequently as she improved physically.

"Mary, Flint and I talked about adding to the house, maybe a wing for us so we'd all have more privacy. What would you like to see done to the house to make it more livable?"

"Oh my, I'd like a lot of things, but there's never the money."

"For now let's not consider the cost. Just tell me what's on your wish list."

"Well, all right. First, we need a wing off the west side with lots of windows for a master bedroom for you and Flint—a big bathroom with one of those Jacuzzi bathtubs and a roomy walk-in shower for Flint. He'd like that. An office for Flint with a view of the mountains would be nice. And a living room for the two of you to get off by yourselves now and then."

She smiled at her future mother-in-law. This woman knew no other way than to care for others. Everything Mary mentioned was for them, but nothing for herself. "Tell me what would make this part of the house more comfortable for you."

Mary glanced around the big kitchen. "Well, now that you ask. A bigger pantry with room for another freezer would be nice. Being so far from town, it's helpful to have space to store extra food. I always wanted a sewing room where I could leave stuff out while I'm working on it. But what I think would make life so much easier is a garage attached to the house, especially in the winter. That makes me think of improving the mudroom so the men could leave their boots there and not track dirt all over the house." She stopped and looked at Stephanie. "Now you've got me going. We always want more than we have, don't we? If nothing got added to this house, we could manage as long as we have the Lord."

She couldn't resist giving the older woman a hug. "You are such a wonderful example to me. Flint has given me the go-ahead to talk to an architect about adding a wing to the house. He's coming out tomorrow to look at the current structure."

"Tomorrow? That's fast. But then I suspect, young lady, that you know how to get things moving." Mary dried her hands. "We've done all we need to in here. Let's go sit in the living room. Flint should be down soon if he can get Allie to lie still long enough to go to sleep. I declare that child has more energy now than all of us adults."

They had just gotten settled in the living room when he came downstairs. "Allie fell asleep quicker than I expected. I think she's still a little tired from the weekend and her party."

Mom nodded. "That and she played hard all day with her new toys." She looked at Dad, reading the paper. "Especially that bicycle. She's already saying we need to take the training wheels off."

He sat on the couch next to Stephanie and put his arm around her shoulders. "Not until the doctor gives the go-ahead. On or off, there's too much danger of falling. For now, she's not allowed to be on that bike at all without an adult to watch."

She looked up at him. "May we tell them our decision?" He tightened his hold on her. "Sure."

"You do it."

"All right. Mom, Dad, we've made some plans and want to see if they're okay with you. We want to get married here at the ranch in a month, the second Saturday of June. Then we'll take a week off for the honeymoon. But that means you'll have to take care of Allie."

Mom glanced at Dad who nodded. "That's no problem. We'll be happy to take care of her. You plan as long a trip as you want. But are you sure we'll have enough room for a wedding here at the house?"

"Stephanie suggested we rent a tent and put it up in the front yard. We can have the wedding out there even if it rains."

Dad nodded. "That sounds like a right smart idea. We can have the food and everything out there and not mess up the house."

Mom punched him in the leg. "We don't care about the house being messed up. How many people do you expect for the wedding?"

She looked at Flint. "I have no idea. You'll have to decide whom you want to invite. Other than Brigitte, Richard, and Nancy I'm not expecting anyone to come from New York. I'll send an invitation to George and his wife, Ivana. Oh, also, Enzio and Maria, but I don't expect they'll come this far, although I'm going to offer to provide the airfare."

He rubbed the back of his neck. "Mom, you got any ideas on how to make a list of who to invite?"

Mom smiled. "You leave it to me. I'll get a list together. I'm going to say at least two hundred."

"You're kidding, two hundred. Do we know that many people?" He could only shake his head.

"Well, think about it. People from church, the fire brigade, and people you went to school with, and people from work. That doesn't count the family. Yes, at least two hundred."

He shook his head. "Is this going to get out of hand and be a bigger deal than I originally thought?"

Dad grunted and nodded. "It already has, son. You might as well sit back and enjoy the ride."

HE FELT EVERY RISE and fall of the ensuing roller coaster ride. When he had given Stephanie the go-ahead to look into adding a wing to the west end of the house, he had no idea she intended to have a work crew clearing the area within a couple of days and the foundation laid within a week. Hammering was non-stop through the day.

She merely called a contractor in Cedar Ridge and offered a bonus if the work was completed before the wedding. The new wing was more extensive than he had anticipated. It included two bedrooms, each with a bath, one for them and one for Allie, a living room, two offices, a small kitchen with a dining area, and a two car garage.

She also had a crew of workmen adding to the other end of the house, which involved a three-car garage, an enlarged mudroom with a bath with a shower, a walk-in pantry, and a sewing room. Some days as many as fifty workmen were swarming around the house.

Two weeks after Allie's birthday, he asked her to go riding with him. As they rode side-by-side occasionally touching hands, he looked at this woman who had agreed to be his wife. "You know how beautiful you are sitting on a horse in the sunlight?"

She smiled. "Breathe in that air. It's gorgeous here. I don't miss the city at all."

He gazed at her face, so serene and at peace. "I wondered if you would. This is a different life in so many ways. At times we go for days having no visitors out here."

She laughed. "You can't imagine because you've always had family around you, but I've spent a lot of time in the middle of one of the world's largest cities feeling lonely. Here, there's always someone around to talk to and do things with."

He frowned. "Is it too much? Would you rather we had a place to ourselves?"

"Of course not. We'll have the new wing of the house, and that's enough. I want to fill the house with family." She cut her eyes over to his face. "I want to have children. Several."

He sighed with contentment. "Me too." He grinned at the thought. "We'll start on that immediately after the wedding."

They rode along in silence for a while. Then he pulled his horse up beside the stream. "Let's walk and let the horses rest." He helped her dismount and then tied the horses so they could reach water and the new, green grass.

She slipped her arm around his waist as they walked along the creek edge. "I want to ask you something, but I want you to be open with me about what you want."

He stopped walking and pulled her close until she was leaning into his side. "Sure, ask away."

"I don't want my wealth to be a problem between us. But I don't really know what to do with it."

He wondered where she was headed. The money had always concerned him as well. "I don't want it to be a problem either."

She nodded. "So what would you say to becoming the director of Firebird Foundation? Quit your job with Booker and Williams and only manage the money. You know what's there and how big a job it is as well as anyone. Ben and Tony can manage the day-to-day investments with our guidance."

"Taking responsibility for the decisions of dispersing the funds from the principle?"

"Yes. Already, as you know, the Foundation has close to a billion dollars in assets, a lot of it in cash. Someone has to take charge, and I don't want to do it. I've worked with corporations for years, but it's never been something I enjoyed." She tightened her hold on his waist. "I want to be a full-time wife and mother—to have time to sit and study my Bible and to have you home in the evenings with nothing else to do but be a family."

He imagined the life she described and knew it was what he wanted, too. "I could work out of the office at the house and set up the rest with Ben and Tony in Cedar Ridge. Being only twenty miles into town, I can go in to work a couple of days a week. What if we set up an advisory board with you as the chair? Then you could guide the distribution of the funds. I'm willing to do the day-to-day management."

"It's settled. You'll manage Firebird Foundation. I've also been thinking about the artwork in storage, my apartment, and several other investment properties I should sell and add the proceeds to the Foundation. I'm not sure about selling the Edge of the Pointe yet."

"Don't get rid of anything until you're ready. I don't see that there's any hurry. We haven't talked about a prenuptial agreement yet. I'm willing to have one drawn up to protect you if you desire."

"No, I don't want a prenuptial, all I have will also be yours. I trust you completely. But I do want us to set up a trust fund for Allie so she'll be taken care of no matter what the future brings."

He pulled her into his arms and caressed her. His heart felt so full of love for this woman, he didn't know if it would burst or not. God had blessed him above anything he could have ever imagined after losing Valerie. The future looked filled with as much promise as a sunrise over the mountains. He lifted his eyes heavenward. *Thank you, Lord.*

He pressed his face into her sweet-smelling hair. His voice, husky with emotion, came out muffled by her hair. "I promise to do everything I can to be worthy of your trust, so help me God."

Chapter Thirty-Nine

DRESSED IN HER WEDDING dress, Stephanie stared into the long mirror. When she and Brigitte had flown back to New York to close the apartment, they'd spent hours searching for the perfect dress. Movers packed and transported her belongings from New York to Colorado. By the time her things had arrived from New York, the new addition was ready, smelling of fresh paint.

Smoothing the lace-covered brocade across her hips, she whirled to admire the mermaid style that flared gently from the knees. Below the bateau neckline scalloped in lace, small pearls highlighted the lily of the valley appliqués of the lace-covered bodice and the three-quarter lace-appliquéd sleeves, which all formed a breath-taking elegance. She picked up the pearl and diamond silver earrings that had belonged to her mother and carefully clipped them on. Brigitte stood behind her ready to put on the veil.

She had chosen to wear her long dark hair loose and flowing the way Flint liked it. Brigitte lifted the hip-length double veil of appliquéd tulle and positioned it.

"I'm glad we decided against the shorter veil, aren't you?" She turned from side to side checking her image. "What do you think?"

"What do I think about what? Your dress is beyond gorgeous, you look radiant, you're marrying a very handsome man. This new wing of the house is fabulous. Should I go on?"

She laughed. "No, that's enough. By the way, you look pretty fabulous yourself."

Her maid of honor also wore a mermaid-style dress, long-sleeved, high-necked emerald green silk that fit snuggly until knee level and then sprayed out with fullness to the floor. Brigitte also wore her hair loose with just a white orchid behind one ear.

"Thanks, I appreciate that you let me choose my dress. This is the most beautiful bridesmaid dress I've ever worn, and I've worn a few."

"Well, I hope you return the favor when you and Samuel marry. By the way, when will that be?"

Brigitte smiled and held up her engagement ring. "We thought September would be a good time. I want to be married in Boston for my mother. Otherwise, we would have it here."

She wanted to give Brigitte a hug but refrained so as not to muss up their makeup and dresses. "I'm so happy for you and Samuel, although I'm still surprised that you're going to live in Alaska."

She jumped at a light tap on the door.

Mary entered wearing a tea-length pale green dress she had bought in Denver during Allie's last doctor's visit. "You girls about ready? Oh my, Stephanie, you are a vision."

"Thank you. Is Allie ready?" She hoped all the excitement wouldn't be too much for the child.

"Yes. Their Aunty Margo is reading a story to the children in Allie's room, and then she will take them downstairs to the tent when you're ready."

She looked around the vast master bedroom with its master bath suite. It was perfect. Tall crème candles spread just a hint of the aroma of gardenia into the room. A large vase of fresh flowers graced the end table beside the bed. Flint had let her decorate the room, which she had done in white and wood tones. That fit her soon-to-be husband's color preference and the blue curtains and velvet throw pillows against the white bedspread matched hers. He had been uncomfortable about moving his stuff in before the wedding, so Mary planned to do that while they were on their honeymoon. With the fireplace and the big bay window facing the high mountains in the west, she had created a retreat filled with everything on their wish list. *When I come back to this room, I'll be a married woman, Mrs. Flint Tucker.*

"I'm ready." She took her bouquet of red and white roses from Brigitte and started down the hall that led toward the living room. There Dad stood dressed in a new black suit and black cowboy boots waiting to escort her down the aisle.

Holly and Vickie stood together in dresses that matched Brigitte's. Allie looked adorable in her matching emerald green dress frilly with petticoats and a big green bow holding her hair back.

Holding her grandpa's hand, Allie pointed with the other one. "Ohhh, look at beautiful Stephanie."

Tears puddled in her eyes as she gazed at the child. *In a few minutes, I'm going to be her mother.* "You look beautiful too, Allie."

Running a finger around the inside of his collar, Tom said, "Let's get this show on the road."

Mary had already gone to let Abe escort her to her seat.

Acting as the wedding director, Nancy Anderson lined them up and signaled the singers from the church.

She felt tears gather into her eyes again as she heard the hymn, *We Gather Together To Ask the Lord's Blessing.* How God had blessed her when all seemed so dark and bleak. To be walking down the aisle as a Christian to meet Flint, a righteous man who loved her, surrounded by this loving family, and to have a future where she would never be alone again was a magnificent answer to prayer. To think that just a year ago she didn't even know how to pray.

Family and friends seated on white folding chairs filled the wedding tent. Hundreds of white and red roses decorated the sides and front of the tent. White tulle draped from the ceiling to the sides of the tent giving an illusion of a chapel. Down the center aisle, white taffeta formed a path along which Allie now strolled carrying a basket from which she dropped rose petals. She then went and waited next to her father, dark brown eyes sparkling. Next came Vickie, Holly and then finally Brigitte as maid of honor.

She glided down the aisle with her arm through Tom's, watching Flint's face as he welcomed her with love as they prepared to join their lives together. Her heart felt as if it would burst from the love for this man.

He stood tall dressed in a black suit and black cowboy boots. She smiled at the memory of the pained expression when he had offered to wear a tux. Glad that she had said no, as he looked great in the ordinary black suit. Next to him stood Abe, Samuel, and Stephen all dressed the same. She glanced at Tom's face glowing with love and pride as he walked her down the aisle toward his tall sons. Yes, he had a right to feel good about what he and Mary had accomplished in raising their children. Would she and Flint have the same opportunity with their own children?

Richard took a step forward. "Who brings this woman to be wed to this man today?"

"I, Tom Tucker and her mother Mary, have the honor." Tom placed her hand in Flint's. He gave them both an impromptu kiss before hastening back to his place next to Mary where he settled his arm around her. She was already wiping her eyes with a handkerchief.

She gazed into his blue eyes and returned his smile. She had never seen such love shining from someone's eyes and felt a tingling all through her being knowing it was for her.

Allie sidled over and leaned against his leg. She played with the ribbons on the empty rose petal basket. He placed his right hand on Allie's head as he held her hand with his left.

The ceremony continued in a blur. She answered when asked if she was willing to marry this man beside her. When David and Richard pronounced them man and wife in unison, she received his kiss with lips that softly responded and held a promise of wondrous things to come.

Hours later as they prepared to climb into his truck for the drive to the mountain cabin for their honeymoon, she hugged Allie. "We'll be back soon, and then we'll be together always."

Allie hugged her back. "You promise? You'll be my new mommy for always?"

She glanced at Flint and smiled. "For always. I promise."

HE PUT THE TRUCK INTO gear and inched down the lane toward the road. Everyone yelled good wishes after them. Glancing over at her, he smiled. It had been a beautiful wedding, but he was happy to be driving away with his new bride.

"How long will it take to reach the cabin?" She undid her seatbelt and scooted next to him.

"It should only take about an hour and a half to get there. I like you sitting close but buckle up please." Indeed, he did like the feel of her warm body next to his.

She found the middle seatbelt and fastened it, and then laid her head on his shoulder. "I'm so happy I fear I'm going to burst. I've heard the expression 'bursting with happiness,' and now I know how it feels."

"Can I presume to be part of the reason?" He kept his hands tight on the steering wheel, although he wanted to take her into his arms. He drove a little faster, anticipating being at the cabin alone with her.

She snuggled up to him and entwined her arms around his. "Yes, you can assume that. Are you happy, Flint?"

How could he express what he was feeling? "I'm happy, joyful, content, anxious, and I'm not sure what else."

"Anxious? What about?"

"I want to give you everything your heart desires and be the man God wants me to be and that you deserve. Only time will tell whether I can do it, but I promise you I will try." He glanced at her and then quickly back to the road. He also had to admit to being a little fearful about whether or not he could meet all of her expectations.

"You just give me your love and guide me toward heaven. God will lead us the rest of the way."

He pulled the truck over to the shoulder of the road and stopped. Taking Stephanie into his arms, he gave her the kiss he had been longing to give her in all the long months of loving her. When he came up for air, he said, "I love you, Steph, and I promise to always be there for you."

"I love you, and I promise to give you all of myself for the rest of my life." She kissed him again with passion and promise.

Pulling back from her, he laughed from the pure joy of the anticipation of their life together. "Let's get to the cabin."

<>

About the Author

A J Hawke is a native Texan born in Spur, Texas who has a passion for exploring the American West and creating stories with Christian based romantic themes. A J Hawke has lived and traveled throughout the American West as well as other parts of the world and enjoys reading, writing, friends, family, and being a Christian. The author's online home at www.AJHawke.com. You can connect with A J on Facebook at www.Facebook.com/AJHawkeBooks and you can make contact at AJHawke@AJHawke.com if the mood strikes you. NOVELS BY A J HAWKEInspirational Historical Western RomanceCedar Ridge Chronicles Series:Cabin on Pinto Creek, Book 1Joe Storm No Longer a Cowboy, Book 2Colorado Morning Sky, Book 3Colorado Evening Sky, Book 4 STAND-ALONE NOVELSMountain Journey HomeCaught Between Two WorldsLance McTavish Home To TexasSIGN UP FOR A J HAWKE NEWSLETTERSigning up to the mailing list entitles you to a free copy of one of my novels. You can get the novel, CAUGHT BETWEEN TWO WORLDS, an inspirational contemporary romance for free, by signing up at http://AJHawke.com.LEAVE A REVIEW ENJOY THIS BOOK? YOU CAN MAKE A POWERFUL DIFFERENCE Your experience as a reader of my novels is powerful as a review affect the choices of other readers when it comes to the decision to purchase. Amazon decides whether a book is worth their attention, as far as advertising, a large part by the number of reviews. Also, if you leave a review for one novel of a series, Amazon does not transfer it to other novels in a series. So a review is appreciated for each novel you read. The type of review is up to you, the reader. The reviews do not have to be long, just a sentence or two, and then a star rating. If you enjoyed CAUGHT BETWEEN TWO WORLDS, I would be grateful if you would share your experience, after reading the novel, which I consider a true gift.

Read more at www.AJHawke.com.